— STAR TREK —
ENTERPRISE®

RISE OF THE FEDERATION
TOWER OF BABEL

CHRISTOPHER L. BENNETT

Based upon *Star Trek*®
created by Gene Roddenberry
and *Star Trek: Enterprise*
created by Rick Berman & Brannon Braga

D1636262

POCKET BOOKS
New York   London   Toronto   Sydney   New Delhi

Pocket Books
A Division of Simon & Schuster, Inc.
1230 Avenue of the Americas
New York, NY 10020

This book is a work of fiction. Any references to historical events, real people, or real places are used fictitiously. Other names, characters, places, and events are products of the author's imagination, and any resemblance to actual events or places or persons, living or dead, is entirely coincidental.

First Pocket Books paperback edition April 2014

POCKET and colophon are registered trademarks of Simon & Schuster, Inc.

For information about special discounts for bulk purchases, please contact Simon & Schuster Special Sales at 1-866-506-1949 or business@simonandschuster.com.

The Simon & Schuster Speakers Bureau can bring authors to your live event. For more information or to book an event, contact the Simon & Schuster Speakers Bureau at 1-866-248-3049 or visit our website at www.simonspeakers.com.

Cover design by Alan Dingman
Cover art by Doug Drexler

Manufactured in the United States of America

10 9 8 7 6 5 4 3 2 1

ISBN 978-1-4767-4964-8
ISBN 978-1-4767-4966-2 (ebook)

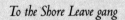

To the Shore Leave gang

There is an ancient human legend: The peoples of their world came together to build a vast tower reaching to heaven, but their god, fearing their potential to achieve whatever they imagined, cursed them with the inability to understand one another's speech and scattered them across the Earth. . . .

The reason humanity has now conquered the heavens is that they finally stopped blaming their god for their own fear of what they could achieve together.

—Anlenthoris ch'Vhendreni,
2161 Babel Conference

2163

Prologue

October 19, 2163
Klingon privateer *Sud Qav*, Kandari Sector

"A LORILLIAN FREIGHTER," Vhelis announced with a feral grin. "Sensors say it carries refined metals—probably duranium!"

Captain Lokog grunted acknowledgment as he studied the hemicylindrical vessel on the viewscreen. "Tell me about Lorillians." He had come across a few at *raIjul wa'maH* and other local trade outposts over the years, but they had never seemed worthy of his notice.

"A weakling race," Vhelis told him from the sensor station. "They were *jeghpu'wI'* of the Vulcans, more or less." Lokog nodded, aware that the Vulcans would have used a less honest label for their conquered subjects—even before one of those subject races, humans, had managed to overthrow Vulcan rule, take over their empire, and absorb the Andorians and Tellarites into it. Though the humans also hid their conquests behind pusillanimous labels like "Federation" and "democracy."

"Has the Federation absorbed the Lorillians?" he asked Vhelis.

"Not yet," she answered. "They trade, and they talk, but that is all."

That must be why the freighter was unescorted. "Armaments?"

"Low-yield particle cannons. Nothing more."

Kalun, the gunner, laughed. "Easy pickings!"

"Assume nothing!" Lokog told the younger Klingon. "Fortunes can turn foul at any time. Never lower your guard." Seeing that Kalun was suitably chastened, he turned to the helmsman. "Attack vector."

"*Luq, HoD!*"

"Ready weapons," Lokog ordered Kalun. "Disable their engines and life support."

"*Yajchu'!*" the gunner barked.

Lokog looked around at his bridge crew. Their fierce, battle-hungry expressions made an absurd contrast with their smooth, infantile foreheads, the brows of weakling races like Vulcans or humans. How he hated the sight of them.

Almost as much as he hated the sight of his own face.

Even after nine years, it shamed him. If only he had unloaded his cargo at the Qe'tran colony and moved on, instead of stopping to avail himself of the local pleasure slaves. By that quirk of fate, he had fallen prey to the virus that had stripped the planet's Klingon inhabitants of their warriors' pride, the cranial ridges that declared their houses and heritage. He had been left half a Klingon, a *QuchHa'*—and forbidden from returning to his ship lest he infect the rest of his crew. He had lost his dignity along with his possessions and standing, all through no fault of his own. His dreams of getting out of the privateer life, maybe buying his way into a minor title and starting a house of his own, had been forever shattered. True, some of the nobles who had succumbed to the same plague had managed to cling to their standing, but a commoner like Lokog had no chance of advancement now that his weakness was written across his very brow.

In the years since, as he'd struggled to acquire a new ship and crew and resume his raiding activities in alien space, he'd come to realize he may have been better off where he was. Most *QuchHa'* in the Defense Force had been reassigned to segregated crews and sent to patrol the borders, given the chance to redeem their shame in battle with the Empire's enemies—or, more bluntly, to die as cannon fodder since the Empire had no other place for them. But there were those who plotted rebellion, convinced that the only way the *QuchHa'* could survive was by seizing the High Council from the *HemQuch* majority. And there were *HemQuch* factions who saw the plague as proof of the current leaders' weakness and plotted their own takeovers. The Council had fought off coup attempts from both directions in the past few years, and the Empire teetered on the brink of civil war. All in all, Lokog found it preferable to stay in unclaimed space, beyond the crush of the Empire's racial politics.

Not that he feared battle, Lokog insisted to himself. It was more a matter of choosing a battlefield where one could concentrate on one's chosen prey without having to worry about getting caught up in someone else's fight.

And the Kandari Sector, as Vulcan charts labeled this region, was a good place for it. This was the *ra-Ijulngan*'s zone of influence, and their trade commission was notoriously broad-minded about the ways their trading partners obtained their goods or conducted business. Granted, they were uncomfortably close to the territory of the upstart Federation. But the Andorian fleet that formed the bulk of its military strength was saddled with patrolling its borders, much like the *QuchHa'* crews back in the Empire, and only explorers and traders traveled this far outside them. The *raIjulngan* traded actively with the Federation and had sought their help half a year ago with the Mute crisis; but they had their own extensive mercantile empire and showed no inclination to be absorbed into another state, so Lokog had no cause to worry about the Federation Starfleet poking its extremities into his private pursuits. Indeed, the *raIjul wa'maH* outpost would be the ideal place to sell the Lorillians' cargo once Lokog had completed his more forceful transaction here. If any Lorillians survived the attack, he might even be able to pick up a little extra profit at the Orion slave market there.

"We've been detected," Vhelis reported in sharp, clipped syllables. "Target emitting distress signal."

Lokog grinned. "Let them bleat. No one here will come to their aid."

U.S.S. Pioneer NCC-63
Approaching HD 19632 system, Kandari Sector

"All right," Tobin Dax said, spreading the *Xiangqi* pieces facedown on the mess hall table. "Now mix them around some."

Across from the diminutive, balding chief engineer, Lieutenant Valeria Williams obliged, scrambling the wooden disks. There were fourteen in all, one of each of the seven different types for each color.

"Look at one," Doctor Dax went on. "Don't show it to me, but remember it."

Lieutenant Commander Travis Mayweather watched over the armory officer's gray-clad shoulder as she lifted one far enough to get a look at it. Mayweather had played Crewman Chen's favorite game enough times to recognize the characters on the Chinese chessmen; this was a red *xiàng* or elephant piece. "Got it," said the auburn-haired Williams, who'd gotten fairly good at the game herself.

"All right." Dax displayed his empty hands, then began stacking the wooden disks with his left. After putting two other pieces atop Val's, the chief engineer moved that hand away to stack another three while his right hand rested upon the first stack, which he then placed atop the one in his left. After adding two more pieces to the stack, he pushed it over to Lieutenant Samuel Kirk, who sat at Williams's right, clad in the cobalt blue of the science department. Along with Mayweather in his command greens, the group represented all four shipboard departments, though Doctor Dax wore a civilian suit rather than the red-brown tunic of a Starfleet engineer. "Now, ah, cut it anywhere you want. Don't let me see." The Trill, who looked like a human in his thirties aside from the leopard-like spots adorning his temples and neck, studiously looked away as the younger blond historian took off the top five pieces, put them on the table, then placed the other three on top of them, squaring off the stack. "Now you, Commander," Dax said to Mayweather. Kirk pushed the stack gently toward the first officer, careful not to tip it.

Mayweather was tempted to pull a trick of his own at this point. He was intrigued, for he'd never seen anyone perform magic with *Xiangqi* pieces before. It combined the moves of coin magic with the selection and location tricks of card magic, an innovative twist. Dax had explained that the *Xiangqi* pieces were similar to gaming tiles that his people used for sleight of hand, so he'd found it easy enough to adapt the techniques. But Travis had learned some card and coin tricks in his youth, growing up on the low-warp cargo ship *Horizon,* where hobbies had been essential to pass the abundant time between planetfalls. Dax's hand positions had tipped Mayweather off to how the trick worked and where the red elephant really was. He could sabotage the illusion easily enough when he made his cut, giving away the trick and embarrassing the performer.

But no. There was a time, a place, and a right kind of target for practical jokes. Tobin Dax, while a capable and reliable engineer, was almost pathologically shy. He'd been part of the crew for six months, but had only recently grown comfortable enough to socialize like this, and still tended to hide behind his magic in the belief that it was the only thing that made him interesting. There was a point that could be made by sabotaging his illusion; if nothing else, Mayweather felt the Trill was too caught up in the mechanics of the tricks at the expense of his patter, impairing his ability to hold—and deceive—an audience. Still, public embarrassment would do more harm than good, undermining what little social confidence he'd gained. Besides, Mayweather wasn't just another crew member anymore; he was *Pioneer*'s first officer, responsible for the morale and performance of the crew.

So he simply did the cut as instructed, splitting the stack right in the middle, and obliged when Dax said, "Now place it in the center of the table." Mayweather deposited it amid the remaining six pieces scattered across the tabletop.

Dax looked at Williams. "Now, ah, Val . . . can you guess where your tile is?"

"Easy," Williams said. Her eagle eye hadn't left the stack, and she'd followed both cuts. She grabbed the top two pieces in her hands and lifted them. "It's right here."

But when she turned them over, the piece she revealed was a black *pào*, or cannon. "No way. I know I counted right." She flipped over the whole stack and spread out the pieces. The red elephant was nowhere in sight. "I don't get it. I had my eye on that stack the whole time."

"Ah, but what you forget," Dax said, his words more confident than his tone, "is that the elephant always moves two points diagonally." He gestured toward a stray piece in roughly the indicated position, keeping his hand well away from it. Val flipped it over to find the red elephant, just where Travis had known it would be.

Mayweather and Kirk laughed and applauded, while Williams just stared, trying to figure out what she'd missed. "Good one, Tobin," Kirk said. "I like how you worked the piece's specific move into the reveal."

"Thank you," Dax said, eyes focused on his hands as they rearranged the pieces.

"But didn't you say the Trill game tokens were more like playing cards?" The engineer nodded. "So that final touch was something you added just for this."

"I guess so. It seemed like a good idea."

"Hey, don't sell yourself short," Mayweather told him. "You're more creative than you think."

"I just want to try that again," Williams said. "I know you switched the pieces somewhere. I just need to figure out where."

Kirk stroked her upper arm gently, right above the *Pioneer* mission patch on her right sleeve. "Relax, Val. They're not Klingon snipers."

She was unmoved by his gesture of affection. "But if I'm not good enough to see through a simple trick, how can I spot a Klingon sniper when—"

The intercom hailed. *"Commander Mayweather, Lieutenant Williams, report to the bridge. Alpha shift, report to stations."* The clipped British tones were unmistakably Captain Reed's. Typically, he was early for his duty shift.

Mayweather rose and walked to the panel by the mess-hall door, activating the intercom. "Mayweather here. What's going on, Captain?"

"We've picked up a distress signal from a Lorillian freighter. They're under attack by Klingons."

"On our way," Mayweather said, and Williams was on his heels as he headed out.

Dax followed them into the corridor. "Wonderful," he moaned. "You just had to tempt fate, didn't you, Lieutenant?"

The distress signal originated more than two light-years from *Pioneer's* position, roughly along the trade route between Beta Rigel and the Xarantine trade colony on Zeta Fornacis VI. Even at the *Intrepid*-class starship's maximum of warp 5.6, it took more than an hour to reach the coordinates. Ensign Grev's attempts to hail the Lorillian freighter produced only static in reply.

"This is taking too long, Captain," Valeria Williams muttered to Malcolm Reed as he paced by her tactical station forty minutes into the journey. "A freighter like that couldn't have held off a Klingon ship, even a privateer, for that long."

Reed gave a grim scoff. "'Privateer.' To be a privateer, you need letters of marque authorizing you to attack a declared enemy in wartime."

The short-haired lieutenant replied with a gallows smirk. "Don't Klingons pretty much consider themselves at war with everyone?"

"They can call it whatever they like, Lieutenant. But these are pirates, pure and simple."

Williams grimaced. "And with transporters, it wouldn't take an hour to beam the cargo over. Sir, what are the odds we'll be able to accomplish anything when we get there?"

"I understand your frustration, Val." Reed spoke reassuringly—something he'd been gradually learning to do as a necessary part of command, but that he still found easier with Williams, who shared his background as an armory officer, than with the rest of the crew. "But one can hardly ignore a distress signal. We can only hope there will be someone left to help."

She held his eyes. "Yes, sir."

But when they finally neutralized warp at the signal's coordinates, the signs were not promising. "The Klingon ship's long gone," Williams reported solemnly. "But there is an ion trail, sir."

"Let's see if we're needed here before we go haring off," Reed said from the command chair. "Rey, any biosigns?"

At the science station on Reed's left, Lieutenant Reynaldo Sangupta replied with unwonted solemnity. "I'm not reading any, sir. The ship is a mess—engines shot, holds blown, half the living space open to vacuum."

"Captain, recommend we pursue the Klingons," Williams said.

"Not just yet, sir," Sangupta interposed, studying a readout on his console. "We need to take a closer look."

"What have you got?" asked Travis Mayweather, who stood at Reed's flank.

"Some of the compartments are flooded with methylacetylene gas. It's toxic to most humanoids, and it'll suffocate you if it displaces the oxygen, but Lorillians have a weird biochemistry. There might still be survivors with biosigns too faint to read from here."

Reed nodded. "All right. Find an intact docking port if you can. Travis—prepare a boarding party."

Sangupta's instincts had been sound. Mayweather's party found seven corpses, all victims of the Klingons' disruptor bombardment, and Sangupta's sensor scans picked up two more bodies drifting in space nearby. But the remaining five members of the freighter crew were found in the methylacetylene-flooded engine bay, their biosigns barely registering but present—though one died before Doctor Liao was able to stabilize him.

Now the rest were in *Pioneer*'s sickbay, where Malcolm Reed and Val Williams spoke to the chief engineer, a middle-aged woman named Dashec. The sandy-haired Lorillian, distinguishable from human only by a vertical cleft between her brows and by the subtle nuances of body language and scent that an experienced space traveler like Reed had learned to pick up on, was weak but deeply relieved by the survival of most of her engine crew—particularly since the three included her "breeding partner," as she called him, plus their adolescent daughter and a cousin of some sort. It seemed Lorillian freighter crews were much like the "Space Boomer" communities from which Therese Liao and Travis Mayweather hailed, living on low-warp ships crewed largely by families. Still, several of the dead had been family as well, and Dashec pleaded fiercely with Reed to hunt down the Klingons and deal with them once and for all. "I'm afraid this isn't a warship," he told her with as much sympathy as he could. "But we'll do what we can for you." It didn't satisfy her. Liao gave her captain a hooded look and advised that the engineer needed rest.

Once they were out in the corridor, Williams made a fist and struck it against her palm. "Those Klingon bastards. We can still hunt them down, sir."

"And do what? We're outside our jurisdiction. This is Rigelian space."

"Barely, sir. You know the Rigelians. They're as happy to do business with pirates and slavers as their victims."

"Still, they're the closest thing to a rightful authority in this sector. We'll gather what evidence we can, advise them to be on the lookout for the stolen duranium. If nothing else, maybe the Lorillian government will put pressure on them to act. They're one of Rigel's biggest trading partners."

"They'd be long gone by then. We can track them ourselves."

"We'd have to put the Lorillians off someplace safe first, and the Klingons would be long gone by then."

"Dashec sounded like she'd be willing to take the risk."

"For herself, Val. Maybe for her partner. But for her daughter?"

Williams stopped walking, her shoulders sagging. After a moment, she ran a hand through her auburn hair. "Why are we even out here if we can't make a difference?"

"Because we're here to explore, not to police," he reminded her. "It was a hard truth I had to face back on *Enterprise* those first few years. Sometimes we came across things we couldn't accept, but our ability to do anything about them was limited. We were just one ship, far from home, nosing about in other people's territory." He stroked his neat goatee, a reminder of how much he'd changed since those early years—which just drove home how much was still the same. "Sometimes we were able to stop them, but often the best we could do was help others learn to defend themselves, or call in help from someone more powerful, like the Vulcans."

The armory officer's hazel eyes held his. "And what if the only ones powerful enough to act refuse to do so, sir?"

Reed had no answer for the lieutenant. Unless the Rigelians could be convinced to get tougher about patrolling their own backyard, things were unlikely to get any safer in the Kandari Sector.

November 10, 2163
U.S.S. Endeavour NCC-06, entering Iota Pegasi system

"Attention, Earth vessel! You are ordered to halt your approach immediately. Any attempt to enter orbit of the asteroid or provide aid to its occupiers will be met with force!"

Captain T'Pol blinked at the incongruity of the message. While the battle cruisers forming a cordon around the large, roughly cylindrical asteroid on *Endeavour*'s main viewscreen were of a type that the Arkonians manufactured and marketed to several known species, they bore the distinct colors and alterations favored by the defense fleet of the United Planets of Tellar—one of United Earth's partner nations in the United Federation of Planets. Apparently that abundance of unity had not yet reached this system.

Others on the bridge crew were similarly nonplussed. "'Earth vessel'?" asked Lieutenant Elizabeth Cutler from the science station on T'Pol's left. "Did someone miss a few years' worth of memos?"

T'Pol turned to the station immediately to fore of Cutler's. "Return channel," she ordered, and Lieutenant Commander Hoshi Sato efficiently complied, nodding a mere second later. "Tellarite vessel. This is Captain T'Pol of the *U.S.S. Endeavour*. Our ship represents the entire Federation, yourselves included. Starfleet Command has sent us to investigate and resolve this conflict."

A dark-haired, stout Tellarite male appeared on the viewscreen. He wore an avocado-green command tunic with three stripes on each sleeve and shoulder strap, identical to her own in design (if not in proportion) except that its left breast bore the hoof-like service patch of the Tellar Space Administration rather than the stylized arrowhead of the United Earth Space Probe Agency, and its right sleeve was adorned with the name of his ship in Braille-like Tellarite script rather than a UESPA-style circular mission patch. *"Captain Brantik, in command of this fleet. Whether you represent Earth or the Federation is beside the point. This system is Tellarite space, and that makes it Tellarite jurisdiction!"*

"We are not here to dispute Tellar's claim to Iota Pegasi," she told him. "But the settlers are human.

This is an interworld matter, the very kind of dispute that falls under Federation jurisdiction."

Tellar had claimed the binary system—which was old enough to have habitable planets but young enough that they lacked complex indigenous life— nearly two decades ago but had made only cursory efforts at developing it until recently, as prosperity resulting from Federation membership had prompted a new mining boom. Yet upon their arrival, the mining and colonization fleet had discovered that in the interim, the crew of the Earth Cargo Services freighter *Voortrekker* had established a colony of their own within the system's asteroid belt, burrowing into one of its larger members and spinning it up to provide simple artificial gravity while building solar collectors, heat radiators, and other necessary machinery into its surface. The Tellarites had ordered the "squatters" to leave, but the Boomers had refused to abandon the home they had invested so much time and labor in constructing. Each side had attempted to convince the other through negotiation, legal maneuvering, and financial persuasion, but each insisted on its own prior claim. Matters had grown increasingly tense, to the point that the Tellarite government had solicited Federation aid in hopes of averting violence.

But no one seemed to have informed Captain Brantik of this. *"You'd like that, I'm sure,"* he said with a sneer. *"Any excuse to push into our territory and throw your weight around. But this is our territory, by law and treaty, and that gives us the right to enforce our own boundaries! You have no authority to prevent us from expelling these interlopers, and if you obstruct our efforts, I promise you we will open fire!"* His meaty hand struck a control, and his image was replaced by that of the well-armed fleet he commanded. Clearly, T'Pol reflected, the adoption of a standardized Starfleet uniform still represented an ideal more than an actuality.

"Captain," Sato said, "we're getting another hail. This one's from within the asteroid."

"Onscreen."

A human female with rough-hewn features and gray-blond hair appeared. *"This is Freya Stark, governor of the Voortrekker colony, to the Federation starship on approach. You'd better turn around if you know what's good for your pig-faced friends! We warned them about calling in reinforcements."*

"Particle cannon fire from the surface!" Takashi Kimura called from tactical. "It missed the lead cordon ship by nine hundred meters. A warning shot."

"You come closer, so does our aim." Stark shut off her transmission.

"Brantik is hailing again," Sato announced. At T'Pol's nod, she opened the channel.

"You see what you've done?" the Tellarite captain bellowed. *"You're just stoking the flames! Turn around now!"*

"Ensign, all stop," the captain ordered Pedro Ortega at the helm station in front of her. "Hold station at this distance from the asteroid."

"Aye, Captain," the green-uniformed ensign replied.

Beside T'Pol, Commander Thanien ch'Revash stroked his blue-complexioned chin, his antennae curving forward with interest. "Odd," said the seasoned Andorian officer. "Both of them think we're here to support the other."

"Return channel to both," she ordered Sato, then spoke. "This is Captain T'Pol of the *Endeavour*. Please understand that we are not here to provide military aid to anyone. We are all Federation members here, and the Federation has mechanisms for dispute resolution between its member governments. The use of force by one Federation member against another is unacceptable and will not be tolerated—in either direction."

Stark appeared on the screen again. *"That's where you're wrong, Vulcan,"* the human female replied. *"We're an independent colony. We never agreed to submit to your Federation's rule. Damn it, the whole reason we chose to settle out here was to get away from your creeping federalism."*

"Your vessel operates under Earth registry, ma'am."

"A flag of convenience."

"Even so, it carries with it the obligation to abide by the laws of the flag state."

"Maybe on a ship, but a colony is no ship. We will resist any attempt by the Federation to impose its will on us, and bringing in a prettier starship to do their dirty work won't change anything. We'll fire on anyone who tries to come down!" She shut off the feed.

Brantik appeared on the screen again. *"They won't listen to your logic, Vulcan. We've been dealing with them far longer than you, so leave this to us. I won't tolerate any interference."* And his channel closed once again.

"This is absurd," Thanien said, shaking his white-haired head. "What do the Boomers imagine they can achieve? They are besieged."

"I don't think it's about tactics, Commander," Sato replied. "It's about pride. They're used to living independently. The Boomer lifestyle attracted people who prized self-reliance and autonomy, who wanted to get away from large civilizations or central authority. They know they're the little guys, and they're fighting to stay that way."

"They're a relic of an earlier era," the first officer said, waving a hand in dismissal. "The frontier is giving way to a proper civilization. They'll just have to learn to live with that."

"So we should just let the Tellarites force them out?"

"Of course not. The Tellarites are behaving as much like renegades as they are. The Federation *does* have authority in this matter. The law is clear on that."

"The laws are new, Commander," the delicate-featured Japanese woman replied. "And most of them haven't been tested yet. We can't expect everyone to be an expert in how they work—or to agree on how they should work."

"Then we should transmit the relevant codes to both sides for their review."

"Both these groups clearly take a lot of pride in doing things their own way."

"All our worlds have had to make concessions," Thanien replied, restrained impatience in his tone. "Our duty is to remind them of that."

"At gunpoint? You saw how close they are to the edge."

"If I may, Commander," Kimura said to Thanien, "if we push them in the state they're in now, a violent response is inevitable. Nothing *Endeavour* couldn't handle, but both of them would be sure to suffer casualties."

"Commander Sato," T'Pol asked, "are you proposing an alternative?"

The communications officer took a moment to gather her thoughts. "The one thing they do agree on is that we're outsiders, that we have no claim here. Maybe we should use that. Present ourselves as a neutral third party that can mediate between them."

Thanien frowned. "But that would be endorsing their denial of Federation law."

"I'd prefer to say it's . . . choosing not to argue with it for now. The important thing is to get them to the table." She turned to T'Pol. "Captain, this is the only common ground they have. It's all we have to work with."

T'Pol judged it a well-reasoned point. But outwardly she merely nodded in acknowledgment, then turned to Thanien. "Commander?"

Grudgingly, the Andorian replied, "Granted, in the short term it could avert violence. But I'm concerned by the precedent it sets. There are enough fringe groups already trying to rebel against the Federation or dismantle it. The separatists on Alrond, the Anti-revisionists on Vulcan, the Centauri First movement—I'm worried enough about their popular support, especially with an election coming next year. And these groups seem like more of the same. I think it's more important in the long term to make a strong stand here."

"With respect, Commander," Sato said, "a crackdown would just provoke more resistance from groups like that. We'd be playing right into their rhetoric that we're an authoritarian state."

After a moment's contemplation, T'Pol said, "Commander Sato is correct. Our immediate priority is to avert bloodshed. We cannot let indefinite future ramifications impede us from fulfilling that duty. And portraying ourselves as a disinterested third party may be our best option in this case."

She could tell Thanien was displeased, but he acceded to her decision. "It will be a challenge to convince them to accept our neutrality," he said.

"This crew has surmounted greater challenges," T'Pol replied. She turned to Sato. "Commander—open a channel to both sides. Let us begin."

November 14, 2163
Starfleet Headquarters, San Francisco

"Both parties have agreed to Commander Sato's proposed resolution, Admiral," T'Pol reported over the monitor on Admiral Jonathan Archer's desk. *"The United Planets of Tellar will cede its claim to the Voortrekker asteroid, and said asteroid will be relocated to the neighboring Ross 271 system."*

Archer smiled at his former first officer. "That's good news, T'Pol. I never thought the Voortrekkers would go for it. It feels . . . like a retreat."

"To planetary inhabitants like ourselves, it would," T'Pol replied. *"Hoshi's insight was in recognizing that Boomers are accustomed to taking their homes with them. All they wanted was to keep the asteroid; where that asteroid is located is secondary. Ross 271 is close enough to the Tellarite-Denobulan trade routes to suit their needs nearly as well as Iota Pegasi."*

Archer shook his head. "Still—moving an asteroid that size across interstellar space won't be easy."

"Lieutenant Cutler has calculated that the asteroid can be accelerated to a maximum of twenty-seven percent of lightspeed before ablation from interstellar dust would become a serious hazard. Allowing for acceleration and deceleration, they should be able to reach the red dwarf within twenty years."

He whistled. "Twenty years. That's a long haul even for Boomers."

"Indeed. It should be interesting to observe how their culture develops over time. It is possible that the generation that comes to maturity once they reach their destination will be so accustomed to living in space that they see no need to remain in orbit of a star."

"Who knows? They wouldn't be the first Boomers to wander clear out of known space." He smiled. "I have a feeling that future explorers are going to find some unexpected human offshoots out there."

"Perhaps."

"So what about the Tellarites?" Archer went on. "They sounded pretty unwilling to give up that asteroid's mineral wealth."

"There are numerous other asteroids in the system, so the material loss is small. I believe their resistance was driven more by pride. Their perception that they have now convinced their rivals to retreat should be enough to let them save face."

The admiral nodded. "I know how important it is to Tellarites to appear strong."

But he frowned as he followed that thought further. "Still," he went on, "Commander Thanien had a point. We can't solve every internal problem by backing down and letting every faction assert its autonomy.

There are already too many groups that would just as soon dissolve the Federation or secede from it. Not to mention how many alien powers would be glad to help them." He recalled the recent attempt by the Orion Syndicate and the Malurians to manipulate the Federation into a military conflict, apparently hoping to provoke the increasingly pacifistic Vulcans into withdrawing from the still-tenuous union. The Orion agents who had been manipulating Federation officials had been flushed out (though actionable proof of the Syndicate's involvement remained elusive), but Archer had his suspicions that some Malurian moles may have gone undiscovered; after all, they were masters of disguise and infiltration.

Granted, it was likely that the separatist and isolationist factions on the Federation's member worlds were simply the kind of opposition parties that would naturally arise in any free, pluralistic society, and that their increasing size and passion was merely a backlash to the growing unity of the Federation, one that would pass once their predictions of dictatorship and dystopia failed to materialize. But even if they weren't being manipulated from without, giving the separatists too much rein could undermine the Federation's tenuous stability. "Sooner or later," he went on, "people are going to have to get used to the idea that Federation law applies to them."

"*I do not discount the commander's concerns, Admiral,*" T'Pol replied. "*But I tend to agree with Hoshi that we can win hearts and minds better through reason and benevolence than through intimidation.*"

Archer noted the difference in the way she referred to the two officers. "I hope you're right, T'Pol. But it's . . . logical . . . to consider other points of view too." He smiled. "I haven't always gotten along with my first officers, but I've learned how valuable it can be to listen to one who disagrees with me."

T'Pol held his gaze for a long moment. *"I see. I will take that under advisement, Admiral."*

Once she signed off, Archer asked his aide, Captain Williams, to contact the Tellarite councilor so he could pass along the good news. That was one fire put out—which meant he had that much more attention to spare for the others that were currently smoldering.

2164

1

February 12, 2164
Verex III, Orion-Klingon Borderland

". . . So WE CAN ALL SEE the benefits to such an alliance," intoned the burly Orion at the head of the meeting table, his gaze taking in each of his two guests in turn. "Working alone, the Vulcans were powerful enough to drive both of your organizations into retreat. Now they are part of a larger, even stronger Federation whose Starfleet patrols increasingly interfere with your efforts to stay in business. What better revenge," the green-skinned man went on in a polished baritone, "than to form a partnership of our own to stand against them?"

"The benefits of allying with your . . . employers are self-evident, Harrad-Sar," replied the Mazarite representative, Eldi Zankor. But then she sneered, the expression subtly stretching the scalloped flaps of skin that extended from her cheekbones to her ears. "But what can Jofirek here provide us? The Vulcans drove his syndicate from Agaron while I was still learning to walk, and he's been struggling for relevance ever since!" Despite the white hair of her temples and eyebrows, a typical trait of her species, Zankor was in the prime of her life, her ambition and ruthlessness—and the government purge of her predecessors some years before—allowing her to rise to the head of Mazar's crime syndicate at a precocious age.

The same could not be said for the wizened, silver-maned Agaron who sat across from her, the characteristic vertical ridge that bisected his people's foreheads almost lost amid a sea of wrinkles. "How dare you!" he wheezed. "My smuggling and narcotics connections span two sectors!"

"Two or three systems in each sector, at best. Why would you even want this fossil in our alliance, Harrad-Sar? He'd just be a drag on us."

"I've had forty years to rebuild *my* organization! Your group is still trying to pick up the pieces after the purge!"

Harrad-Sar spread his hands. "Please, please, my friends," he said. "The Federation's strength comes from its unity—its ability to set aside its members' differences in pursuit of their mutual interests. Our respective syndicates will be better able to stand against them if we learn from their example. This joint venture can benefit from Jofirek's experience, the connections and markers he's accumulated over the decades, as well as from the fervor and resources of the Mazarite cartel."

Watching through a pane of one-way glass from the next room, Navaar smiled at her slave's performance. "He's doing well," the merchant princess purred, absently twirling a lock of her luxuriant black hair around a slender green finger.

"He always was a quick study," replied her sister D'Nesh as a muscular male slave—bigger and younger than Harrad-Sar, with fewer and less elaborate metal adornments piercing his bare scalp—brushed her curly hair for her. "I guess you were right not to kill him after all."

"I knew he had it in him to redeem himself for his failure." In her private thoughts, Navaar admitted the truth: the failure to capture Jonathan Archer all those years ago, in retaliation for his disruption of the Orion Syndicate's slave market on this very planet, had rested as much with herself and her sisters as with their chief slave. Not only had Archer's officers somehow managed to overcome the Three Sisters' powerful pheromonal control, but Earth and its allies had learned the truth about Orion women: that they, or at least their most pheromonally potent elite lineages, were the actual rulers of Orion civilization rather than the slaves they pretended to be. On top of everything else, the Starfleet crew had crippled the warp drive of Harrad-Sar's ship and forced him and the Sisters to limp home at sublight; it had been nearly a year before their distress signals had reached another Orion ship, and the Sisters had spent much of that year punishing Harrad-Sar for his failure. D'Nesh had wanted to tear out all his piercings and keep tearing until there was nothing left but a pile of bones and organs. Maras would have been happy to watch and join in; the youngest Sister was a woman of simple pleasures.

But Navaar had recognized the truth: that they had simply been making Harrad-Sar the scapegoat for their own failure, driven by their fear of the consequences when they finally returned in disgrace. She had convinced her siblings that they would need to stick together more closely than ever to survive, to draw on their slaves' loyalty to the fullest rather than discarding them and trying to start fresh. Harrad-Sar had recognized in turn—with a little persuasion from his owners—that his own best chances of survival had come from helping the Sisters survive, and if anything, it had been the bonds the four had formed during that long trek home that had enabled them to weather their disgrace, emerge stronger, and eventually rise to their current leadership roles in the Syndicate.

"Your arguments are all well and good," Jofirek was saying to Harrad-Sar, "but I'm too important to deal with middlemen. When do I get to meet your employers?"

Zankor scoffed. "Restrain your lust, old man. Just the sight of them would probably give you a heart attack."

Navaar smiled, both at the compliment and the irony. While the Sisters' existence and importance were known to the higher-ups in other syndicates, few knew them on sight. Thus, Zankor and Jofirek were unaware that Maras was in the room with them, posing as one of the junior attendants who played a menial and generally decorative role in the proceedings—while a massive, nearly nude male slave tended to Zankor's needs. Although Maras's skills, to put it kindly, were far more in the physical sphere than the mental, she knew enough to avoid getting too close to Zankor, aware that pheromones as potent as the Sisters' could have an irritant effect on humanoid females. Zankor was confrontational enough without such a hormonal boost. But Maras sat near enough to Jofirek to make him aroused and suggestible, ensuring that he would do whatever Harrad-Sar asked in the Sisters' name.

Right now, Sar was assuring the old man that he was fully empowered to speak for the Syndicate. But Navaar was distracted by a grunt of displeasure from the being who stood to her left, also watching through the mirror. "Something troubles you, Garos?" she asked.

Dular Garos turned his broad, gray-scaled face to hers. "I share Zankor's skepticism about Jofirek's usefulness," the Malurian intoned in his deep, resonant voice. "In fact, negotiating with either is a waste of time. Both their organizations are in ruins, struggling for relevance. What can they possibly provide you that the Raldul alignment cannot?"

Behind them, D'Nesh laughed. "You're just jealous."

"I'm surprised at you, Garos," Navaar said with a gentler smile. "You understand our long-term objectives as well as anyone. To beat the Federation at their own game, we need to enlarge our alliance, draw on every resource we can. We need to be able to strike at them from all sides."

"Right," D'Nesh added. "And it can't hurt to have a couple of sacrificial beasts to throw their way if we need to."

Garos threw her a skeptical look. "Just so long as Maluria doesn't turn out to be the sacrifice."

"Garos, Garos," Navaar said, stroking his arm. "Do you really think we would have revealed ourselves to you so openly if we didn't value you as our closest ally?"

"You only revealed yourselves to me because you know Malurians respond to dominant females." As always, he was frustratingly unmoved by her instinctive efforts at seduction. Not only did his reptilian origins make him immune to Orion pheromones, but Malurian males were irrevocably bonded to the large, polyandrous females who generally remained on their homeworld, Malur. Garos was an exile from Maluria—the system containing Malur and its three colony planets—and every action he took was driven by the hope of returning home in glory one day.

"But you have seen us do the same with others of sufficient importance. The Basileus from Sauria, for example."

"Only when he failed to accept me as your representative," Garos said with irritation, still stung by the humiliation of Maltuvis's dismissal.

Navaar faced him squarely. "What would reassure you of our commitment to our partnership with Raldul?"

"Perhaps your attention to a matter of higher priority," he replied.

D'Nesh gave him a cute pout with steel behind it. "Such as?"

"Such as the situation with the Rigelian Trade Commission. The Lorillians and Axanar have been pressuring Rigel to enact more aggressive security and anti-piracy patrols in the Kandari Sector—even to join the Federation so they can have Starfleet protection! The Commission has already invited the Federation in for talks. And if Rigel joins them, then others will be quick to follow." He gestured at the negotiators on the other side of the mirror. "What good will it do to bring these minor players into our circle if the Federation nearly doubles its own size while our attention is elsewhere?"

"Come, Garos," Navaar said. "You worry too much about short-term concerns. We're playing a long game here."

"You may be. The Syndicate's territory is large enough that you can easily afford the loss if Rigel cracks down on crime and piracy in Kandari. But my alignment depends far more heavily on those revenues."

Navaar smiled. "And that is the benefit of our partnership! It lets us direct our attentions toward several goals at once. You are more than welcome to address the Rigel situation yourself if it troubles you so. We trust Raldul to have the skill and resources to carry out such a venture."

Garos sneered. "While you waste time playing seduction games with relics like these."

"You know better than that, my friend," Navaar told him, turning back to watch as both the crime lords finally acceded and affixed their thumbprints to the document of alliance. "This is a small piece in a much larger puzzle. And other, far more important stratagems are already in motion."

February 25, 2164
Patorco Harbor, Narpra, Sauria (Psi Serpentis IV)

Patorco had made Antonio Ruiz fall in love with darkness.

The harbor city was built into a vast, partly submerged lava tube on the edge of Narpra's largest island, its homes and businesses carved into the living rock of the walls. Dozens of tiers of dwellings arched over harborside paths worn smooth by eight millennia of webbed footsteps, and over heavy wooden piers that could be pulled up to serve as dikes when Sauria's frequent, fierce storms flooded the cavern. Far overhead, Ruiz could glimpse the mesh of carefully bred, broad-leafed plants that spanned the gaps in the roof, filtering the sunlight during the day to shield the Saurians' vast nocturnal eyes while storing its energy in a calorie-rich vegetable oil used as both a fuel and a culinary staple. But at this time of year, Psi Serpentis A was in the sky for only a third of a day at this latitude, and only the faint illumination of its distant red-dwarf companion, about as bright as a crescent moon on Earth, currently showed through the leaves.

Yet the water shimmered, its bioluminescent algae casting a gentle blue glow up from the harbor. Overhead, highly polished sheets of gold, silver, and bronze, plus more modern mirrors, caught and redistributed the light from the harbor, while streetlamps full of bioluminescent insects added a mix of gentle hues to the light. It was dim by human standards; Ruiz and his fellow Federation consultants carried night-vision visors as a matter of course, and he made sure to spend a few hours a day in a bright room and take daily melatonin supplements to stave off darkness-induced depression. But in his months on Sauria, he had learned to make do with the crepuscular lighting the Saurians favored, so that he could see this city's beauty the way it was meant to be seen. Everything about this place was a triumph of engineering, both mechanical and biological. As an engineer himself, Ruiz had to appreciate that.

Of course, the company was the other main draw. Narprans were an exuberant, friendly people, and they evoked those qualities in others. Ruiz certainly found Narpra more agreeable than M'Tezir, the first Saurian nation where he and his fellow mining engineers had been sent to teach environmentally sound techniques. The geological forces that had created the narrow M'Tezir continent—essentially one vast mountain range thrusting out of the ocean—had also brought the dilithium, duranium, and rare earths in the planet's mantle closer to the surface there than just about anywhere else on Sauria, making it the main focus of Federation mining efforts. But the new wealth the deal had brought to the formerly impoverished land mass had yet to trickle down to M'Tezir's commoners, whom Ruiz had found furtive, somber, and wary of outsiders. Their ruler, an old-style warlord called Maltuvis, was making nice with the Federation and the Saurian Global League in order to profit from the trade agreement, but that hadn't yet extended to improving the way he treated his subjects—people who hoarded what little they had and saw outsiders as potential competitors, a xenophobia that Maltuvis readily encouraged. Ruiz had been much happier upon relocating here to Narpra, a Global League member whose constituent islands arced between M'Tezir's northern tip and the west coast of the planet's largest continent. Not only was the cooler climate more comfortable for Ruiz—still tropical by Earth standards but not too different from his native Cuba—but the social climate was far warmer. He and his colleagues had been readily incorporated into their Narpran protégés' social lives.

Ruiz grinned as Redik's, the miners' favorite sauna bar, came into view. The local miners had been bringing the humans here for weeks, and Ruiz had taken to it readily. The Saurians were already famous across the stars for their brandy, whose potent charms Ruiz appreciated, but he'd developed a particular liking for Narpran rum, a dark and flavorful spirit distilled from a seaweed cultivated by local divers. He also had a definite fondness for the hot spring–fueled sauna and steam room facilities in the back, particularly since Laila Alindogan partook of them regularly—and was considerably more comfortable with the local custom of group nudity in saunas than Ruiz was. On more than a few occasions, the two of them had ended up going home together after a few lively hours drinking and sweating with their friends. (Not that Saurians sweated, of course, but they benefited from the heat and humidity in their own way.)

But when the group entered Redik's this time, they

found the mood oddly subdued, the patrons muttering quietly. Some threw furtive glances toward Ruiz, Laila, and the other offworlders as the group came up to the bar. In the darkness, it took a moment for Ruiz to figure out what else was wrong with the scene. "Where's Karep?" he asked. The lanky, golden-brown Narpran male was a fixture here, a seasoned rumweed diver and mariner with a seemingly endless supply of tales of adventure and debauchery accumulated over a century and a half of life. Ruiz didn't yet know enough about Saurian history, oceanography, or sexuality to judge how much Karep embellished his accounts; but he often thought that, in a way, he'd be disappointed if they turned out to be true in every detail, for the old salt was an artist with their telling, at least once you got a few liters of rum into him. Saurian biochemistry made them resistant to most toxins, so they could hold their liquor far better than a human, but they still found it relaxing and stimulating—at least when it was suitably strong.

The bartender, a pink-complexioned female named Bavot, lowered her bulging orange eyes and wiped down the bar. "Karep is out tonight."

"Out?" Ruiz protested. "He's never out! He practically lives here!"

Another regular, a big, red-hued longshoreman called Naralo, threw the human a surly look. "He's not here. He's . . . sick."

Ruiz was as startled as the rest of his group. In all the months he'd been here, he'd never seen a Saurian come down with so much as the sniffles. No wonder everyone was so quiet.

"Well . . . well, then," Ruiz said after a moment, "Bavot, a round for everyone, on me. We'll drink to Karep's health."

Narálo blinked in confusion. "You mean . . . drink until he's healthy again?"

"No, no, it's a toast. It's a way of wishing him a speedy recovery."

The big Saurian tilted his egg-shaped head. "And you humans believe that our having drinks will somehow make him healthier?"

"Well, no, not really. It's just . . ."

Laila came to his rescue. "It's just a way of paying tribute. Expressing our shared concern and sympathy."

"Sounds more like you're using his misfortune as an excuse to drink," Naralo grunted. But then Bavot put his own free drink in front of him, and he studied it for a moment. "But I didn't say it was a bad custom. To Karep's health, then!"

The mood soon lightened—the group was still subdued, but sociable, and the drink loosened them up. Eventually, as was customary, they headed back for the saunas. But in the changing room, Naralo suddenly staggered, nearly knocking the half-undressed Laila over. Ruiz caught her arm to steady her. "Hey," he said, chuckling. "I think for once I'm more sober than you, big guy."

"No, this is. . . . My head hurts. I need . . ." The big Saurian breathed heavily, emitting a wheezing sound.

Laila guided him to a bench, then frowned and felt his forehead. "You're feeling a bit warm. Do Saurians get fevers?"

"I never . . . have. Just . . . let me rest, I'll be fine."

She felt his pulse. "Are you sure? Your hearts are racing." Ruiz was still just sober enough to resist asking which one was winning.

Another bar patron, a female bearing the distinctive lilac skin tone of the M'Tezir, stared at Naralo. "I've seen this before. Karep had the same symptoms. It's spreading!" She turned an accusing glare on Ruiz. "You! You humans were sitting next to him. And you were in Karep's sauna the other night!"

"Come on, Rolanis," Laila said, "there's no reason—"

But Rolanis was backing away in alarm, retrieving her clothes. "Stay back! It's you offworlders. Bringing your weakness, your disease! Contaminating us!" She ran out, ignoring the calls from her friends to calm down.

Laila was now helping Naralo get dressed, offering to escort him home. Ruiz looked around at the other Saurians, noting their unease. "Maybe I'd better go, too."

"No," one of his miner friends assured him. "It's just the ravings of a drunk. M'Tezir aren't used to indulging as much, can't handle it as well."

The other Saurian miners chimed in, assuring Ruiz that they didn't take Rolanis's accusations seriously and would still gladly share a sauna or a drink with him. After seeing off Laila—who promised to return once she'd gotten Naralo home safely—he acceded to his friends' invitation.

Still, Ruiz caught some furtive looks from the

other patrons in neighboring saunas, and a few chose to give him and the other offworlders a wide berth.

March 16, 2164
Starfleet Headquarters, San Francisco

Danica Erickson gazed out the window of the Starfleet commissary and sighed. "Do you ever miss it?"

Jonathan Archer followed her gaze, taking in their elevated view of the San Francisco coastline and Marina Boulevard. "Miss what?"

She turned her strong-featured, dark-complexioned face back to his. "Being able to go for a walk on the Promenade or have lunch at Fisherman's Wharf without needing a security detail to keep the reporters at bay. Just being Jon and Dani instead of the great admiral and the 'daughter of the transporter'."

Archer nursed his iced tea for a moment. "I guess I'm used to it. This is my life now, and I can still make the best of it, even if it's not the life we had when we were young."

Her big dark eyes widened in mock outrage. "Hunh! Young*er*, please!" They shared a chuckle, but her mirth faded swiftly. "At least you have something real to accomplish. Me, I don't have any answers for them. I'm not the transporter genius my father was. But that never stops them from asking me how long it'll be before it's safe to use transporters again. I feel I can't even go out in public anymore."

Archer nodded, understanding her refusal to have

anything to do with transporter research after all the losses her family had suffered as a result of her late father's work developing the technology. She'd only stayed with Emory Erickson as long as she had in order to care for him after the transporter accident that had crippled him.

But then Dani caught herself. "Oh, I'm sorry, Jon. I realize my petty problems don't compare to what transporters did to you . . ."

He gently waved off his childhood friend's concern. "It's okay. It's barely even a problem anymore. Phlox's latest treatments have pretty much halted the nerve damage and repaired most of it. I'll never be quite back to top fighting form, but then, I probably wouldn't be anyway now that I'm not . . . young*er* . . . anymore," he finished, echoing her emphasis.

"Well, that's good to know, at least." She shook her head. "I'm almost glad Dad passed on before he found out about this. The thought that his invention was hurting people because of something he missed—"

Archer reached out and rested his hand atop hers. "Hey. It wasn't anyone's fault. The assembly errors are cumulative, gradual. Nobody could've known until transporters were in heavy use for years."

"He still would've blamed himself. You know that. You know how obsessive he could be about—" She broke off, remembering how her father's desperate experiment to retrieve her lost brother from transporter limbo had led to the accidental death of one of Archer's crew and Erickson's own incarceration for the final years of his life. Danica herself had not been held accountable for her involvement, partly due to Archer's advocacy; but it had scuttled her ambitions for joining Starfleet, forcing her to settle for a civilian engineering career.

He squeezed her hand more firmly for a moment. "It's okay. We caught it in time, you know. Nobody's died from it. And I'm sure we'll crack the problem sooner or later. For now, we just have to get places the old-fashioned way—in skimmers and shuttlepods."

She chuckled. "Just like our primitive forebears."

"That's right." He was glad to see her bright smile again. "Oh, speaking of travel," Archer went on, hoping to distract her further from her regrets, "I'm going to be heading out on *Endeavour* next week."

"Oh! Back in space again, good for you! Where to this time?"

"The Beta Rigel system. Since we helped them with the Vertian crisis last year, the Rigelian Trade Commission has been more receptive to the possibility of joining the Federation, and President Vanderbilt wants me to help convince them."

"The Trade Commission?" Danica asked. "How is it their decision?"

"They're the de facto government of the Rigel worlds—at least, the allied ones. The individual planets and colonies have their own local governments, but it's the Trade Commission that's managed commerce and communication among the inhabited worlds of the system since it was founded six hundred years ago. So it's evolved into the administrative body that holds the alliance together."

"Sort of like the way the British East India Company ran the British Empire's colonies."

"Something like that, but more egalitarian and not for profit. Almost like the Federation in some ways, just on a more local scale. That's part of why the president thinks they're a good prospect for membership."

"They're big, too. Multiple planets and . . . how many species?"

"Three native intelligent species. Let's see, there are the Jelna from Rigel V; they're the ones with the gray skin and green and black facial tattoos. There are the Zami from Rigel IV—that planet isn't part of the trading community, but they have a large expatriate population on Five and on the Rigel II colony."

"They're related to Vulcans, right?"

"They're very similar, though we're not sure how or if they're related. They have less pointed ears and generally have lighter hair—many of them could almost pass for human." He took a sip of his tea. "And then there are the chelonian bipeds from Rigel III—basically big shell-less tortoises. Their name is hard to pronounce, so we call them Chelons."

"But they all like to be called Rigelians."

"That's right—even the colonists from other races like the Xarantines and Coridanites. Don't get me wrong, they value their cultural plurality, but they take pride in the larger community they're part of. They usually see themselves as Rigelians first and different species second." He gave her a wry grin. "Plus it doesn't hurt to present a united front to the rest of the galaxy—or to play up Rigel's reputation as an economic powerhouse."

"Something tells me that reputation is why the president is so keen to have them join."

"True, it would help boost the Federation's economic and political standing. And maybe add even more names to our roster—since Vanderbilt hopes that where Rigel leads, its trading partners will soon follow. He's determined to see the Federation grow and solidify itself before his term ends. Plus, with Vega Colony applying for membership, adding a multispecies community like Rigel at the same time would help ease concerns about humans becoming too dominant in the Federation."

"Well, the more, the merrier."

"Anyway, I've still got my work cut out for me," Archer went on. "Joining the Federation would mean adopting certain laws and regulations about interstellar commerce and security. But the Rigelians pride themselves on their so-called 'tolerant' trading practices, which means they'll deal with just about anybody and not be too picky about the legalities. That's one reason why it would mean so much to get them to join—it would help curb interstellar piracy and groups like the Orion Syndicate. It would—" He noticed that Danica's eyes were glazing over a bit. "I'm sorry, I'm boring you."

"It's not that, exactly," she said. "I was just thinking . . . all you ever seem to talk about anymore is your work."

He shrugged. "They do keep me pretty busy around here."

"I know, but . . . don't you ever feel there's

something missing? I can't remember the last time I heard you talk about going on a date or being in love. At least, not since . . ."

She trailed off, but he completed her thought. "Not since Erika."

"Jon . . ." Now she reached out and took his hand. "I know how much she meant to you, but it's been seven years. Sometimes I worry about you. I'm afraid you're going to end up alone."

"It's not . . . that I'm not open to the possibility," he said. "It's just . . . other things keep getting in the way."

"You were always busy," she said. "You're the most driven man I know. But you didn't always let that keep you from having a social life."

"No. But . . . it kept it from getting too deep." He reflected back on Margaret Mullin, the woman he'd loved in flight school. She'd turned down his marriage proposal on the grounds that he cared more about Starfleet than about her. He'd been devastated at the time, but it hadn't affected his absolute commitment to Starfleet, and he'd since come to realize that he would never have been able to commit to her as much as she'd deserved. He'd had other flings in subsequent years—Caroline, Rebecca, even Ruby from the 602 Club, though she'd been equally "close" to quite a few other flyboys. The one other woman he'd grown truly attached to was Erika Hernandez, but they'd had to break it off when he'd been promoted above her. Once aboard *Enterprise*, his only romantic fling of note had been with the intrepid scientist Riann on the Akaali homeworld; after that, the only women he'd been involved with were either illusions created by shapeshifting aliens or spies sent to extract information.

Then Erika had become captain of her own *NX*-class starship, *Columbia,* and she and Archer had rekindled their relationship at last. But *Columbia* had been lost in the first year of the Romulan War. Since then . . . since then there had only been his work.

He shook his head. "I'm not the young hotshot I used to be, Dani. These days . . . after what I had with Erika, what I—when I think about what we could've had if she'd lived . . ."

She smiled in sympathy. "I understand, Jon. It'd have to be something deep enough, meaningful enough, to compare to that."

"And I'm just not sure I have the attention to devote to that now. Not while there's still so much work to do to get the Federation through its growing pains."

Her brows rose wistfully. "But is there ever going to be a time when the work ends?"

Archer had no reply. Instead he tried to brush it off with a smile. "Hey, don't worry about me. I've still got Porthos."

It did little to reassure her. She knew as well as he did that Archer's beloved beagle was getting on in years, and even modern geriatrics could only do so much. Porthos might still have a few good years in him, but nothing lasted forever.

They spent the rest of lunch talking about inconsequential things. When they parted, Danica hugged him longer and tighter than usual. After she'd left,

Archer found himself wondering if there'd been a sub-text to her talk of romance that he'd overlooked.

Dani? No way. They'd been friends since childhood, more like brother and sister than anything else. Sure, she was smart and beautiful and warm, a good catch for anyone, but there was no way she could think of him in that way.

Is there?

2

T'POL PAUSED on the threshold of her groundside apartment, sharpening her senses. She wasn't familiar enough with the environment to judge if anything was out of place; though Starfleet maintained it for her use when *Endeavour* was at Earth, Admiral Archer allowed the vessel to spend more time abroad on exploratory or diplomatic missions than was typical for an admiral's personal flagship. Still, she sensed something that did not belong in an unoccupied dwelling. As she advanced into the main room, allowing the door to close behind her, she refined her impression . . . soon realizing that what she sensed was a familiar presence, and a welcome one.

She turned just in time to see a lanky figure in black coming up behind her. "Trip," she greeted in the most casual and unsurprised tone she could muster.

The light-haired human whom she knew as Charles Tucker (despite his having abandoned any open use of that name upon feigning his death nine years before) rolled his eyes, though he was smiling as well. "Shoulda known I couldn't sneak up on you."

She did not soften her stance. "How did you get in here? The door was locked."

Trip smirked. "Maybe I beamed in."

T'Pol gave him a disapproving glare. "That would be most unwise. You realize the damage is cumulative, and you have been transported more than most."

"I said 'maybe.'" He shrugged. "Guy's gotta have some secrets."

She turned away. "That is not amusing."

After a moment, she felt his hand on her shoulder. "Hey. What is it, T'Pol?"

She hesitated briefly, then her hand went to his. "I . . . your safety is a source of ongoing concern to me. I have . . . had unusually many opportunities to fear your imminent or actual death."

She didn't have to see him to know he was giving an understanding nod, narrowing his lips. "And you're upset about my line of work puttin' me in danger."

"There is more than that." She walked away, not to distance herself but merely to release tension. She paced around him, a body in orbit—the bond that drew them together balancing the momentum of her motion. "This ongoing pretense of your nonexistence. Having to meet only in secret or through our tele- pathic bond. Keeping the truth from Hoshi and other friends." She stopped and turned to face him. "How long can we sustain this, Trip?"

He stared. "Is this the talk?" he said at length. "The 'where are we going' talk?"

"It is a valid question to consider." She tilted her head, eyes darting and lips pursing. "There has been a certain . . . stimulation . . . to the challenge of main- taining a relationship in secret. In the short term, it does have its fascinations. But have we no goals beyond the short term? Have you?"

"I . . . I dunno," Trip replied. "Like you said, I've kinda gotten used to not plannin' on a long-term future. Not . . . that I'm in any hurry to give up breathin'," he assured her when he saw her reaction. "I just—I've learned to make the most of livin' in the moment."

He underlined his position by kissing her, drawing her into his embrace. She found it agreeable to indulge his professed philosophy for now. It had been too long since they had been together in the flesh. Her ability to sublimate her emotional responses was limited at the best of times, but her feelings for Trip strained her Vulcan disciplines to the breaking point. Her need for release was not nearly as intense as the compulsion of *pon farr*, but it was close enough.

Once they were sated, they showered together briefly, after which she stepped into the air-drying tube. "Hey, why not stay here a while longer?" Trip invited.

She closed her eyes, concentrating on the sensation of the powerful air flow against her skin. The laminar current was quiet enough that she could speak normally. "You know that Vulcans do not thrive in conditions of high humidity."

"Come on, live a little. It'll be fun."

She opened one eye to give him a sidelong glance. "More of your 'live in the moment' philosophy? Enjoy the here and now, even if it harms you in the long term?"

"I guess so."

"Is it not more logical to attempt to optimize all future moments, rather than simply the current one?"

He shut off the shower and came to join her in the air tube. "So what are you suggesting? Where do you plan for this to go? We can't exactly have a close relationship as long as you're a starship captain."

"You could reveal yourself. Resume your Starfleet commission." He winced. "I know you feel you have changed too much, compromised too much. I know you are reluctant to face your former friends."

"You've been talkin' to Jonathan."

"I've been sharing minds with you," she riposted.

"All the more reason you should understand why I can't come back." He fidgeted. "Top o' everything else . . . if I did come back to Starfleet, explained what I've been doin' all these years, I'd serve out my whole tour on a penal asteroid."

T'Pol had to concede he had a point. The agency he worked for had ambiguous legal authority at best, relying on a certain interpretation of the imprecise wording of Section 31 of the Earth Starfleet charter—a section that, perhaps suspiciously, had been copied without alteration into the Federation Starfleet charter upon the merger of the founder worlds' space services. Officially, their actions were performed without the knowledge or sanction of Starfleet Command, and thus they had no legal protection if their actions were exposed.

She sighed, stepping out of the tube and turning to face him. "So this is all we can have? The status quo?"

He came out to join her, meeting her eyes. "Can you live with that?"

"That remains to be seen."

Recognizing that they were at an impasse, they let the subject drop, helping each other into light robes before leaving the 'fresher. Trip tried to steer the conversation onto a new topic once she had reached the bedroom and begun brushing her shoulder-length hair. "So how soon before you and Jonathan ship out to Rigel?"

She quirked a brow. "You are aware of *Endeavour*'s itinerary?"

"I keep current."

"We leave in two days," she said. "Are you available for the duration?"

"Far as I know." He stepped closer. "By the way, we've been pickin' up some chatter from those parts. The Malurians have put out some feelers to the First Families on Rigel IV. We're concerned they might want to sabotage the Federation talks."

"That is neither anomalous nor surprising. The Malurian crime syndicate has had dealings in Rigelian space for decades."

"All the more reason they'd want to try to screw up this agreement. T'Pol, you remember what a mess Garos caused last time. He shouldn't be taken lightly."

She turned to him. "I am doing nothing of the sort. I simply question why this is any business of your section."

He sighed. "I know, I know. I get it enough from you and Jonathan both: the section's about dealin' with extraordinary threats, so why butt into everyday Starfleet problems?"

"Exactly. The Federation's safety is our responsibility. Your 'Section Thirty-one' is an adjunct at best. Yet sometimes it seems as if you perceive that relationship in reverse."

"It's not that," he said, stepping closer. "It's just . . . I worry about you, T'Pol. I want to keep an eye on you, make sure you're safe."

She put down the hairbrush and rose, staring at him. "You believe that makes it better? Trip, I am the captain of a Starfleet flagship. I am not a damsel in distress from one of your antiquated movies."

"That's not what this is about! I'm just . . . tryin' to help out. To do what I do now, but on your behalf. Because you're someone important to me."

"'Someone important.' A nebulous characterization. Why should I accept your unsolicited intervention when neither of us even knows how our relationship is defined?"

"So now you're mad at me because I care about you?"

"Because you seem to care more about your secrets, your evasions, and your games of deceit."

"It's my life now. I can't help that."

"And what kind of life is it? A life without truth is illogical. Surak wrote that the truth is simply the actual state of the universe. To live at odds with the truth is to be in conflict with reality itself. Such an existence is unsustainable."

Trip threw up his hands. "Good ol' Surak, a quote for every occasion. Like Vulcans are some great paragons of truth. What about that Kolinahr thing Surak preached? Purging all emotion forever? You and I both know there's no such thing as a Vulcan without emotion. Where's the truth in that?"

She gave him an icy glare. "You are attempting to offend me in order to avoid confronting my questions about yourself."

"Well, evasion seems to be what I do now, doesn't it?" He began pulling on his pants under his robe. "Maybe I better just be true to form and slink back into the shadows."

"If that is where you are most comfortable."

He tossed the robe aside and pulled on his shirt. "If you don't mind, I'll show myself out."

"Technically, I never invited you in."

He gave her a meaningful stare. "Now, we both know that's a lie."

T'Pol merely stared back in silence until he left.

Then she curled up in bed, alone, and longed for sleep that never came.

March 24, 2164
U.S.S. Endeavour, Kandari Sector

"The Rigelians are hiding something," said Aranthanien ch'Revash.

Captain T'Pol studied her first officer from across the situation table at the rear of *Endeavour*'s bridge. "Why do you say that, Commander?"

They stood around the table with Lieutenant

Commander Hoshi Sato and Lieutenant Elizabeth Cutler, discussing the scientific surveys they would undertake of the Raij'hl system (which humans called Beta Rigel to distinguish it from their soundalike name for a more distant star) while Admiral Archer handled the political negotiations. The system was astrophysically unusual—not necessarily for having multiple planets in its habitable zone, for many star systems were similarly densely packed, but for having all of them be Minshara-class and actually inhabited. Not to mention that its primary star Raij was a type-A subgiant and thus should not be long-lived enough to host life-sustaining worlds. The Rigelians' leading theory, Cutler had explained, was that it had originally been a binary pair of smaller, slower-burning stars that had merged together shortly before multicellular life arose in the system—the resultant upheavals possibly prompting faster evolution as life was challenged to adapt.

But Thanien's interest was in the twin-world system currently displayed on the situation table, Rigel VII and VIII. The latter was a barren, heavily cratered and ridged ice planet, like some of the sister moons of Andoria; any liquid water it held was buried a thousand kilometers or more beneath its icy crust. But the larger Rigel VII was a more terrestrial world, beyond the habitable zone but heated by internal radioisotopes and tidal kneading from its sister planet's gravity, and thus warm enough to host sparse but stable oceans and a viable ecosystem—as well as an indigenous humanoid population. "The databases they have sent us say almost nothing about these Kalar. Nothing about their origins, their biology, their government. Why so little information?"

The science officer pursed her lips. "Well, the Kalar aren't part of the Trade Commission, sir, and aren't even spacefaring like Rigel IV. And there's a total ban on contact, so the other Rigelians wouldn't have much sociological information."

"Even so, there must have been enough early contact to give them reason to forbid subsequent interaction. Yet the information here is not even commensurate with that. There is no data on how the other Rigelians became aware of these Kalar in the first place." He frowned, antennae curving forward and wide in wariness. "It smells of secrets. Once we reach the system, I recommend we investigate. Conduct extensive scans of Rigel VII, perhaps send a shuttlepod to conduct a clandestine survey."

"Is that wise?" Sato asked. "We're in the middle of some pretty delicate negotiations with the Rigelians. We don't want to risk offending them."

Thanien turned to her. "Nor do we want to risk inviting them into the Federation without knowing what it is they wish to hide from us, and why."

The communications officer nodded. "Granted. It's worth trying to find out. But we should find a way to broach the subject delicately, give them the chance to tell us themselves. If they seem to be hiding something, then we can look into diplomatic avenues to convince them to be more open. We shouldn't just go sneaking around."

Thanien closed his eyes for a moment and sighed. "You are being naïve, Hoshi. All governments spy on other governments, even potential allies. It is a natural part of the vetting process."

"We should at least show them the common courtesy of asking first."

"That would tip them off to our interest."

"Of course we're interested! That won't come as a surprise to them."

"Nonetheless—"

"Commander." T'Pol spoke softly, but it was enough to bring Thanien up short. "Hoshi is correct. At this point, the nature of the Kalar is a matter of scientific curiosity, nothing more. Without good reason, there is no logic in risking the disruption of our diplomatic relationship with Rigel in order to sate our curiosity. I am sure that Admiral Archer will agree."

She delivered that last comment pointedly, aware of the esteem in which Thanien held the admiral. Yet that did not mollify him. If anything, it made him feel manipulated. He held his peace as the briefing continued, but once it ended, he requested to speak with the captain in her ready room.

"How may I help you, Commander?" she asked as the bare metal door closed, securing them within the compact, Spartan volume of the captain's office.

He replied with care. "Captain . . . *I* am here to help *you*. As your first officer, my responsibility is to be your chief advisor."

"I am aware of your job description, having held the position myself."

He knew she did not mean to be snide, but it did not seem like her to retreat behind Vulcan literalism. Perhaps she was simply puzzled, in which case it would be best if he got to the point. "But it seems to me that you more often default to Commander Sato's advice. I am aware you have served together for many years . . . that you consider her a friend and confidante. On a personal level, you are wholly entitled to that relationship, of course. Yet it sometimes feels to me as though you allow that friendship to get in the way of the proper chain of command."

T'Pol studied him icily for some moments. "I see. Then let me assure you that is not the case."

"I would be assured by your actions, not your words."

"Commander—Thanien—while I understand your concern, the fact of the matter is that it is unwarranted. While I would need to review ship's logs to compute a precise figure, I would estimate that in those instances when your advice and Commander Sato's have come into conflict, I have favored hers no more than . . ." She paused, eyes drifting upward for a moment. ". . . fifty-seven percent of the time."

"More than half."

"You are not in competition with Hoshi, Thanien. I consider advice from all my senior staff and other relevant advisors in making my decisions. Just because I do not make a choice aligning with yours, that does not mean your input has not been valuable to my decision-making process." Her mouth quirked slightly, a brow along with it. "In my time as Jonathan Archer's first officer, he frequently arrived at decisions that went against my recommendations. Sometimes, he was even proven right." Thanien knew T'Pol well enough by now to recognize the deadpan humor in her delivery. "Yet I came to understand that I was of value to him as a sounding board and a source of alternatives, even when we did not agree. Indeed, those experiences led me to the opinion that a first officer who is routinely in agreement with their captain is somewhat . . . redundant."

She rose from her desk and stepped closer to Thanien. "If your suggestions do not routinely win out, it is because your training is that of a military officer, while this is a vessel of exploration. Yet it is precisely because of that difference in perspective that I shared Admiral Archer's belief that you would make a fine first officer for *Endeavour*. I find our command dynamic similar to that which I shared with Malcolm Reed while he was my first officer—though of course you bring your own unique perspective."

Thanien considered her words. "Very well. I understand, and I appreciate the explanation."

T'Pol studied him. "Yet you still seem uncertain."

"I accept that you appreciate my place in the chain of command. I still wonder whether Commander Sato does. You and she have served together longer than anyone on this crew save Phlox. It sometimes feels to me that she assumes a special standing in the crew as a result."

"I have perceived no indication of that," T'Pol said. "For myself, I have no reason to doubt her appreciation of the proper chain of command. Any problem you have with her, Commander . . . I suggest you resolve with her."

When Thanien arrived in sickbay, still mulling over his talk with the captain, he found Doctor Phlox feeding the menagerie of strange creatures that the physician kept on hand for medicinal purposes. Generally Thanien liked to time his arrival to coincide with the end of the feeding process; he found several of the creatures unnerving and didn't like to lose his appetite just before taking the doctor to lunch. He knew he'd been on time as always, so Phlox must have been delayed. Perhaps the news broadcast playing on the main sickbay monitor was the cause.

"Ah, Thanien!" the cheery Denobulan called. "Forgive the delay—I've been caught up in listening to the news. A major development in the presidential race today—T'Nol is throwing her support behind Councilor Thoris!"

The news was startling enough to make Thanien's antennae recoil slightly. "That seems unlikely."

"Listen for yourself," Phlox replied, gesturing to the monitor.

Indeed, the subspace news feed was replaying a press conference held earlier in the day (according to the caption) by Professor T'Nol, leader of the Vulcan Anti-revisionist Party and—until today—one of multiple candidates for Federation president in the election that would be held later in the year. This would be the first presidential election under the rules recently ratified by the Federation Council, the first whose winner would serve a full four-year term. And the sitting president, Thomas Vanderbilt of Earth, had chosen not to run for re-election. Thus, the stakes were high and the field was wide open. Every group with an agenda had someone in the race, making for a lively campaign.

But this was the last development Thanien had expected, and the question asked by Earth journalist Gannet Brooks reflected his own thoughts. *"Professor, your movement up to now has advocated rolling back the post-Kir'shara reforms on Vulcan and restoring the High Command and its policies—including its antagonistic stance toward Andoria. How do you reconcile that with backing Councilor Thoris's candidacy?"*

T'Nol, a stern-featured and rail-thin Vulcan woman just past middle age, gave a measured reply. *"It is true that there are many points of conflict between the traditional Vulcan values we represent and those of the Andorian Empire. But one thing on which we agree is our right to preserve that very freedom of dissent—the right of every world, every species, to retain its unique and separate identity. On every world in the Federation, movements have arisen in protest of the haste with which the union was imposed upon us. Yet the voices that advocate greater consolidation and homogenization of our disparate societies have the intrinsic advantage of being united behind a single movement, a single candidate. Those of us who seek to defend our racial independence against that spreading federalism cannot hope to succeed so long as we act separately. Thus, the logical solution is to cooperate in standing against that which we all oppose, at least until we have succeeded in its defeat.*

"*I have assessed the relative standings of the various Planetarist candidates and have determined that the candidate with the highest probability of victory over Councilor al-Rashid is Councilor Thoris. He is an experienced and respected statesman and is better known on an interstellar stage than other candidates such as myself. He has a sizeable coalition backing his efforts already and a well-organized support structure for fundraising and message promotion. If the Anti-revisionists, Lechebists, and other Planetarist and pro-independence factions combine their support behind Anlenthoris ch'Vhendreni, our estimates show his odds of victory to be at least sixty-one percent, based on currently known variables.*"

"Quite a stimulating twist, isn't it?" Phlox asked with relish. "I wonder if they'll actually be able to make a partnership work, or if their traditional rivalries and resentments will scuttle the whole thing."

"People like that are generally poor at tolerating those they disagree with," Thanien replied, his current mood inclining him to cynicism. "I doubt it was so easy for the Anti-revisionists to set aside their hatred of Andorians. I'd just bet that T'Nol's 'logical' calculation was helped along by some generous concession or payoff from Thoris's camp." Phlox simply chuckled at his cynical assessment and continued feeding his Calrissian chameleon.

Now the broadcast had switched to an excerpt from Councilor Thoris's response. Andoria's erstwhile ambassador and foreign minister was a thin-faced, aging *chan* with a reedy but commanding voice. "*I am grateful for this endorsement,*" he said, "*not only for how it affects my political chances, but because it shows that despite our different views, goals, and ways of life, the races and cultures of the*

Federation are able to choose to work together when it is in our common interest. And that is precisely why the centralization of government that we see occurring with such haste is unnecessary, and why it must be halted before it compromises our planetary sovereignty. The members of the Federation rushed into union in the wake of the Romulan War, out of the desire for a strong and united defense. But while such mutual defense is certainly of value, in our haste we failed to consider the negative consequences of entrusting too much power to a central state. The Articles of Federation contain too few provisions for protecting planetary rights and resisting cultural homogenization. Starfleet has been given too much power of enforcement in matters that should be the purview of the members' own security forces. Is it right that we even have a combined, consolidated Starfleet? Is it not better for each member world to bear responsibility for its own defense, to have forces specialized for its own particular needs?"

Thanien's mouth twisted in scorn. It was a small-minded, ignorant objection. Starfleet was still quite a diverse organization, with each member world's space agency assigned to its own particular specialty: exploration and diplomacy for the United Earth Space Probe Agency, border defense for the Andorian Guard, operational support and supply for the Tellar Space Administration, and so on. But that mix of specialties benefitted all the member worlds equally. And Thanien had learned as much from his fourteen months aboard *Endeavour*—an Earth-built, human-crewed ship with a Vulcan captain and a Denobulan chief medical officer—as he had from his thirty-two years in the Guard.

"And is it right," Thoris continued, *"for the Vanderbilt*

administration to be in such haste to enlarge the Federation by pressuring the Rigel system to join along with the Vega Colony? The current member states must already compete for standing and resources with five other members. How much more will each of our influence and independence be diminished if we must compete with seven others? Or ten, or twenty? How much further will our individual cultures be eroded away, subsumed within a mixture of so many ingredients? And what precedent does this imperialistic fervor set for the future?"

"Sad," Thanien observed. "Thoris was one of the strongest advocates of cooperation against the Romulans. His willingness to share Andorian technology was critical to Earth's victory." He shook his head. "To see him pandering to the voices of fear and isolation just to win an election—it's pitiful."

"Try not to be so hard on him," Phlox said, "or them. There's value in considering all points of view. That's the key to democracy!" He grinned widely.

The feed was now showing a rebuttal from Thoris's principal rival, Earth's Councilor Haroun al-Rashid. *"What candidates such as my fellow councilor and Professor T'Nol are overlooking is that the type of loose partnership they advocate has already been tried, and failed, as the Coalition of Planets. History has shown us that we need a partnership strong enough that it will not disintegrate at the first sign of trouble. And last year's incident between the Tellarite and Boomer colonists at Iota Pegasi shows that we need clearly defined guidelines for managing disputes and delineating rights and responsibilities among our members. We need institutions in place that will guarantee and facilitate our cooperation while still protecting our sovereign rights."*

Phlox finished up his feeding rounds and moved to

the monitor. "Shall we go to lunch now, or would you like to keep watching?"

"No, I have no interest in hearing more," Thanien said.

Phlox shrugged and shut off the news feed. "Your loss," he said as he and the first officer exited through the frosted double doors into the corridor beyond. "I find this whole noisy political process most entertaining. We Denobulans, you know, are a patient bunch—slow to anger and slow to change. Politics for us is a cautious and deliberate affair; we're sometimes too slow to adapt to a change in circumstances."

"A pervasive problem, it seems," Thanien said. "I, for one, find it an embarrassment that so many of my people are so irrationally frightened of the new era the Federation has created. That even lunatics like the Lechebists are being taken seriously is a source of shame for all Andorians." It had been a year since Lecheb sh'Makesh had been elected governor of Alrond, a colony world in Andoria's home system, and declared it the seat of the Andorian Empire in exile, in defiance of Federation authority. At first it had seemed to be mere words, with the Alrondian government pursuing no aggression but simply wishing to be left alone. But as the election drew closer, the rhetoric from Lecheb had become increasingly confrontational, helping to fire up the Planetarist and isolationist factions that sought to weaken or dismantle the Articles of Federation that they claimed had been forced upon them. Thanien still wanted to believe these were just a small fringe of the Federation population, a disproportionately vocal minority too small to have any real impact. But he feared that they might be more than a mere nuisance.

The thought made him embarrassed about his sense of rivalry with Hoshi Sato. Making the interspecies relationship work had been difficult, sometimes turbulent, but that was no excuse to fall into bickering. The last thing Thanien wanted was to be anything like the Lechebists and their ilk.

I'm being a fool, he decided. There was no need to confront Sato about his concerns; he would simply set them aside and do his duty. This, he resolved, would be the end of it.

"They're simply trying to cope with the rapidly changing world they live in," Phlox was saying. "So much has happened so quickly these past few years . . . it's natural that there'd be some turbulence as a result. It's certainly livelier than Denobulan politics, and I'm finding it endlessly entertaining. I'm fascinated to see how it will play out." He grinned. "Especially if Admiral Archer succeeds in getting Rigel to join before the election. That will certainly put the Pyrithian moon hawk among the bats," he finished with a dramatic chuckle.

"I can understand their reticence," Thanien said, "given the unfriendly reception they're getting from those like Thoris. It must be unclear what we have to offer the Rigelians at this point. We're not exactly putting our best face forward at the moment."

"But that's exactly what we are doing," Phlox replied, still grinning. "For when it comes to diplomacy, the Federation's best face is the one on the front of Jonathan Archer's head."

March 26, 2164
Tregon, Beta Rigel V

"You must understand our confusion, Admiral Archer, Commissioner Soval. Why should we accept your current president's offer to join your Federation when your next president doesn't even want us?"

"Let me clarify that, Director," said Jonathan Archer. He strove for patience in his reply to Director Jemer Zehron, the Jelna member of the Rigelian Trade Commission's governing board, whose four members sat across from the Federation delegation in the ornate council hall within the Commission's Tregon headquarters. Along one wall was a large picture window looking out on the coastline of Rigel V's most prosperous city, beyond which was the flotilla of icebergs that the currents drove through the Tregon Sea at this time of year. Rigel V was near the outer edge of Tau-3 Eridani's habitable zone, making it prone to long winters and chilly springs and autumns.

"Councilor Thoris is just one of the candidates for president," Archer went on, aware that he was addressing a live viewing audience across the Rigel system as well as the board members in this chamber. "We have a democratic process much like those found on your own member worlds."

Soval, the Federation Commissioner for Foreign

Affairs, leaned forward in his seat on Archer's right. "By the same token," the silver-haired Vulcan added, "whoever is elected president will not be able to dictate policy unilaterally. He or she will govern in partnership with the Federation Council—a council on which the Rigel system will gain representation should you agree to join."

"You say the system," intoned Sajithen, the Chelon director representing her homeworld Rigel III. At least, Archer thought "her" was the correct word; Phlox insisted the Chelons were hermaphroditic, but all of the ones Archer had met presented themselves as either male or female. Regardless, Archer couldn't tell them apart; like all her kind, Sajithen was massive and broad-bodied with a thick, leathery green hide, a beaked face that evoked a tortoise and an eagle about equally, and clawed flippers that were more dexterous than they looked. While the more humanoid representatives sat in fairly normal chairs, the less flexible Chelon leaned forward on a *glenget*, a cushioned frame on which she rested her knees and abdomen. "Do you imply that the Rigel worlds warrant only one seat on your council?"

"My intent," Soval told her smoothly, "was simply to reflect the fact that the number of seats Rigel would gain is a matter for future, more formal negotiations, in the event that you choose to pursue membership."

Boda Jahlet, the Trade Commission ambassador who moderated this meeting, shifted her weight, rattling the elaborate wooden beads draped over her shoulders and chest. "This would be the ambassadorial conference you spoke of, on the planetoid designated Babel?" the sallow-skinned, craggy-faced Jelna exofemale asked.

"Correct," said Soval. "A neutral ground where representatives from both sides can conduct final debates and negotiations and then vote on the question of admission."

"Yes, yes, but that is the question," Zehron interposed. The director—representing the colonies on Rigel II and the inner asteroids, despite belonging to the native species of Rigel V—was of the Jelna's endomale sex, differentiated from an "exo" like Jahlet by paler skin, softer facial features, and red eyes. According to Phlox's merry lectures about Rigellian sexuality, the exomale and exofemale sexes—distinguished by an extra Z chromosome and outnumbering the "endosexes," the more typical males and females, by better than two to one—were the more robust and aggressive ones from an evolutionary-behavioral standpoint, adapted to handle the hunting and gathering while the endosexes stayed in camp to nurture and defend the young.

But you'd never know it from listening to Zehron; the supposedly gentler endomale had been closed-minded and confrontational from the start. "What are the chances of our admission when so many voices in the Federation protest the very idea?" he hectored. "We have had our own interstellar community for longer than you humans have known how to split an atom. Why should we seek entry into your upstart organization when we are not even welcome there?"

"Many people in the Federation do want you to join," Archer said. "The Federation is built on inter-stellar partnership and plurality. If the majority of voters on our founding worlds agreed that it was a good idea to partner with each other for the greater good . . . well, then they recognize the value of part-nership with other worlds, too." The admiral chose his words circumspectly, not wanting to overreach with his promises. "Yes, there are some who feel differently. But like Rigel itself, the Federation is dedicated to freedom of belief and expression. Those voices of protest are there because we respect their right to be heard."

"Noble words, Admiral." This time the speaker was Director Nop Tenott, a male Xarantine who repre-sented the Rigel Colonies, as the various alien com-munities that had settled in the Rigel system over the past two centuries, mostly on the moons of Rigel V and VI, were known. He tilted his high-crowned, hair-less yellow head, a skeptical expression on his noseless face. "But if you have such a commitment to plural-ity of thought, why do you insist that we compromise our traditions of cultural freedom and tolerance by adopting the Federation's uniform strictures on com-merce and business?"

Archer tried not to read an ulterior motive into the director's words. He'd had a bad experience with a Xarantine emissary during the Vertian crisis last year, but he reminded himself that, whatever his species, Tenott was a Rigelian by birth and citizenship. Then again, that was hardly a guarantee of ethical business practices, which was the root of the problem.

Soval replied before Archer could. "The policy changes necessary for Federation membership would only be in certain areas. The outlawing of slave trading, the halting of piracy, the restriction of business practices that would endanger sentient lives or planetary ecologies, the guarantee of basic rights for all workers, and so forth."

The final director, Sedra Hemnask of Rigel V, now spoke. "I appreciate the principle," said Hemnask, a relatively young female belonging to the Zami species, with long, wavy cinnamon-brown hair and a fair complexion. She was humanlike enough that Archer found her very attractive, and the subtle points of her ears did nothing to detract from that. "Certainly there is good reason to wish for the effective control of unethical practices and threats to life and limb. The First Families and their ongoing depredations are a continual thorn in the Commission's side." Hemnask spoke with restrained passion, and Archer wondered if, despite her birth and upbringing within Rigel V's large Zami community, her genetic kinship with the natives of Rigel IV inclined her to take the piratical behavior of its ruling families personally.

"But our peoples have learned over the centuries that there can be danger in taking such intervention too far," Hemnask continued. "Well-intentioned meddling in other cultures can become heavy-handed and invasive, a threat to their rights and independence."

"Absolutely," Sajithen declared in her gravelly Chelon tones, punctuating it with a series of sharp clicks from her rigid beak. "Four centuries ago, the Jelna's overzealous attempts to 'modernize' my ancestors led to a rebellion that flamed for generations, until we finally forced the Commission to give us equal representation."

Zehron yawned. "And listening to you, one would think the rebellion was still going on."

"My people have long memories, Director. And that was not the final time we were exploited by outsiders. We consider it prudent to remain alert to the risk."

"Believe me, Directors," Archer said to Sajithen and Hemnask, "I understand your position on this matter. For centuries, the Vulcans have practiced a similar philosophy toward contact with other races. It helps guide my own beliefs about the Federation's responsibilities in interspecies contact." Soval gave him an appreciative nod—though not without a trace of irony, given all the times through the years when he had found Archer's embrace of the non-interference policy to be insufficiently rigorous.

"But we believe that's for dealing with those outside your own community. Don't get me wrong—we value the diversity of customs and beliefs among our own members. But there are some principles that need to be agreed on by every member of a society for it to function. Some basic standards of ethics and individual rights. Like laws against murder and slavery, violent assault and theft. Laws that protect people's fundamental right to exist and to live free from violence, coercion, or oppression."

"So how do you preserve such freedom," Zehron

countered, "if the state itself coerces the people to follow its rules?"

"Rather," Soval replied, "the people mutually consent to abide by those rules for their own collective benefit. They ensure their own safety and liberty by agreeing to respect others' safety and liberty—even when that requires making compromises. Absolute, unfettered freedom is only possible for one who lives absolutely alone. When one is part of a community, one must balance one's own freedoms and rights with those of others. There are constraints on freedom, but only to the extent that different individuals' freedoms come into conflict. It is the responsibility of the state to moderate those conflicts equitably."

"Or, as a famous human jurist once said, 'The right to swing my fist ends where the other man's nose begins,'" Archer added.

"And what about the rights of businesspeople," Tenott asked, "to conduct their business in the most profitable manner, without the government dictating limits?"

"Where's the profit if there's nobody to protect them from being attacked, robbed, or enslaved themselves?" Archer countered. "It's not just the Federation government that wants this. Many of your own trading partners have been asking for more protection from Orion and Klingon and Nausicaan raiders. They want guarantees that their merchants and freighter crews will be safe when they pass through Rigelian space."

Archer looked around at the board members.

"There can't be true freedom for anybody . . . unless they have freedom from fear. Unless they know their right to live, to choose, to love, and to hold on to their possessions won't be taken from them by force, whether by a government *or* by other people. In any free system, there have to be some basic standards of behavior that everyone agrees to abide by, some basic protection for their lives and their rights—and they have to agree to empower somebody with the authority to enforce those standards if anyone violates that social contract. It's not enough just to trust the marketplace to balance everything out. You can see that isn't working."

"Don't presume to lecture us on how well our system works, Admiral," Zehron sneered. "We have our own mechanisms for ensuring fair trade and preserving the security of Rigel as a whole. It's a system that's served the Rigelian peoples well for centuries, since even before first contact."

"But the Rigelian peoples had centuries to work within those principles and find a healthy balance in their application," Soval replied. "While those who immigrated here," he went on, nodding to Tenott, "did so because they found your system agreeable and chose to live within it. It is in the best interest of all the permanent inhabitants of Rigel to make the system work in a way that does not disrupt the social order."

"Although," Director Hemnask muttered with displeasure, "the First Families have not been constrained by that logic."

"That is true. Nor are they alone in that regard. As the Rigelian trading community expands farther into the galaxy, there will be more who choose to abuse the license you grant them—who will not see the benefit of restraining themselves for the good of the greater market and will simply exploit the lack of law enforcement and worker protections to serve their own selfish interests."

Zehron tilted his head back. "So you're telling us to be afraid of outside impositions from others so that we'll accept outside imposition from you. How would we be any less exploited by the Federation?"

"Because you'd be members of it," Archer stressed, "participants in the decision-making process just as each of your worlds is a participant in the Rigelian community."

"So why should we join you," Tenott asked, "instead of you joining us? Why should we, the older community, take second place?"

"It is not a question of first or second," Soval told him. "While your community is quite cosmopolitan, it is based primarily in one star system. You trade and travel widely, but your own system provides such abundance of worlds and resources that you have never needed to colonize others. The Federation, by contrast, is already an interstellar power encompassing multiple systems—a partnership of several nations like your own."

"There's another reason," Archer said. "At the risk of blowing my own horn, that reason is Starfleet. Starfleet's strength is why Rigel and a number of its trading partners turned to the Federation for help with the Vertian crisis last year. And Starfleet's skills in science and diplomacy were key to ending that crisis peacefully. If you joined the Federation, you'd know that Starfleet would always be there for you when you needed it."

"But the Vertian threat is over," Zehron countered.

"We have reason to suspect that threat was engineered by the Orion Syndicate, in partnership with the Malurians' leading criminal organization, to undermine the Federation. We foiled that effort, but there are signs that they're trying to recruit more allies, to build an alliance of their own. A criminal empire like that could threaten all of us."

Soval's gaze took in the directors. "The Federation was not founded until after the Earth-Romulan War ended. Yet the reason it formed so swiftly thereafter is that its members belatedly realized their mistake in not uniting earlier. Had they joined against the Romulans from the start, it would have been easier to end that common threat with far less loss of life. It is wiser to anticipate problems than merely to react."

Archer's gaze took in the directors. "We're not trying to pressure or scare you into joining. I firmly believe there are far more constructive reasons for our worlds to unite, and I believe we've spelled out those reasons today. But if we stand together, we will all be stronger for it—and safer when threats do arise."

As the bright blue-white disk of Raij sank below the icebergs, Ambassador Jahlet suggested an adjournment for the evening. "You have offered us much to consider, Commissioner, Admiral. Now the board must deliberate on these matters and discuss them with the larger Commission."

Archer could hear the subtext. Once he and Soval had made their polite farewells and been escorted out, the admiral turned to the commissioner and spoke with resignation. "We're not gonna get an answer this trip, are we?"

"Perhaps not," Soval said. "But I sense we have gained more ground than in previous discussions over subspace. I believe you made our case well, Admiral."

"Thank you, Soval." There was a touch of irony in Archer's smile as he recalled how hard he'd had to work to earn the Vulcan's trust and respect . . . and how little he'd wanted it in the first few years of their acquaintance. He took heart in the thought. If the two of them had gone from bitter rivals to partners within the space of a few years, then there was hope for winning Rigel over after all.

He just hoped that would happen before the Orion situation escalated out of hand.

3

From: Jeremy Lucas, Interspecies Medical Exchange relief mission, Narpra, Sauria

To: Phlox, Chief Medical Officer, *U.S.S. Endeavour*

Draft saved: April 26, 2164, 16:43

Dear Doctor Phlox:

Sorry I haven't responded to your last letter before now. The situation on Sauria has grown even more dire since the IME was first invited in. Here in Narpra, the country where the illness was first reported, the rate of incidence had reached the level of an epidemic by the time our team arrived. We've had our hands full just trying to keep the Saurians alive, let alone determine the etiology or transmission vectors of the condition. So far, the mortality rate is only around fourteen percent of affected individuals, but for the Saurians, who have little experience with diseases this severe, even that rate is seen as shocking.

Unfortunately, that shock and fear have made it difficult for my people to do their jobs. Given the timing of the outbreak, many Saurians are convinced that exposure to offworlders is the cause of the disease. Naturally that was one of the first possibilities we examined, but we could find no solid evidence to support it. The infectious agent doesn't correspond to any known Saurian pathogen, but there are no proteins identifiable with the biochemistry of any alien race currently on Sauria. And the only correlation we've found between morbidity and exposure to extra-Saurian organisms is in public places, where both Saurians and outsiders would congregate anyway, and where any number of other factors could be in play. There's no sign of correlation among Saurians who've interacted with offworlders in more private venues. But the public nature of so many patients' interactions with offworlders just reinforces the Narprans' fears and makes cooperation difficult.

Which, as you can imagine, Phlox, is disappointing to me for more than medical reasons. The Saurians are a remarkable race biologically, with an incredibly robust physiology: a quadruply redundant circulatory system, a respiratory filter that cleanses toxins from inhaled air like our livers cleanse blood—and don't get me started on the amazing efficiency of their actual livers. And their adaptations to nocturnal existence are fascinating. But more than that, they're a lively, passionate people with a rich, ancient culture. I relish the opportunity to get to know them and explore their world, but their fears of disease have made it difficult.

Still, I'm making the best of it. My team and I have been lodged with the Federation mining consultants—since their lodgings have been equipped with bright lights, thermal controls, and other ame-

nities we fragile mammalian types require—and
the lot of them have been welcoming to us, probably as grateful for friendly company as we are.
And a few of them have managed to hold on to
the trust of the friends they've made among the
Saurians, though it's tenuous in some cases. One
fellow in particular, Antonio Ruiz, has made a
number of friends at the local taverns, and he and
his clique have treated us to a few memorable
nights on the town. I think his gregariousness has
helped balance out some of the fears and propaganda that . . .

"Doctor? Doctor Lucas! You need to come quick!"

The urgency in the voice coming through the door
of his hotel room—and the repeated chimes of the
door annunciator that accompanied it—distracted
Jeremy Lucas from his letter. Heaving his portly frame
out of the chair and twisting his walrus-mustached lip
in annoyance at Sauria's high gravity, Lucas made his
way to the door and opened it, recognizing the Fili-
pina woman on the other side. "Laila, what is it?"

Laila Alindogan pulled on his arm. "Come on,
something's happening outside! The police are here!"

Lucas followed her out into the corridor carved
from the igneous rock of the city. Once they reached
the hotel entrance, they found the Narpran police arrayed around it in sizeable numbers, with several offworlders including Antonio Ruiz facing off against
them. "Look, are you gonna tell us what's going on?"
Ruiz asked. "What have we done to get evicted?"

The local police chief, Densri, responded in a patient voice with a hint of apology. "It's the new policy, sir," she said. "Due to the . . . concerns of infection, we're asking offworlders to leave as a precaution."

"Come on, that's ridiculous!" Other voices raised in protest alongside Ruiz's.

Lucas strode forward, putting all his authority into his voice and bulky presence. "Excuse me!" The crowd subsided, turning to him. "Chief Densri, I can assure you, my people have found no evidence that this disease is being caused by non-Saurians. We need to be allowed to work closely with your people if we're to help you find a cure."

"That will not be necessary," came another voice. A wiry, violet-skinned Saurian male strode forward. "Colonel Kurvanis, M'Tezir Royal Command."

"Doctor Jeremy Lucas, Interspecies Medical Exchange. What are you saying, Colonel?"

"I am saying that a remedy for the disease has already been discovered—in M'Tezir."

"What? How can that be?" It would be wonderful news if true, of course. But Saurians had so little experience with illness that it seemed doubtful their medical science could crack this problem faster than the Federation's or the IME's—particularly given that the M'Tezir nation had historically devoted its sciences more to military applications than medical ones.

"Perhaps," the colonel said loudly enough to be audible to the crowd accumulating along the boardwalk and peering out the windows in the adjacent rock face, "your people have been reluctant to find a cure lest it prove your culpability in bringing alien diseases to our world."

"I've already explained that that's not the case."

"And we have confirmed that it is."

"How? M'Tezir kicked the offworlders out almost as soon as the disease appeared, even though none of the cases were on their soil. If we were causing the disease, how could you identify and cure it without studying us?"

"Doctor," Chief Densri said as if breaking bad news, "the medicine is real. I have seen it work."

"Then isn't that all the more reason to work with us to administer it to your people?"

"It is all the more reason to keep you away from our people," Kurvanis told him. "It is a treatment, not a vaccine. It does not preclude re-infection from further exposure."

It still sounded fishy to Lucas. "I'd like to study your research. There's no point in doing anything rash."

Chief Densri spread her hands in a Saurian gesture of negation. "Doctor Lucas, the government's decision has already been made. M'Tezir has agreed to mobilize their military for a medical relief mission. But the only way their troops can set foot on our soil without it constituting an act of war against the Global League . . . is if we sever ties with the League. And its allies."

"That's crazy," Ruiz protested. "Why not just send in civilian doctors?"

"Only the military has the resources, numbers, and

efficiency to get the job done," Kurvanis declaimed with pride. "And they are already on their way. The decision is final. We are doing you a courtesy by allowing you to stand here and argue at all. But it is best if you are gone by the time the troops arrive. They are . . . dedicated to protecting their people from all threats."

Laila Alindogan turned to Densri. "So this is it? All we've taught you, all the generosity and welcome you've shown us . . . it ends at the point of a gun?"

"So long as you cooperate, there will be no need to make this . . . unpleasant," the chief said, though she clearly did not wish it to be this way.

"Don't worry, your Federation won't lose its precious minerals," Kurvanis said, misreading Alindogan's concerns. "M'Tezir will continue to honor its deal with the Federation, but it will now be managing Narpra's resources instead of the Global League . . . as soon as the terms of alliance are finalized."

"Getting ahead of yourself, aren't you?" Ruiz asked.

"I need not justify myself to you. Your only concern at this point is packing your belongings and leaving. That is a government order." He turned to Chief Densri. "Which you will now enforce. Correct?"

Densri glared at him. "I know my job, Colonel. Even if I don't take the pleasure in it that you do." She turned to Lucas. "Please, Doctor. On behalf of Narpra, I thank you for your service. But I now require you to leave."

Lucas looked around at the police troops—big, strong, incredibly durable Saurian police troops—and knew there was nothing he could do. He still had nightmares about that horrible day a decade ago when a band of genetically enhanced human Augments had held him hostage at Cold Station 12, torturing him and threatening the lives of others—even killing Deputy Director Iyer before his eyes—to force him to hand over the hundreds of Augment embryos stored there. He had done his best to be brave, only to ultimately succumb in order to save his friend Phlox's life . . . rendering Iyer's sacrifice essentially meaningless, a guilt that had stayed with him ever since. As much as he wanted to stand up to this intimidation and redeem his shame, he knew he couldn't bear to risk any more lives if he could avoid it. His fellow offworlders were better off cooperating with the Narpran police than they would be if they waited for Colonel Kurvanis's forces to arrive.

So with a heavy sigh, he turned to Ruiz, Alindogan, and the others. "We have to do as she says."

"But, Doc—"

"It's their decision, Antonio," he said, nipping the young Cuban's tirade in the bud. "We have to respect it even if we don't agree with it. That's part of being a good guest."

"So . . . so where will we go?"

"There are still other countries in the Global League where we should be welcome." He tilted his head back and took one more lingering look at the beautiful lava-tube city. The sun was just rising, and the light filtering through the plant canopies above gave the city a verdant glow like the depths of a rainforest. He lamented that his stay in Narpra had been so brief. "But there's nothing more we can do here."

May 12, 2164
U.S.S. *Pioneer*, orbiting Kaferia (Tau Ceti III)

Malcolm Reed smiled at the familiar face appearing on his ready room monitor. "Admiral Archer! To what do we owe the pleasure, sir?"

"*Good to see you, Malcolm,*" the admiral said. "*And you, Travis,*" he added to the man who stood on Reed's left.

"Always good to see you, sir," Mayweather replied.

"*So . . . any luck with the Kaferians?*"

"No, sir," Travis reported. "They're grateful for our offer to help shore up their planetary defenses, but they're still not interested in Federation membership. They hardly even have any kind of government to negotiate with."

"*I understand. I guess I'm not surprised.*" The insectoid natives of Tau Ceti III had never had a problem with the erstwhile human colony on the neighboring fourth planet (confusingly called Outer Kaferia, with the third being Inner Kaferia; the system's first explorers and settlers, the Kaferi family, had lacked both imagination and modesty when it came to naming things). Far from the stereotype of the insect hive mind, the Kaferians were fervent individualists content to let everyone, even alien colonists, go their own way so long as they stayed peaceful. But when the Romulans had conquered Tau

Ceti IV and destroyed the NX-class vessel *Atlantis*, the Kaferians had offered safe haven and medical care for the starship's survivors—including one Lieutenant Travis Mayweather. After the Starfleet crew had been evacuated, the Romulans had invaded Inner Kaferia in retaliation. Luckily, the Kaferians had evolved the ability to hibernate underground to survive the frequent asteroid impacts the system was prone to, so most of them had managed to sleep out the four-year occupation undetected. Otherwise, the Romulans would probably have exterminated their entire race as they had the human colony.

Now, *Pioneer* had been sent to the sole remaining Kaferia in the hopes that Mayweather could build on his past relationship with the natives and find some basis for a higher-level partnership. But while the Kaferians had been as friendly as ever, they were still just as determined to stand alone. "They'll be good trading partners, Admiral," Mayweather concluded, "but a formal alliance is too much to ask."

"Then that'll have to do," Archer said with a sigh. *"I have no doubt you did your best, Travis."*

"Thank you, sir."

"Fortunately, I have some better news on another front. The Rigelians have finally issued a formal petition for Federation membership."

Mayweather beamed. "That's great!"

"Excellent news, sir," Reed added. "Congratulations. I take it the next step is an ambassadorial conference?"

"That's the next step for me," Archer said. *"T'Pol will be*

escorting Commissioner Soval and myself to Babel aboard En-deavour. But I have something a little more interesting in mind for Pioneer." The admiral paused before continuing in the deliberate, almost lecturing tones he sometimes adopted. *"I've realized that there's still a lot we don't know about the Rigel system, both its planets and its peoples. And there's still a lot they don't know about us, too. If we're going to become partners, it's a good idea to have a cultural exchange. You know, get to know the new neighbors."*

Mayweather chuckled. "I'll tell the steward to get started on a green bean casserole for ten billion."

"Very funny, Travis. But there's more at stake here. A lot of Rigelians still have doubts about us, questions about what the Fed-eration's really like. And, let's face it, a lot of people in the Fed-eration have doubts and misconceptions about Rigel—ones that the presidential campaign isn't doing much to clear up."

Reed nodded. "And you want us to bring more facts to the table. Let people see what Rigel's really like."

"That's right. I've only seen parts of the system myself. We've all been to Rigel X more than once, but that's an independent port run by the Xarantine. And I've been to Rigel V a couple of times now, done the tourist thing when I had the chance . . . this last time I got around to visiting the cabarets on Rigel II." He gave a conspiratorial grin. *"We'll . . . talk about that sometime when we aren't on an official channel."* Reed and Mayweather ex-changed an intrigued look.

"Still, Admiral, since you called on me for this mis-sion, I assume you'd like us to be more than just tourists." *Pioneer* may have been a ship of exploration, but there were other captains better suited for pure science or di-plomacy. Reed was still a soldier and defender at heart.

Archer grew more serious. *"That's right, Malcolm. There are some security concerns worth exploring. For instance, the First Families of Rigel IV. They're not part of the trading community, and they're basically pirates and gangsters. But they have a strong influence on much of Rigel II and the Colonies. I'd like to know if their corruption spreads even farther, and how much of a threat it poses to bringing Federation law to Rigel."*

"Understood, sir."

"There are also some lingering questions about the Trade Commission. They say they do have some mechanisms for regulating commerce—and despite appearances, their methods can't be completely hands-off or the system would be in chaos. But they're reluctant to go into specifics, and nobody else seems eager to talk about it either. Whatever it is they're doing, I think it's important to know about it before we invite them in the door."

Reed nodded. "Of course, Admiral."

"Also . . . there's the mystery of Rigel VII."

"Still no luck getting the Rigelians to tell us about its natives, sir?"

"That's right. I'd like you to look into it—but discreetly. If we're treading on some cultural taboo, then we need to approach it with care. But we still need to find out if there's anything going on there that could affect the Federation's decision about granting membership."

"I understand, Admiral." Federation membership entailed certain ethical standards. If the Rigelians had some reason for being ashamed to talk about the Kalar, then it would be incumbent upon *Pioneer*'s crew to find out.

"But don't get the wrong idea, Malcolm. Your main mission, as always, is exploration. True, this time you're exploring a system

where humans have gone before, but it's such a large, complicated system that there's still plenty left to discover. And there are plenty of people there who are eager to learn more about us."

Reed straightened. "Sir. I'm honored that you're entrusting *Pioneer* with such an important responsibility. However . . . to be honest, sir, I'm concerned that a diplomatic assignment of such delicacy is . . . well, a little outside my wheelhouse."

"I have confidence in you, Malcolm. You know the sector, you've got a good crew, and you've been by my or T'Pol's side for many diplomatic missions. I wouldn't have chosen you if I didn't think you were the best captain, and crew, for the job."

Reed's chest swelled at Archer's praise. "Thank you, sir. We won't let you down."

May 15, 2164
Trykar Palace Hotel, Kefvenek, Rigel II

Dular Garos gazed out the tinted panoramic window of the hotel suite, taking in the view from the fortieth story of the massive pyramidal structure that was the Trykar Palace. The garish Kefvenek Strip below was festooned with blinding lights, a compensation for the generally dim daylight in the terraformed polar regions of the planet. Not only did Raij never rise very high above the horizon, but the fierce white sunlight that baked most of the planet's surface was blocked here by the edges of the valley in which the city was ensconced, by the dense, high rainforest of imported Rigel III vegetation beyond, and by the near-perpetual

clouds and mist in the sky above—a mist supple-
mented by the thousands of tall, chimney-like seed-
particle launchers arrayed around the region when
evaporation off the rainforest was insufficient.

Even so, a few vivid sunbeams had managed to
push their way through the obstacles and shine down
on the Strip, casting unexpected and no doubt un-
welcome light on the sordid activities it hosted. Casting his brown eyes skyward, Garos saw extraordinary
beauty . . . but it wasn't enough to efface the sleaziness
of what lay below.

But then, that's always the way, isn't it? As much as one
aspired to heights of purity and light, the ugly business in the trenches was an unavoidable fact of the
universe, and accepting it was usually necessary to get
anything done.

"Spectacular, isn't it?"

Case in point, Garos thought as he shifted his gaze
to the man beside him. Vemrim Corthoc was a Zami
Rigelian, and his ornate robes and the elaborate, jew-
eled coiffure of silver-blond hair atop his head (largely
concealing the blunt points of his ears) marked him
as a member of the elite First Families of Rigel IV.
Any fleeting illusion that Corthoc was appreciating
the same view as Garos was quickly dashed, for his
proud gaze was directed toward the casinos and flesh-
pits below, toward the garish, flashing signs and wall
displays whose shifting, multicolored lights did more
to obfuscate the actions of the Strip's patrons than to
illuminate them. "Just look at all those tourists down
there just waiting to be fleeced. This was a desert just

a few centuries ago—now it's a fertile, umm, plain where we can farm . . . well, harvest the riches of the galaxy."

"By putting all those people through a thresher," Garos replied.

Corthoc laughed in what he imagined was agreement. "Exactly! See, that's what I was going for, a, what is it, metaphor thing about farming."

"Yes, I gathered that." Garos controlled his reaction, regretting that Malurian masks were such technological marvels, responsive to the subtlest cues from the faces within. The Zami mask he wore now was not much different from the mask he'd worn during his months on the Akaali homeworld before his exile: smooth, pink, and fleshy with thin arcs of hair over the eyes, but without the Akaali's forehead grooves and with somewhat sharper tips to the ears, plus a paler, longer, golden-brown wig. It was a convenience to the maskmakers that so many humanoids defaulted to that smooth, babyish appearance (the biology alignment back home attributed it to the evolutionary pressure toward neoteny), but it was an annoyance to Garos that he so often had to don such an unflatteringly bland visage. Particularly since it increasingly reminded him of the human species and Jonathan Archer, whose interference on the Akaali world had led to Garos's exile, and who had played a key role in foiling his Vertian stratagem last year.

"I think what Corthoc is trying to say," came a feminine voice, "is that it represents all we have to lose should Rigel align with the Federation."

Garos turned to Retifel Thamnos, a tall, middle-aged Zami woman with pleasantly sharp features and a mane of red-gold hair, which she wore in a less elaborate, more unruly coif than Corthoc's while somehow making it look considerably more elegant. He smiled at her, a more sincere response than he had granted Corthoc. "Exactly the position I have come to you to advocate." The Thamnos family had fought its way to prominence more recently than the Corthocs, building its wealth and power on the exploitation of the offworlders who had come to Rigel II over the past two centuries, and cunningly wielding that power to undermine one of the entrenched ruling families and usurp its rule of a substantial portion of Rigel IV. As such, its members had not had time to grow as decadent and inbred as the Corthoc line, thus retaining their capacity for intelligence and calculation. The Corthocs had sent Vemrim as their representative to the Malurians because it got the dullard out of their hair for a time, but Retifel had volunteered to represent the Thamnos clan because she was ambitious and politically savvy.

"The First Families," Garos went on, speaking mainly to Thamnos, "are the strongest rival bloc to the Trade Commission—the only native rivals with interests spanning multiple Rigelian worlds and including interstellar business partnerships. Thus, you are in the best position to undermine the Federation's attempts to co-opt the Commission."

"We know all that," a bored Corthoc replied. "But what do *you* have to offer us?"

"The Raldul alignment is a powerful interstellar cartel," Garos told him, "and we have powerful allies such as the Orion Syndicate. We are skilled at infiltration, deceit, and sabotage. We can get into places even you cannot easily reach. And we can offer you a lasting partnership, much like the one the Federation is offering your Commission foes—albeit without the moralistic restrictions the Federation seeks to impose."

"Now, that appeals to me," Thamnos said, inhaling on the long narcotic stick she held between her fingers. Mercifully, her narcotic of choice gave off no disagreeable smoke or odor, but it surprised Garos that this canny, self-possessed woman would allow herself to be subjugated to one of the same addictive chemicals that her family used to entrap and control those they considered their lessers. "The Federation's idyllic promises have made their way even to the ears of our serfs," she went on, "despite our best efforts to limit their outside contact. It's filling their minds with dangerous notions about rights and freedom."

Corthoc gave a commiserating sigh. "Oh, that's so irritating, isn't it? We've had to maim or execute so many useful workers this past quarter. And somehow that just seems to make the rest of them *more* rebellious." ·

"Of course it does, you fool," Thamnos spat. "The one thing stronger than fear is hate. Make them see you as the source of pain in their lives and they'll just fight you harder." She smiled. "Subtlety is the key. Put the latest strain of the fever virus into their water supply, weaken and kill enough to take the fight out of them, then when they're at their lowest, announce you've found a cure and come to their rescue. Earn their gratitude and they're yours."

Garos controlled his reaction tightly. As refreshing as Thamnos's intelligence and charm may have been after spending any length of time with Corthoc, she was ultimately just as selfish and decadent, her power built on the backs of her people. They would both gladly sacrifice the well-being of their planet and its inhabitants if it brought them more power. They weren't so different from the entrenched alignments that ruled the Malurian system, preservers of the planetbound laws and traditions that hampered the race's efforts to compete and flourish in an interstellar age. Those like Garos and Raldul, who recognized that Maluria needed a galactic presence to stand against external threats—even to preserve the race against disaster on a global scale, the Holy Mother forbid—were ostracized and treated as criminals, and thus forced to become criminals to survive. In truth, Garos felt more affinity toward the rebellious peasants of Rigel IV than toward the First Families that so cavalierly subjected them to torture, addiction, disease, and outright murder at a whim, and that hoarded offworld technologies and medicines to themselves while the masses toiled in virtually preindustrial conditions. He despised everything Thamnos and Corthoc stood for.

But he served the good of the Malurian people, not the Rigelians. The Raldul alignment needed the wealth and influence that their extralegal dealings in the Kandari Sector made possible, and Maluria, whether the system's leaders admitted it or not, needed Raldul to keep it strong and safe. Rigel had to be kept out of the Federation for Maluria's sake, even if it meant Rigelians had to suffer and die. Even if it meant Garos had to climb down into the trenches with filth like the First Families.

So he made his mask feign a suitably devious smile. "That's exactly the kind of cunning I'm looking for, Retifel. Exactly what we'll need if we're to thwart the Trade Commission and the Federation."

Thamnos took what she evidently imagined to be a seductive drag on her narcotic stick and smiled back. "And that's why I'm glad you're here, my dear Dular. We've had designs against the Commission for decades, but acquiring the resources and support to make it happen has remained a problem. Now, perhaps, that can change."

Garos widened his smile. "Whatever designs you have imagined, I encourage you to think bigger. What do you want most of all?"

Thamnos spread her arms expansively. "This. I want Rigel II. I'm tired of having to control it piecemeal, a casino district here, a bought politician there. I'm tired of having to share it with the Jelna and the Chelons and the outworlders. We are the First Families, born to rule unopposed. We should *own* this planet. That is what I want, Dular. And I want the Trade Commission to be so hobbled that it can't do a thing to stop us."

"Nothing is beyond us if we work together, my

friends." Garos led her—and, as an afterthought, Corthoc—over to the table. "Now . . . let us discuss how we may get you what you wish."

May 17, 2164
San Francisco

"The latest report confirms our intelligence from two months ago," Charles Tucker informed his superior. "A high-ranking Raldul member, maybe Dular Garos himself, met with First Family representatives on Rigel II. They're planning to derail the membership talks."

"I see." His superior, a square-jawed, gray-haired man who went by the name Harris, took in his report calmly. "And what do you recommend we do about it?"

Tucker considered for a moment, then sighed and set his mouth grimly, recalling a past argument and the others that had followed. "We . . . don't do anything. We let Starfleet and the diplomats deal with the problem."

Harris studied him for a long moment, his gaze revealing nothing. It lasted long enough to put Trip's teeth on edge before the older man relented and gave a slight smile. "You're absolutely right. Or should I say, Captain T'Pol was right." Tucker glared, but he was past being surprised at the lack of personal privacy in the life he led now. "The Federation is more than capable of taking care of itself . . . most of the time. It has laws, defenses, countless skilled professionals more than capable of dealing with the vast majority of its problems, and usually we serve the Federation best by staying out of its way.

"Not to mention that it's in our own best interests not to involve ourselves in more situations than we absolutely have to. Each intervention increases the risk of exposure." Harris smirked. "As a wise school of philosophers once observed, the first lesson of not being seen is not to stand up. So our, ah, services should be the last resort, not the first."

Tucker gave him a sidelong look. "Then what are we doing here? Why are we going to all this trouble, abandoning our lives, hiding our identities, when most of the time there's no point?"

"I understand your frustration, my friend. You want to feel that all this secrecy, all this deception and denial, serves a purpose. But our purpose," Harris went on, "is to watch . . . and to wait. To be ready for those—hopefully rare—situations that the Federation can't resolve through legal and aboveboard means. Situations that only the invisible and unaccountable can address.

"I know it's not very glamorous or rewarding. But it's our life. You've said yourself, we have to be careful not to take things too far. What we do often isn't pretty, so the less we have to do it, the better."

"I know, I know. I guess sittin' by and watchin' has never been my style. That's why I joined Starfleet." Tucker sighed. "In another life."

Harris contemplated him for a moment. "You know . . . one of the things we are meant for is to take care of matters outside the authority of those official institutions. Situations beyond Federation jurisdiction that might someday pose a risk to the Federation."

Sensing that Harris was about to make him an offer, Tucker perked up. "I like to travel."

"Good. We need a fact finder for a . . . troubling situation that's developing. It may be strictly a local problem, but it could affect Federation interests." He tilted his head. "And it's a fair distance in the opposite direction from Babel."

He thought it over. It wasn't as if he were eager to flee from T'Pol. He wasn't sure quite what the range limitation on their telepathic bond was, but they seemed to connect less often the farther they were from each other. But if what she needed was to be trusted to solve her own problems, then he'd give her the necessary space. He just wasn't sure yet if that path would lead around to bringing them back together. For now, he supposed that was her decision to make.

"Sounds perfect," he told Harris. "Just tell me what the weather's like there so I can pack."

4

D'NESH ENTERED the medical section of the Three Sisters' estate to find Jofirek on a bed in the treatment area, harassing a Boslic nurse. Luckily for the nurse, the elderly Agaron crime boss lacked the speed or energy for much more than verbal advances. Still, D'Nesh chuckled at the slave's plight. As far as she was concerned, females who lacked the power to keep males under control deserved whatever happened to them.

Of course, D'Nesh did not have to wait for service, so she was promptly shown into the adjacent exam room and Doctor Honar-Des arrived moments later, as soon as he could abandon the patient he'd been with and run his hands through a sterilizing beam. Des was a smallish, elderly Orion, only half a head taller than D'Nesh, with a fully bald and unadorned head. He eschewed body piercings for what he called sanitary reasons, though D'Nesh had to wonder how he reconciled that with the full gray beard he wore. "What's Jofirek in for?" she asked him idly as he pulled the curtain shut over the doorway. "Did Zankor try to kill him again?"

"Well, he came in seeking performance enhancement. Apparently he's having difficulty maintaining enough stamina for the celebrations. But I've advised him that we need to stabilize his heart first."

"Ugh." She grimaced. "That's why it's better to die young and pretty."

"So what can I do for you today, Mistress?"

D'Nesh spoke reluctantly. "I'm feeling a little tired myself. Like my . . . my game is a bit off."

"In what context?"

"You know. *The* context." It was difficult to get the words out, to admit that her sexual allure and potency were at anything less than full strength. After all, her power as an elite depended on that.

But Navaar had gathered the members of her alliance here on Orion to discuss their future plans, and naturally she'd thrown the expected bacchanalia to cement their loyalty—and to celebrate the successful progression of her long-term plan for Sauria. In the past month, Maltuvis had consolidated his control of Narpra and had moved his "medical relief" troops into a second disease-ravaged neighbor, effectively conquering both nations without firing a shot. He now controlled almost all of Sauria's mineral wealth, and there was nothing the Global League or the Federation could do about it. And it was all thanks to Orion medical science. Plagues, as Navaar had gloated, could be very useful tools. And they had a way of spreading.

D'Nesh had joined in the festivities gamely, as usual, but had noticed that she was getting less attention from the available partners than Navaar or Maras. Of course, she could always order the slaves to do as she bade them, and yet . . . "One of the bed slaves . . . I told him to do this thing I like and . . ." She set her jaw. "He said no. Just once—all I had to do was raise my voice and he cowered nicely—but he still said no."

"Well, let's take a look at you, Mistress." She disrobed for the examination, annoyed that Honar-Des took the sight of her spectacular body in stride. True, he had been chemically castrated, or he would have been unable to control his urges enough to do this job. But not being gawked at when nude was somewhat humiliating. It made her feel powerless.

"You're perfectly all right, Mistress," the doctor told her once the exam was finished. "Nothing wrong except a minor hormonal deficiency, which is perfectly natural in someone of your—maturity."

She stared at him in outrage. "I am *not old!*"

"No, no, of course, Mistress, I never meant to suggest—"

"Navaar's a year older than me. There's nothing wrong with her hormones!"

The doctor's eyes turned away. "Well . . . each individual is different, Mistress. I assure you," he said, meeting her gaze again, "this is a minor inconvenience, easily remedied."

She grabbed the collar of his coat. "Remedy it, then. Now!"

"I'll be just a moment." He left the room for the dispensary, and D'Nesh put her clothes back on—which didn't take long. When Honar-Des returned, he gave her a container of gel capsules. "These are a standard hormone supplement for Orion females. They help restore the natural hormone levels that your body is . . . producing in lower quantities now."

She stared at the pills. "So this is just for now, until I get my full strength back?"

"Well, we'll monitor your situation and see how it goes."

D'Nesh could tell he was handling her. He was rightly afraid to state to her face that she was getting older, that she needed chemical help to remain as irresistible as an elite female needed to be. She'd never admit it, of course, but it was a fear she'd had to live with ever since Maras had hit puberty and begun displaying signs that her pheromonal potency would surpass that of her older sisters. If the girl hadn't been too stupid to have any ambition, D'Nesh would have had her sold into slavery in a Klingon torture pit years ago. But the little twit wasn't completely useless; as much as it galled D'Nesh to admit it, the two elder sisters benefitted from having Maras's chemical allure reinforcing their own. If they had rejected Maras or sold her, then some rival elites might have co-opted her, manipulated her into acting against them. So D'Nesh could understand the practical, strategic reasons why Navaar kept the three of them inseparable. What ate at her was the way Navaar genuinely seemed to like the child, to dote on her and indulge her dull-witted antics. She'd never allowed D'Nesh to get away with half as much. *"It's because I expect so much more from you,"* Navaar had explained on many an occasion—but it didn't make it sting any less. D'Nesh felt she was forced to work harder than anyone else to earn Navaar's respect.

And now with this happening, her potency starting to fade . . . she could never tell Navaar about the supplement, or she'd never live it down. To be losing her natural potency while her older sister was still—

"Wait," she said to Honar-Des as he showed her out of the exam room. "Navaar's already on these pills, isn't she? She gets a little performance boost of her own to stay on top, doesn't she?"

Honar-Des looked terrified. "Please, Mistress . . . I'm obligated to keep all my mistresses' medical information confidential. I beg you not to make me reveal . . ."

She laughed. "Don't worry, little man. You just told me what I need to know. Get back to your patients."

Honar-Des thanked her abjectly, ignoring Jofirek's loud demands that the doctor pay attention to him now. D'Nesh left in a better mood, reassured that she could still make men grovel at her feet. Where seduction failed, there was always cruelty. If anything, she enjoyed that even more.

June 9, 2164
Mount Dleba Observatory, Rigel V

"This is where Rigel began."

Rehlen Vons, assistant director for Rigel V, gestured proudly at the antique telescope mounted in its carefully maintained brass fittings. "It was through this very telescope," the craggy-faced Jelna exomale went on, "that Lovar Dleba first detected the fires that the Zami of Rigel IV used to manage and clear the forests of their world. Her studies over the ensuing years confirmed the regularity and design behind the fires, and eventually she refined the instrument enough to detect the smaller fires of their permanent settlements and migratory bands. This proof that intelligent life existed on their neighboring world inspired Jelna science and engineering as we sought to develop the means to communicate with our neighbors. In time we realized the natives of Four were not advanced enough to detect us in return——but within two centuries of Dleba's discovery, a robotic probe bearing her name made the first landing on Four and sent back the first images of the Zami people."

"Incredible," breathed Lieutenant Samuel Kirk. "It took humans over three hundred and fifty years between Galileo's first telescopic observations and the first robot probe landing on Mars."

"Maybe if we'd had proof of intelligent life on the world next door," Travis Mayweather told *Pioneer*'s historian, "we'd have been motivated to develop spaceflight faster, too."

"But we did assume there was intelligent life on Mars for centuries," Kirk replied. "Remember Percival Lowell's so-called canals? We didn't abandon the idea until the space probes of the nineteen sixties revealed the truth."

The first officer shrugged. "Assuming is one thing. Actually seeing it? That's always a stronger motivator."

"Very true," Vons replied. "But that was only the beginning. Over the generations that followed," the pale-haired assistant director went on, "the Jelna established ongoing trade relations first with the Zami, and later with the Chelons of Rigel III. We shared our technology and medicine in exchange for the local goods and the unique art and literature of each species. Naturally there were turbulent times— cross-species diseases, political oppression, wars—but through those hard lessons, the Rigelians learned the value of trade without judgment, cooperation without cultural domination. We learned to respect one another's autonomy and freedom of choice, and it only brought us closer. The Trade Commission oversaw a peaceful, prosperous Rigel system for over a century and a half before the Coridanites made first contact."

Kirk traded a look with Mayweather, aware of the bias that informed the board member's account. As the most junior member of the board of directors— Sedra Hemnask's assistant, filling in for her now that she was en route to Babel—Vons had been tasked with the assignment of shepherding *Pioneer*'s crew on their fact-finding tour. Yet he had made it clear enough that, unlike Hemnask, he was skeptical of the benefits of Federation membership and reluctant to abandon the Commission's traditional laissez-faire policies.

True, it was Hemnask herself who had gone to represent the RTC at Babel. But Babel was the Federation's side of the equation. The Rigelians would conduct their own vote on the membership question. And Vons's attitude, alongside the skepticism of Directors Zehron and Tenott, made it clear that *Pioneer*'s crew would have to make a strong case for the Federation.

But that struck Kirk as a good sign. A healthy, open debate could be very beneficial for social progress.

Not to mention that it would make his account of this historic event that much livelier. Generally, a Starfleet historian's job was to study the recorded history of the alien worlds they visited—and Beta Rigel was a mother lode in that regard, three distinct planets with their own independent histories as well as a millennium of mutual interaction. Yet Kirk now had the opportunity to write new history as it happened.

But his gaze darted to Valeria Williams, *Pioneer*'s fetching and fiery armory officer, and he wondered if such an achievement would improve his standing in her eyes. It seemed unlikely, though; while they had bonded last year in the aftermath of a serious warp accident, the lieutenant had subsequently shown no more than friendly interest in Kirk. Indeed, though her physical relationship with Reynaldo Sangupta had ended even before then, she still responded more passionately to the brash young science officer than to the quiet Lieutenant Kirk, even if that passion usually took the form of argument. Right now, Val and Rey were lingering beneath the antique telescope, carrying on a hushed debate while Vons led Commander Mayweather out of the chamber, the sound of the Jelna's rattling beads echoing in the hallway beyond. "You're kidding," Williams was saying. "You support Rigel's admission? I thought you Planetarists were afraid it would trample your cultural autonomy or something."

"Hey, I'm not just a label," Sangupta countered. "Sure, I want the member worlds to hold on to their autonomy, but I don't see why letting more worlds in would hurt that. I mean, space is really big. Even with warp drive and subspace radio, it takes a lot of time and effort for different worlds to interact. That's *why* a more centralized government won't work—the worlds are going to go their own ways just by being so far apart. So why not let Rigel and other worlds join?"

"Maybe. But what's the rush?"

"Wait, wait. You're against admission? I thought you backed al-Rashid."

"I do, but that doesn't mean I agree with Vanderbilt forcing the issue just so he can leave a legacy," Williams told the science officer. "I'm all for a bigger Federation, but let's choose our members wisely. That's why we're here, right? Because there's so much we still don't know. What's really going on inside the Trade Commission? What aren't they telling us about Rigel VII or the corruption on Two?"

"What makes you so convinced they're up to something?"

"Because I don't trust corporate government. You know what happened on Earth when the corporations got too much power. Political parties used as fronts for dismantling environmental and ethical regulations. Justice becoming a commodity to be bought. The wealthy few impoverishing the masses, the homeless walled inside Sanctuary Districts."

Sangupta held up his hands to quell her increasingly fervent tirade. "All right, all right, no need to convince me. But in case you've forgotten, the RTC's a nonprofit corporation. Like a charitable foundation.

The board members are elected by their worlds. They get paid a stipend so they aren't motivated by profit."

"Sure, in theory. But they do business with a lot of companies that are definitely out for profit, and they don't worry too much about keeping their excesses in check. What if they're just as corrupt as the people they deal with? The Federation should've taken the time to learn all this *before* inviting them to Babel."

"Well, that's what we're here for now, isn't it?" Sangupta replied breezily, leading the way outside after Mayweather and Vons.

Williams rolled her eyes and turned to Kirk, implicitly inviting him to join her as she followed the science officer out. "So what do you think?" she asked him. "In or out?"

Kirk replied carefully. "I just think I'm lucky to be here to witness such a historic decision in the making. Even better, to be the one to chronicle it firsthand. It's quite a privilege."

Williams smiled. "Lucky you. We all get so caught up in the politics of the moment—you have the perspective to see the big picture. I guess that makes all our arguments seem a bit petty."

The historian smiled back. "Without those arguments, my job would be more boring."

She chuckled. "But you're right. When all this is said and done, it's your words people will read to learn about this. Students for centuries to come will know your name."

He flushed. "It's names like Jonathan Archer and Malcolm Reed that they'll remember. I might get mentioned in citations here and there, but that's not the same as being famous."

She clapped his shoulder. "It's not about fame, Sam. Fame is fleeting. It's about making a lasting impact."

Kirk gazed after her fondly as she pulled ahead to join the rest of the group. They had emerged into the large circular plaza surrounding the observatory, a plaza that was one vast orrery representing the Beta Rigel system. The observatory dome itself, painted bluish-white, represented Raij. Rotating slowly around it, driven by the oft-repaired antique clockworks under the plaza, were models of each of its planets. Williams jogged past the large blue orb representing the hot Jovian Rigel I, preceded and trailed at sixty-degree intervals by arc-shaped sculptures representing the Trojan asteroids held in orbit by the interaction of the Jovian's gravity with the sun's. Kirk followed her across the closely packed orbits of the planets within the habitable zone, though most of them were elsewhere in their courses at the moment. He paused to study the intricate mechanisms driving the multiple moons that circled Rigel VI, a Neptune-type giant whose rocky satellites hosted several of the Rigel Colonies along with some of the system's most prominent mining and shipbuilding facilities.

Kirk caught up with the others as they approached the model of Rigel VII, a harsh, volcanically heated world nearly half-covered in oceans, and its co-orbital partner Rigel VIII, a cratered ice planet akin to Saturn's Rhea or Tethys but far larger. Beyond them, Rigel IX was a Jovian with a vast ring system, and the rocky Rigel X was a frigid world that had needed partial terraforming and atmosphere processing to enable even a small portion of its surface to be made habitable.

The orrery ended there, for the distant, cold worlds beyond had not been discovered until after Dleba's era, and there was insufficient room on the plateau to expand the plaza. Perhaps this was fitting, for the Rigelians had designated everything from Rigel X's orbit outward as beyond their territorial interests, free for others to settle or exploit as they chose. Rigel X itself had become a significant free port for the Kandari Sector, but as of yet, no one had found the worlds beyond it worth the effort to develop.

But Commander Mayweather was still lingering by the models of Seven and Eight, and Kirk could tell he was trying to find a diplomatic way to broach the topic of the Kalar without treading on any local taboos that might make Rehlen Vons more hostile than he was already. Leave it to Rey Sangupta, then, to breeze right up to them and ask, "So what's the story with these Kalar?"

Mayweather and Williams both glared at the science officer. But while Vons hesitated for a moment, he simply gave a sad tilt of his sallow-skinned head before replying. "Yes, it was inevitable that this would come up eventually. In truth, it isn't something we like to talk about. It reflects a dark chapter in our system's history." He sighed. "But sometimes we value our secrets too much. This is a truth we should not hide, for it informs who we are and what we believe."

The first officer kept his handsome features calm and nonjudgmental. "We're here to learn, sir."

"The Kalar were originally a racial group native to Four, alongside the Zami." Kirk had gotten used to hearing Rigelians refer to their planets by number, a custom adopted to avoid favoritism toward any one people's language. "But they were larger, more aggressive. They terrorized and enslaved their neighbors. In the first century of interplanetary contact, as the Jelna pursued economic development on Four, the Kalar were a major obstacle. As Zami prosperity grew from offworld trade, the Kalar coveted what they had, and chose to take it by force." He shrugged. "Or maybe they felt threatened by the Zami's growing power. In any case, they became a greater threat to both species' interests. And so the Jelna and the First Families mutually agreed to relocate the Kalar to Seven."

He went on solemnly. "The Kalar resisted fiercely but could not prevail over Jelna technology. They were transported in chains, in terrible conditions, for months as they made the crossing from world to world. Afterward, the relocated . . . survivors . . . were understandably resentful toward outsiders. Ever since, the Kalar have maintained a policy of total isolationism. Any offworlder who sets foot on Rigel VII cannot expect to live for long."

Williams grimaced. "I can't say I blame them."

"The Jelna and the Zami both paid a penalty for our actions," Vons replied. "As a result of different species spending so long in such conditions, disease organisms crossed species and mutated, and the plague you know as Rigelian fever evolved. The Kalar were immune, but the fever ravaged both Four and Five. Even with the best of medical care, tens of millions died on both worlds. Which hit Four harder, since it had a much smaller population and less advanced medicine, but it was a cataclysm for Five as well. The result was chaos and war on both worlds for generations, until the Zami expatriates on Five discovered the cure.

"It took generations more for regular space travel to resume, but when it finally did, it brought renewed prosperity to both worlds—and Rigel had learned a harsh but necessary lesson about the dangers of imposing our will on other societies. Ever since, we have respected the Kalar's isolation, and they have remained apart from Rigelian society." He gazed at the painted globe representing Rigel VII and sighed. "This is our greatest shame—but it is why we are so loath to judge and impose upon others."

"That's a remarkable story," Kirk said after a respectful silence. "Humanity has been through similar ordeals in its history. When explorers from Eurasia began regular contact with the isolated American continents, their diseases wiped out nearly its entire population, destroying many great civilizations and leaving most of the survivors too weak to resist conquest for long. History might have been very different if the infections had gone both ways." He gave a sad smile. "Perhaps we would've learned a lesson in tolerance far sooner—before we, too, began abducting people and forcing them to spend weeks chained in the holds of slave ships."

The assistant director pondered. "Your candor is much appreciated, Mister Kirk. It demonstrates your commitment to building closer ties, and it gives me more cause to trust your people."

Kirk smiled. "As has your own candor about the Kalar tragedy."

Vons returned the smile. "You came here to learn about our people, and I think that if there is any prospect of our becoming true partners, then such learning needs to go beyond the superficial tours and texts. I would invite you to visit the Commission's private archives. There are records there, original documents from the founding of the Commission onward, that are found nowhere else. Some of them are . . . sensitive, reflecting aspects of Commission history that we are not proud of. We keep our own secrets, just as we respect our business associates' right to theirs." Kirk nodded. "But establishing a closer relationship often entails the sharing of such secrets, as necessary to create mutual . . . understanding."

"I'd be honored." After a moment's thought, Kirk turned to Mayweather. "That is, sir, if it's . . ."

The commander chuckled. "Absolutely, Sam. That's what we're here for, after all."

Kirk snapped his fingers. "You said original documents. Untranslated?"

"Oh." Vons frowned, recognizing the problem. "I'm sure we could provide translators to assist you . . ."

"No—that is, thank you, but it would be more beneficial for me if I could bring Ensign Grev with me. He's a skilled translator and linguist, and he's more familiar with my language, so he could do a better job translating things for my benefit."

The assistant director spread his arms. "Certainly. He is welcome as well. It might take some time to get the necessary clearances . . ."

"Not a problem," Mayweather said, smiling. "We're in no hurry to leave. There's still a lot of Rigel left to see, and we're enjoying your hospitality."

Kirk's heart raced in anticipation as the group moved on. Williams punched him in the shoulder as she went past, and he realized what a silly grin he must have on his face. "Careful there," she said. "If you decide to float back to the ship, remember not to hold your breath. It'll rupture your lungs."

5

K'SHINARI WAS ONE of Antonio Ruiz's favorite patients to tend to. Although the elderly Saurian had been hit hard by the plague, she never lost her good spirits, never failed to muster up the energy to regale Ruiz with stories about her dozens of grandchildren and great-grandchildren . . . and never looked at him and his fellow offworlders with suspicion or fear. It had been some time since he'd felt such uncritical acceptance on this world.

He smiled as he approached her cot with her dinner tray in hand, anticipating the look on her bulbous-eyed face when he showed her the piece of *pevrig* cake that her youngest grandson had managed to smuggle in to him. True, it went against doctor's orders, but Ruiz firmly believed that a positive state of mind was as vital to health and healing as physical condition. K'shinari had been in this increasingly crowded treatment wing for weeks, lacking the comforts of home, and Ruiz believed the favorite family recipe could work wonders for her.

But he slowed as he reached her cot and saw Doctor Sobon and his nurse standing solemnly over the motionless figure who lay there. Sobon was a renowned xenomedical specialist from the Vulcan Science Academy, and his arrival had given Ruiz hope that a cure for the plague would now be within reach. But the doctor turned to him, his kindly, middle-aged features showing a sympathy unusual for a Vulcan. "I'm sorry, Mister Ruiz," he said. "K'shinari expired just moments ago. We made her final hours as peaceful as we could."

Ruiz had known this was a possibility, even a likelihood. Still, it hit him harder than he would have expected—perhaps because he'd fooled himself into hoping. He heard himself muttering some kind of thanks to the doctor, then turned away, took a step or two into the aisle . . . and just stood there, having no idea what to do next.

"Here, lemme take that." A pair of hands firmly but gently eased the tray out of his own, and Ruiz belatedly realized he had been about to let it fall. "Hey, are you gonna be okay?"

As the new arrival put a solicitous hand on Ruiz's arm, he finally had the presence of mind to look up. The other man had a lean, light-complexioned face with a sharp nose and chin and protruding ears, giving him a slightly gawky quality. "Uh, thank you," Ruiz said, pulling himself together. "Thanks, I'll be all right. It's just . . ."

The other man nodded. "I get it. This is a rough gig. And if we were the type who could just turn off our feelings about it, well, I guess we wouldn't be here in the first place."

Ruiz gave a hollow chuckle. "I guess you're right. Um . . . I'm Antonio. Antonio Ruiz."

"Albert Sims. Call me Al." They shook hands. "You look like you could use a cup o' coffee. How about it?"

"That'd be good, thanks."

Once they were in the cantina, away from the abundance of full cots and the overabundance of freshly empty ones, Ruiz was able to relax somewhat. "If you don't mind my asking," Sims said, "those don't seem like the hands of a medical professional."

Ruiz rubbed his callused fingertips together. "Good catch. I came here as a mining engineer. But all the mining countries got the plague and then M'Tezir moved in and kicked us out. I could've just gone back home to Cuba, but . . . well . . . I couldn't just leave these people."

"I get it." Sims studied him. "Cuba, huh? Was . . . is your family from . . ."

Ruiz sensed what he wasn't saying. No one from Earth would ever forget that day in March 2153 when the Xindi weapon had carved a path of devastation through Florida, Cuba, Jamaica, and parts of Colombia and Venezuela. "No, my family's from farther west, near Havana." He lowered his gaze. "But I had a girl in Santa Clara."

"I'm sorry, man."

"You lost somebody, too, huh?" Ruiz asked. He had noted a trace of the American Southeast in Sims's voice.

"No, I . . . I knew people who did," Sims replied. Ruiz found it hard to believe that the haunted look in his eyes could have come at second hand. Well, maybe he was just that compassionate. He'd come here, after all.

Ruiz tried to avoid sending a bitter thought Laila Alindogan's way. She had been unable to cope with the spreading plague and the growing hostility from the Saurians, so she had left two weeks ago for an asteroid-mining job in the Vega system. He couldn't decide if it was because she'd lacked the compassion to stay or been too empathetic to bear any more of it. Either way, whatever relationship they shared hadn't meant enough to Laila to make her stay. *One more casualty,* he thought, before chastising himself for such an insensitive comparison.

"I've done a bit of engineering myself here and there," Sims was saying. "Well, spaceship maintenance. I came here on an ECS freighter, nursemaiding the computers. Saw what was goin' on here and decided to lend a hand. Besides, I may have had a bit of a . . . flirtation goin' with the first mate's wife, and it woulda made the return trip pretty uncomfortable."

The man made the latter confession a bit too easily, making Ruiz suspect he was downplaying his own selflessness. Or maybe Ruiz just needed to feel optimistic about something. "Well, good for you, friend. The Saurians need all the help they can get."

Sims frowned. "Yeah, about that. This Maltuvis guy's supposed to have a cure, right? So why hasn't he spread it around? Shared it with everyone on the planet?"

Ruiz grimaced. "Well, first, it's just a treatment—it keeps the symptoms at bay, but you have to keep taking it. Which, according to *el Rey* Maltuvis, means it's awfully expensive to make enough to treat everybody.

So it's only *practical* to give the cure to countries willing to pay for the privilege—and willing to accept M'Tezir troops on their soil to 'coordinate' their missions of mercy." He scoffed.

"Well, if that don't just . . . Why not just share the damn formula with the rest of the planet?" Sims demanded.

"He says it'd take too long to train other doctors in the necessary skills."

"He also says the countries have to kick aliens out so we won't re-infect people. You buy any of that?"

Ruiz sighed. "I don't know. Doctor Lucas, Doctor Sobon, all the others, they insist there's no evidence of cross-species infection. But somehow the disease keeps cropping up in the cities where offworlders are living—and the places that have kicked them out are doing okay. That's why so many countries have agreed to Maltuvis's terms. They can see how fishy it looks, but they're afraid to take the chance. And you know how people get when they're scared."

Sims puffed breath through his lips. "Damn. I'm amazed they even let us stay here in Veranith."

"Well, the Veranith are old enemies of M'Tezir. They don't trust Maltuvis and they're not about to let his troops on their soil." Rúiz stared at his coffee cup for a moment. "But not everyone here feels the same. They're scared, too."

"That explains the protestors outside."

"Well, at least they keep their distance. If they get too close, we just have to cough at them and they back away." The two men shared a chuckle.

"If you ask me," Sims said, "this whole disease sounds awfully convenient for Mister Maltuvis."

"Yeah, most of us have thought that. But how to prove he's behind it? He's got an answer for everything. And the fact is, the docs are sure the Saurians don't have the medical knowledge to create a disease like this." He drained the dregs of his cup. "But I'll tell you this: If Maltuvis didn't cause the plague, he's sure got a handle on how to profit from it. The vulture."

Sims pondered his words. "Isn't there anything the Global League can do about it? Or the Federation?"

"Like what? There's no proof. Every country M'Tezir's sent troops to has invited them in, and frankly they look pretty heroic saving all those lives. For every Saurian who thinks Maltuvis is behind the plague, there's one or two more who'd say he was right all along and the Global League was foolish to invite aliens in."

"That's not how I remember it," Sims said. "Maltuvis was just as eager for the trade deal as the League was—he just wanted to be the one that got the most out of it."

"Yeah, well, people have short memories." He snorted. "Half the politicians in the galaxy depend on it."

The man called Albert Sims—or, as he was still known to certain intimates, Charles "Trip" Tucker—pondered Antonio Ruiz's words. The man's account tallied with others he'd heard during this fact-finding mission. Tucker found it inconceivable that Maltuvis hadn't deliberately engineered the disease as a tool to occupy other nations and sever their ties to the Global League. The Saurians were so unaccustomed to disease on this scale that it was a perfect tool for gaining leverage through terror—but terror toward others rather than M'Tezir itself.

The irony was that it didn't seem to be hurting Federation interests. While the open democracies of the Global League were susceptible to the growing popular pressure to sever ties with aliens—a direction in which even Veranith seemed to be heading—the autocratic Maltuvis could maintain his own trading ties with the Federation by fiat, while also assuming control over the trade goods from the other countries he allied with. So even as the Basileus of M'Tezir gained greater power on Sauria, he made the Federation increasingly dependent on him for the resources a growing interstellar nation demanded.

The question was, how? Ruiz was right—as far as Tucker could determine, there was no way the M'Tezir could've engineered a plague so alien to Saurian experience yet so resistant to Federation medical knowledge. It seemed likely that Maltuvis had help from aliens, but who, and why? It was possible the Basileus had hired some offworld contractor with medical expertise, such as Ajilon Prime. In that case, identifying the source and cutting them off could cripple Maltuvis. But what if Maltuvis was simply a pawn in some interstellar power's great game? Was this another salvo by the Orions and the Malurians? Could the Romulans be trying to make an end run around the Neutral

Zone and the treaty that had created it? But what would any of them have to gain, given that helping Maltuvis gain power wasn't hurting Federation trade? If not the Federation, who was being targeted? Indeed, how would any offworlders benefit from turning the Saurians *against* offworlders?

Tucker gave his head a convulsive shake, drawing a glance from Ruiz. "Are you all right, Al?"

He smiled sheepishly. "Just tired."

"Yeah, this place does that to you. How long till your shift ends?"

"A few hours yet. And I should really get back to work now."

"I guess I should, too," Ruiz said. "I lost a friend today . . . but there are still others I can help."

"That's the spirit."

Tucker headed back out to the treatment ward with determination. He'd shaken off his earlier thoughts out of disgust at himself for treating this like some cosmic chess game when real people were suffering and dying here on the ground. That was the kind of attitude he was trying to keep Section 31 from succumbing to.

Meeting Antonio Ruiz had been a valuable reminder of what he was fighting for. Like Tucker, the Cuban had lost someone he cared about in the Xindi attack, had seen his community overshadowed by fear and loss. And it had motivated him to do what he could for other victims of loss and tragedy. How could Tucker do any less, if he wished to honor the memory of his sister? As painful as it was, he needed to go out there with the sick and dying Saurians, to look each and every one of them in the eyes, and to remember what he was really fighting for.

June 14, 2164
Planetoid "Babel," orbiting Gliese 283 B

Director Sedra Hemnask of the Rigelian Trade Commission surveyed the barren surface beyond the viewport of Babel Station's reception dome: an expanse of cratered rock and regolith dimly illuminated by the tiny red dwarf it orbited, half of an obscure, unclaimed binary system whose primary star had long ago sloughed off its atmosphere and left behind a white-dwarf corpse and a smattering of burned, lifeless worlds. "An unlikely soil," she mused, "for sowing the seeds of new nations."

"I see what you mean," Jonathan Archer told the Zami Rigelian as he gazed out the port with her. "But it's got quite a history behind it."

"Really?" Her large green eyes lit up with interest.

He smiled and began to tell the story. Interstellar histories that were half-legend told of a pair of starfaring civilizations, Menthar and Promellia, locked in an intractable holy war for generations. Some eight centuries ago, after their worlds had been devastated and their populations reduced largely to refugee fleets, a last-ditch peacemaking effort was undertaken. Both sides recruited a neutral race to build an outpost on a lifeless subplanet in a small, dead star system hundreds of light-years from either species' territory—a place that neither side would have any reason to fight over, and where they could negotiate far removed from factions seeking to co-opt them or sabotage their efforts. This outpost, they hoped, would be the site of a decisive peace conference that would save both civilizations from extinction.

Yet before the outpost was even completed, the Menthar and Promellian fleets had converged almost by accident around the final surviving colony, in an as-yet-undiscovered system that the histories called Orelious. The resultant unplanned battle had escalated to the point that both sides had gone all in, every surviving ship called in as reinforcements. Even the peacemakers had been grimly obliged to join the fight in defense of the few survivors. "And nobody in local space ever heard from them again," Archer finished. "Some legends say they both got caught by a doomsday weapon that destroyed the planet they were fighting over. Some say one deliberately destroyed itself to take the others with them."

"How awful."

"Well, some historians think the survivors just scattered, finding new homes and taking new names. I hope that's the case, but nobody knows for sure. All we know," he said, gesturing around them, "is what they left us. A grand creation that fell apart because its creators couldn't get along. Like the Tower of Babel in Earth mythology."

"Ahh, hence your code name for it," Hemnask said. Pausing for thought, she smiled. "I can guess—this site is used for diplomatic talks as a reminder of the cost should those talks fail."

"Exactly," Archer replied, impressed by her sharp mind. "Starting about four centuries ago with the Ramatis Choral Debates. The people of Ramatis succeeded in staving off war and are admired as great diplomats to this day. Since then, a number of civilizations have used Babel as neutral ground to hash out their differences and negotiate treaties. Like the Andorians and Tellarites a decade ago, when they asked Earth to mediate a trade dispute." He told her how the Romulan stealth attacks intended to disrupt that conference had backfired, prompting Earth, Andoria, Tellar, and Vulcan to come together against their common foe. Those first Babel talks had led to the formation of the Coalition of Planets the following year; then, after the war, the planetoid had hosted the preliminary talks for the formation of the Federation—although the final signing ceremony had been held on Earth, since founding a nation here would have undermined the sanctity of this neutral ground.

"It's wise to have such reminders of history's grim lessons," Hemnask told him. "The Governing Board is based in Tregon for much the same reason. Centuries ago, it was the site of a great massacre of my Zami ancestors by the Jelna. My people had only been on Five for a few generations then, and when Rigelian fever spread across both our worlds, the Jelna came to see aliens as unclean and drove us from their cities. The fact that the fever ravaged Four even worse mattered little to them. And by driving us out, they probably delayed a cure, for it was Zami physicians who eventually discovered how to treat the fever with ryetalyn. Tregon has stood ever since as an object lesson for tolerance and cooperation. It reminds us that all our people are equally Rigelian, whatever world they come from."

Archer's appreciative reply was drowned out by shouting from nearby. He turned to see Rogra jav Baur, the Tellarite ambassador, engaged in a vocal confrontation with his counterpart from Mars, Mikhail Kamenev, while the Earth and Alpha Centauri delegates stood on their respective flanks. "Excuse me," he said to Hemnask, embarrassed that the representatives of his own Federation evidently needed a refresher in that same lesson.

As he approached, Archer could hear the gist of the argument. "Racist!" Baur was crying. "You just can't stand letting more nonhumans into the Federation. You're no better than Terra Prime or those fanatics on Alrond!"

"How dare you?" Kamenev shouted back.

"Just like a Federalist to demonize the opposition," chimed in Ysanne Fell, the prim and shrill-voiced Centaurian ambassador. "Can you blame the Lechebists for their fear of cultural assimilation? Hopefully the Rigelians won't be fooled into surrendering their autonomy to the state."

"Yes, cultural assimilation is exactly the issue," Kamenev insisted. "Our worlds will lose their uniqueness if too many are blended together in one homogeneous mass."

"Yet you don't seem to object to letting Vega Colony join!" the Tellarite riposted.

"Because they deserve to stand on a level playing field, not as a dependency of Earth! I feel the same about any colony world, such as Alrond or Iota Pegasi."

"Oh, really? And would you flirt with their representatives the way you have with that girl from Vega?"

"You leave Tamara out of this!"

Sensing that words were about to give way to blows, Archer moved forward—but before he could interpose himself between the two large men, he saw that someone else already had. A rather small someone else, in fact: a Vulcan woman several centimeters shorter than T'Pol. Yet her stance made it clear that she was not to be moved from where she stood. She held each ambassador's gaze coolly and firmly for several seconds, and each man in turn stood down. "Gentlemen," she said in a soft, serene voice that contrasted with the coiled-spring poise of her body. "I submit that the conference table is a more appropriate venue for policy debates. Perhaps you will grasp each other's positions more clearly without the influence of distracting libations."

Deciding to back up her peacekeeping effort, Archer stepped closer. "Is there a problem here?"

The ambassadors proffered various mumblings about the absence of problems and returned to the havens of their respective factions, which seemed equally matched, with three ambassadorial parties in each. He turned to the Vulcan. "Thanks for your help."

She studied him. "I believe your characterization is

inverted. *Your* assistance is appreciated . . . albeit unnecessary."

He tilted his head in concession. "Point taken."

"Both of you deserve thanks." It was Director Hemnask, coming up alongside Archer once again. "Admiral, would you introduce me?"

Archer studied the Vulcan's refined features, trying to place her name. "I . . . know you're with Ambassador Solkar's delegation, but . . ."

She rescued him from further embarrassment. "T'Rama. Formerly of Administrator T'Pau's security detail."

"That would explain it," Hemnask said. "You are here to protect the ambassador?"

"I retired from security once my husband and I committed to starting a family. The ambassador is my husband's-father, however, and he required a personal aide when he chose to come out of retirement to participate in this conference."

"I understand," Archer said. "He's . . . had quite a storied career."

T'Rama gave him a frank look that was not entirely ungrateful. "You mean he is quite elderly. Yes. But he intends the admission of Rigel to the Federation to be the concluding achievement of his career. I intend to help him see it through." She threw the ambassador a look across the room, a look that Archer would have called affectionate if she weren't Vulcan. "Our family has produced statespersons and diplomats for generations. Yet Solkar's only offspring, my husband, Skon, found his calling in mathematics instead."

Archer snapped his fingers, trying to remember. "Skon. I've heard of him. I read his English translation of *The Teachings of Surak*."

She nodded. "Yes, linguistics is his avocation."

Hemnask furrowed her brow in puzzlement. "I thought it was Admiral Archer who recovered Surak's writings only a few years ago."

"The *Kir'Shara*, yes. What my husband translated were the Analects—secondhand or reconstructed accounts of Surak's original teachings."

"I see. And has Skon undertaken a translation of the *Kir'Shara* yet?"

"He has plans to do so, as his teaching career permits."

"I look forward to reading it," Archer said. "I've read the computer translation, but it's missing something."

"Indeed. At any rate, Skon's duties precluded him from assisting Solkar in this concluding achievement to his career, so I undertook the task. I have considered entering the diplomatic field myself, once our child is old enough not to need constant care."

Hemnask frowned. "If your child isn't old enough yet, then why leave them now?"

"I have not." She placed a hand on her belly. "He is in my care at every moment."

The Zami woman stared, then broke into a radiant grin. "I . . . Congratulations! I had no idea. What a blessing this is!"

"Yes, congratulations," Archer said, trying to keep his tone subdued so as not to embarrass the Vulcan woman with an emotional outburst. "How . . . if it's not rude to ask, how far along are you?"

"Far along . . . ? Ahh, yes. Approximately one Terran month, or one-thirteenth of the gestation period."

"And he's already begun his glorious diplomatic career," Hemnask joked. Then she looked at T'Rama more seriously. "I envy you. The way you've managed to balance your professional duties with your family obligations."

"It has not been completely effortless," T'Rama conceded. "But Vulcan kinship structures and traditions have evolved over the millennia to provide an orderly framework for managing such responsibilities. My former employer T'Pau is also a member of Solkar and Skon's clan. Thus, my transition to a new career is facilitated, and my requirements as an expectant parent are accommodated."

"All very logical," Archer said.

"Thank you."

Hemnask shook her head, impressed. "If only it were so easy for the rest of us. My people, the Zami . . . we place great importance on our family bonds, and on the obligations that come with them. Perhaps that is why we have retained our cultural distinctiveness after so many centuries living among other Rigelians. Yet I have often found it . . . difficult to reconcile my duties to the Rigelian people with my duties to my family."

"Perhaps because your people encompass so many cultures," T'Rama replied. "It is possible Vulcans may face similar dilemmas in the future as members of the

Federation." She threw a look at Kamenev and the other Planetarist-leaning delegates. "Certainly there are already challenges in finding common ground. Yet Surak taught that diversity in combination can be a source of great dynamism and progress. Even through our conflicts, we can learn and grow stronger." She quirked a brow at Archer. "One hopes."

Hemnask laughed, and T'Rama seemed surprisingly untroubled by the response. Archer found her atypically laid back for a Vulcan; he wondered if it was something hormonal, or if she was always like this.

At any rate, Hemnask was right: the Vulcan woman's seeming ability to balance family and career was impressive. Archer found himself thinking back to his earlier conversation with Dani Erickson. Was he using his career as an excuse to avoid personal entanglements? Margaret Mullin had dumped him all those years ago out of fear of becoming a "Starfleet widow." Had he taken her fear to heart and made it a self-fulfilling prophecy? If a Vulcan could be a wife, daughter-in-law, expectant mother, and diplomat without seeing a conflict, why wasn't Archer even dating anyone? True, he believed he had a mission, even a calling, to ensure that the Federation achieved the future he knew it could have, and to defeat the forces that sought to deny that future. But did the future need his attention around the clock, every day? Was there no room for his own needs in the present?

It was particularly hard to ignore such thoughts as he watched Sedra Hemnask laugh, tossing back her mass of golden-brown hair to expose a delicately pointed ear which, combined with her delicate features and large green eyes, gave her an elfin beauty. And when those eyes met with his and her smile widened, he found himself wanting to forget about the future for a while.

6

STUDYING IN the RTC's secure archive wasn't turning out to be quite the historical mother lode Samuel Kirk had expected. For security reasons, the Commission forbade recording or communication devices within the archive—a massive vault carved deep within a mountain on Rigel V's southernmost continent—and live guards were a constant presence to ensure nobody tried to sneak out with a historical relic. Ensign Grev hadn't even been allowed to bring in a text translator unit; he had to rely on his own weeklong study of older Rigelian dialects, and on the assistance of an elderly Zami interpreter who worked for the archive. Kirk was only allowed to take handwritten notes about the documents that he and Grev observed. True, it was a privilege to have access to them at all, but it was frustrating that he wouldn't be able to provide primary-source support for his account.

Moreover, they weren't even granted full access to the archive. One particularly heavy-looking (and heavily guarded) door had attracted Kirk's interest, but his guide, Assistant Director Vons, had made it clear that his invitation to the historian did not include access to that part of the facility. "Those are more recent secure records," the Jelna board member had explained. "Matters where confidentiality is still important to maintain."

Grev, as usual, took an understanding tone, suggesting that greater access might come once Rigel and the Federation had formed closer ties. But Kirk was starting to think the Rigelians' love of secrecy might hamper their participation in a society as open as the Federation.

During a lull in their work, while Vons went off to take a call and the archive interpreter worked to retrieve some ancient settlement accord from the darkest corners of the stacks, Kirk noticed Grev staring at him inquisitively. "What?" he asked the chubby young Tellarite.

"So?" the communications officer asked. "You and Val. How's that going?"

Kirk's gaze reflexively darted toward Crewman Mishima, the security guard that Williams had assigned to accompany them. Mercifully, the tall, gray-shirted man seemed engrossed in a staring contest with the archive guards who stood watch over them, one a massive Chelon and the other a wiry but muscular man of Coridanite ancestry. "What do you mean?" he asked softly, hoping Grev would get the hint.

He did; the young Tellarite leaned forward, elbows on the table, and continued in a more conspiratorial tone. "I mean, have you thought about asking her to dinner?" Kirk stared, but Grev just smiled.

"It's not that hard to see you like her, Sam. And she likes you!"

Kirk fidgeted. "As a friend, sure."

"Friendship can be the start of a lot of things."

"Or it can be the end of them. I'm not the kind of man Val looks at in that way."

"Maybe you just haven't given her a reason to yet."

Kirk threw the young ensign a glare, annoyed at his attempt to stir up false hope. "Come on, Grev. Even if she were interested, you know where Captain Reed stands on fraternization."

"He's been mellowing. And you're not a bridge officer like Rey. It's not likely an armory officer and a historian would be part of the same chain of command. Maybe it'd be okay."

"Maybe." He shook his head and scoffed. "As if it wouldn't be enough of an uphill battle just getting Val's attention."

"Fortune favors the bold, my friend."

"Yeah, and that's why I'm a lowly ship's historian. Boldness is Val's specialty."

"You wouldn't be in Starfleet if you didn't crave challenges."

Kirk threw him an irritated look. "Are you really interested in this, or are you just being Tellarite and looking for an excuse to argue?"

"Who says it can't be both?" Grev replied with aggravating good cheer.

Before Kirk could reply, a muffled thumping sound came from some other part of the stacks. "What's that?" Mishima asked, suddenly on the alert.

"I'll check it out," the Coridanite guard said. "Stay here." Kirk noticed they left the bigger, more dangerous guard to keep watch on him and Grev. Chelons weren't very flexible or fast-moving, but he understood that they could secrete a highly lethal contact toxin from their skins if provoked. Not that he would've wanted to provoke this one anyway.

"Ooh, I hope Mister Vons didn't knock over something valuable," Grev said. "He's just shifty enough to pin the blame on us."

"What makes you think he's shifty?" Kirk asked.

"There's just something off about his body language," Grev said, leaning forward and whispering again. "Like he's trying too hard not to seem like he's trying to hide something." Kirk just stared, trying to parse that, and Grev shrugged. "I notice these things."

A scuffling sound came from beyond the stacks, followed by a more resounding thump. "Tastra!" the Chelon called, her beak clicking in concern. "Tastra, respond!" When no response came, she heaved her formidable bulk forward. "Wait here," she told the *Pioneer* personnel.

"We should stick together," Mishima said. Kirk and Grev rose from the table, moving toward him.

"Do as you will," the Chelon replied. "I need to see to the vault." Kirk realized the sounds were coming from the direction of the heavy vault door.

The Chelon led the way, Mishima behind her, and the other two stayed safely in the rear. When they arrived at the vault, all seemed normal. A contingent of four armed guards flanked the vault door, and Vons stood alone nearby. But someone was missing. "Where is Tastra?" the Chelon asked.

Vons looked unconcerned. "Isn't he with you?"

"He came this way moments ago. There were noises."

"Ahh, yes," Vons said, smiling. "We did our best, but some noises are unavoidable."

Suddenly the Chelon convulsed and clutched her throat—and Kirk realized there was a very large knife stuck in it. He thought he saw a glimpse of motion by Mishima, but by the time he turned his head, he only saw the crewman—falling to the floor with a knife in his upper chest, his phase pistol only half-drawn. Kirk and Grev recoiled in horror. Kirk sensed more movement around him—a faint shuffling step, a puff of moving air, a shadow in the corner of his eye—but he could see nothing but the archive stacks.

"I advise you not to run," Vons told them in a bored tone. "Let me show you why."

The Jelna clicked his tongue several times, and the scene changed. Kirk blinked in confusion, seeing the chamber anew as if he had just woken from a dream. He and Grev were surrounded by several large Zami armed with knives and guns—and by something else. By Vons's feet were two large, six-legged lizards, maybe a meter eighty from snout to tail tip and a third of that in height. Their swaybacked pink bodies, frilled necks, prominent overbites, and upturned mouths gave them a comical, Seussian appearance—in striking contrast to the horror of the scene surrounding them, where not only Mishima and the Chelon but

Tastra and the four vault guards lay bleeding out on the floor. One of the lizards blinked its yellow eyes at him lazily, as unconcerned by the carnage as Vons himself.

"What . . . what's going on here?" Grev demanded, trying and failing to put steel in his soft tenor voice.

"Oh, don't worry, you won't be joining them," the assistant director replied as he moved toward the vault. "We require your services—or will once we obtain what we're here for." He placed his hand on the vault's biometric interface, then let it scan his irises and repeated a code phrase to verify his voice-print. Then one of the Zami assassins placed Tastra's hand on a scanner at the guard station. For a moment, nothing happened, but then the vault door unlocked and began to swing open. "That's a relief," Vons said. "Just enough of a pulse left. For a moment there, Damreg, I thought you'd miscalculated how long he'd take to die."

"We know our business," the fair-haired, pointed-eared assassin said, letting Tastra fall hard to the floor. Kirk turned away before he hit.

Vons led two of the assassins into the vault while the others kept watch over Kirk and Grev. Finally the criminals emerged carrying what looked to Kirk like some kind of computer servers, boxy hexagonal units just small enough to be tucked under an arm and adorned on one edge with indicator lights, most of which were dormant. "What are those?" Kirk asked.

"Be patient, Mister Kirk, you'll find out. We could use your help breaking the encryption on their contents. Well, mainly Mister Grev's help, but your own skills could prove useful in evaluating what he decrypts."

"And what makes you think I'd help you?" Grev insisted, crossing his arms.

"Well, how about this?" Vons gestured to a darker-haired assassin with rounder ears than the rest, and suddenly Kirk was in the Zami's grip with a knife edge tickling his throat. "I said he could prove useful, but I was being polite. Mainly he's a hostage for your cooperation. Do we have an understanding?"

Kirk rallied his courage. Whatever was in those servers was important enough to warrant extensive security—and important enough to kill for. It couldn't be allowed to fall into the wrong hands. "Don't help them on my account, Grev!"

"Noble words, Mister Kirk, but think it through. If he refuses to cooperate, we'll have to kill you both anyway. That would make the decryption somewhat more challenging for us, but really, what choice would we have?"

But Grev was already looking at Kirk with concern and apology. "I'm sorry, Sam. I can't let them hurt you." He sighed. "I'll go with you, but you have to let him go."

Vons looked annoyed. "You really don't grasp the situation, do you? I don't 'have' to do anything. I'm the one with all the power here. Which means *you* have to do what I say you have to do." He shook his head. "Honestly, why am I trying to convince you? You're both coming anyway, because that's the plan."

He turned to Damreg. "Is the relay in place?"

The assassin checked an interface device in his hand. "Online and ready."

Vons nodded. "Place the charges."

The other assassins removed small packs of what looked like plastic explosive from their belt pouches, positioning them strategically. Kirk reflexively started to protest, horrified by the imminent loss to history, but the knife against his throat reminded him of a more pressing set of priorities. He cursed himself for his helplessness; no doubt Val would've known several dozen moves for disarming the assassin and getting the drop on the others.

Once the charges were set, Vons ordered their activation. Grev stared in dismay at the Rigelian numerals counting down on the detonators. "But . . . but that doesn't give us enough time to get out!"

Vons gestured theatrically to Damreg, who began pressing buttons on his interface device. "Except."

He didn't need to continue the sentence; the tingling sensation that engulfed Kirk's body a moment later spoke volumes. He squeezed his eyes shut, hoping that whatever transporter technology his abductors were using was more reliable than the Federation kind. . . .

June 18, 2164
U.S.S. Endeavour, orbiting Babel

"Apparently Crewman Mishima lived long enough to disarm one of the explosive devices," Malcolm Reed reported from the

bridge's main viewer, a mix of pride and anger leavening his disciplined voice. *"It didn't save him, but it reduced the blast damage just enough to let us recover some of the evidence they were hoping to obliterate. We've been able to determine that most of the attackers were Zami Rigelians, and that they had help from Assistant Director Vons, who has now disappeared."* He took a breath. *"Moreover, we've verified that there are no remains from Ensign Grev and Lieutenant Kirk. Apparently they've been abducted, though we're not sure why."*

The bridge personnel around Archer showed relief. But Archer's eyes were on Sedra Hemnask, who was here along with Ambassador Jahlet to hear Reed's report, as it concerned their system. He thought he caught a hint of realization in her expression. "Director?" he prompted. "If there's something you want to tell us about what was stolen from that vault . . ."

"What they took . . . were potentially the most valuable and most destructive things in our possession," she replied softly.

"Some kind of weapon?" Captain T'Pol asked from her command chair.

Hemnask gave a faint chuckle. "In a sense—though the Trade Commission's most potent weapons have never involved physical force. No, our power comes from the secrets we hold." She shook her head. "Or so I thought. It seems Rehlen Vons had deeper secrets than I imagined. That he would do this to us . . . betray us to the First Families. . . . What hold could they have over him?"

"Director, please," T'Pol went on. "In hostage situations, time is of the essence."

Hemnask shook herself. "Yes, of course. Let me explain." She took another moment to gather her thoughts. "We hear what your delegates say about our system," she said. "That the Trade Commission does not pay attention to the misdeeds of our business partners, that we allow them to get away with all things. The truth is . . . we take note of everything. Every action they take, every crime they commit, every violation and exploitation we can document. We see it all, and we remember it all. And that is our weapon."

After a moment, Takashi Kimura spoke from the tactical station. "It sounds like you're talking about blackmail."

"We see it as . . . leverage," Hemnask told him. "We must balance our commitment to the self-determination of Rigel's worlds and communities with the stability of Rigel as a whole. And so we watch. Normally watching is all we do. But if someone threatens an act that could destabilize the system, then we let them know what we have seen . . . and we encourage them to be more cooperative, lest certain uncomfortable truths come to light.

"For example: Many officials on Rigel II are in the pocket of the First Families. They are implicated in many criminal and corrupt acts—acts that violate local planetary laws, or that would alienate their customers, partners, or power bases were they to become known. So long as they have an incentive to keep those ties secret, we can pressure them, keep them from acting too aggressively to increase the Families' power. As long as they are free to serve the Families' interests to a limited extent, it mollifies the Families enough that they do not push too far. But if the officials' ties and other secrets were exposed, then they would no longer have a check on their behavior, and neither would the Families."

"That's . . ." Archer stopped himself from saying it was crazy. He supposed many things in human political history would seem just as irrational to an outsider. "How did a system like that ever come about?"

Ambassador Jahlet fielded that one. "It is a legacy of our history," the beaded Jelna said. "The early Trade Commission was stabilized by the mutual exchange of secrets. The members used the leverage of those secrets as a hedge against betrayal, a deterrent against corruption and exploitation. It has actually served over time to reduce such selfish actions, to encourage us to be forthright and ethical toward one another. The keeping of secrets is a mutual responsibility for the good of all. Many of those secrets are innocuous now . . . but there are still some that hold power and danger, especially those involving the Families and others outside the united Rigel community."

"Those who need greater 'leverage' to be kept in check," T'Pol interpreted.

"Exactly," Hemnask said. "But the stolen files could expose other secrets, secrets that are necessary for any business. Patented designs, proprietary formulas and techniques, the particulars of confidential deals and agreements. Information about a company's health or future profit potential which could lead to insider trading or disruptive runs on the market. The

Families could use this information to blackmail countless businesses across Rigel and beyond—or to intentionally destabilize them. They could cripple Rigel's economy and weaken our ability to keep their piracy and corruption in check."

"*Or weaken your defenses,*" Reed said from the screen. "*Admiral, our forensic scans show evidence that the assailants beamed themselves and their captives out of the vault. They're working with someone who has transporter technology. Maybe the Orions, the Malurians, even the Klingons. Whoever it is, they must have something to gain by undermining the RTC.*"

Jahlet frowned. "But the vault is deep inside a mountain. Even transporters should not penetrate."

Reed's science officer, Lieutenant Sangupta, fielded that one. "*They had a portable transporter relay stationed near the entrance to the mountain. It beamed them out of the vault and into its own buffer, and from there to a waiting ship.*"

"Have you identified the ship?" T'Pol asked.

Sangupta grimaced. "*Unfortunately, it sent out decoy signals to half the ships in orbit, several of which left orbit minutes later.*"

Reed's armory officer, Valeria Williams—whom Archer knew well, for his right-hand man Marcus Williams was her doting father—elaborated. "*We and the Rigelian authorities have already searched and cleared several of them—we think they were uninvolved and just had signals beamed to them to throw us off. But we think most of the rest were deliberate decoys. And several of them made stops at other planets or stations in the system before they could be searched. They've had plenty of time to move their captives elsewhere—especially if they're using transporters. Grev and Sam could be anywhere in the system by now, if they're even still in the system.*"

"It doesn't help that this attack has elements pointing to multiple worlds," Reed added. *"Vons is from Rigel V, the killers used knives made by the hill people of Rigel IV, and the DNA evidence suggests they got past the guards using a reptilian creature native to Rigel III—something called a hypnoid, which can project telepathic illusions. Not to mention whatever offworld power provided the transporter. Our problem, Admiral,"* he finished, a grimace distorting his goatee, *"is that we have too many leads."*

Archer frowned, taking in the bad news. "But why would they take our people?" he asked.

"The secure files are heavily encrypted," Hemnask replied. "Even Vons would not be able to access them without at least two other directors' codes. Starfleet communications officers are renowned for their skills with language and translation. Code breaking is a similar art."

"And, sir," Hoshi Sato said to Archer, "I know Ensign Grev. He's got a real gift for languages, and he's studied all my methods for translation and decryption—even improved on a couple."

T'Pol considered. "The historian may have been taken to help assess the context and relevance of the deciphered data. Or perhaps he is simply a hostage for Mister Grev's cooperation."

"They are friends," Reed verified. *"But then, most everyone on Pioneer is a friend of Grev's. We're determined to get him back any way we can. And Mister Kirk, of course."*

"You will have the Commission's full cooperation," Hemnask told him.

"I appreciate the gesture, Director," Reed said. *"But we both know your highest priority is the recovery of your archives."*

"And it must be yours as well, Captain," T'Pol told

him, "given the risk to the stability of the Rigelian system if they are not recovered in time."

Reed exchanged a look with her for a moment, then nodded. *"Of course, Captain. I understand."* Archer knew that Malcolm Reed would be the first to remind him of a Starfleet officer's duty to sacrifice oneself for others. If Grev and Kirk had absorbed any of their captain's values, Archer knew they would both place the archive's rescue—or destruction—over their own survival, given the need to choose. But being captain, Archer also knew, had a way of changing a person's perspective. Sacrificing those under one's command was a far harder call to make than sacrificing oneself.

But he shouldn't have to bear that burden alone, Archer decided. He turned to Commander Sato. "Hoshi, contact Babel and have them send up a shuttlepod for myself and the Rigelian delegates." As Sato acknowledged the order and began to carry it out, he turned to T'Pol. "Captain, as soon as we disembark, I want you to head for Rigel, best speed. You're going to join *Pioneer* in searching for our people."

On the viewer, Reed looked hurt. *"I see. Well, if you think that's necessary, sir . . ."*

Archer could guess what Malcolm was thinking. He hadn't been a captain very long, and T'Pol was his former commanding officer. And Reed always had been prone to a certain insecurity. "I have every confidence in you and your crew, Malcolm," Archer assured him. "These are your people, and there's nobody who'll fight harder to bring them home safe.

But you know the situation. Rigel's a huge system, so the more ships we have searching, the better our chances."

Reed straightened and nodded stiffly, not looking very reassured. *"Understood, sir. You'll have our full cooperation, Captain T'Pol."*

"Thank you, Captain Reed."

Archer smiled at T'Pol's emotional insight—stressing Reed's title to demonstrate her respect for his authority. *Speaking of which* . . . He turned to the Rigelians. "That is, if it's all right with you."

"Of course, Admiral," Hemnask said. "Starfleet sensors are significantly more sensitive than any we have. A second starship is more than welcome."

"Thank you, Director. Shall we?" At Hemnask's nod, he escorted her and Jahlet to the turbolift. "Good luck, T'Pol. Malcolm."

The captains acknowledged his benediction and he left. Once in the lift, Hemnask studied him. "Do humans truly believe that luck guides the outcome of events? That such a blessing will bring some favorable cosmic influence to bear?"

"Once, I guess. These days it's more just an expression of hope. Letting someone know that you wish them success." He thought for a moment. "Personally, I think success comes from the effort and determination we put into achieving our goals."

"Then should you not say 'good effort'?"

He smiled. "That's just it. With captains like T'Pol and Malcolm Reed, I don't have to say it. I already know I'll get it."

Tregon, Rigel V

"We do not need outside assistance," Jemer Zehron insisted. Though the Jelna endomale's words were nominally addressed to his fellow directors, he was all but glaring toward Travis Mayweather. As this was an impromptu emergency session, Mayweather and the board members were in a small, secure meeting room rather than the council hall, and while there was a table present, the four had all chosen to stand. "This is the Commission's responsibility, and we should deal with it ourselves."

"Do not be obtuse, Jemer," intoned Director Sajithen. The Chelon clicked her beak and clutched the hems of her ornate robe. "We need every available resource to search for the missing archives." She peered through hooded eyes at the other two directors present. "And there are other factors to consider."

"That's right," Director Tenott agreed, gesturing with a stubby yellow finger. "*Pioneer* personnel were taken as well. They have a stake in the search themselves."

"Thank you," Mayweather told the Xarantine.

"While that is true," Sajithen acknowledged, "it is not what I meant. This raid was an inside job. Vons may not be the only one who was compromised. He may not have been working alone."

Tenott scoffed. "Surely you don't mean to suggest that Sedra was involved! She has more reason to hate the Families than any of us."

"We all have our secrets—as you well know, Nop. Like certain payoffs for an environmental inspector on Colony Three to look the other way?"

Tenott wrinkled his noseless face. "You know I made amends for that mistake years ago. I worked hard to restore the dome's stability. What, what about Jemer?" the colonial director went on, gesturing toward his counterpart from Rigel II. "He's taken kickbacks from Family-run businesses before."

Zehron ignored the charge, instead keeping his red-eyed gaze on Sajithen. "And you're so pristine, you sanctimonious reptile? If certain radical ties were to come out—"

"As I said," Sajithen interrupted, bowing toward him with sardonic courtesy, "we all have secrets. This is the value of accepting Starfleet assistance. An outside, neutral party—"

"And are you so sure their hands are clean? Undermining our authority could serve their interests, open a power vacuum they could fill. Maybe they faked the abduction to conceal their collusion."

"Excuse me," Mayweather said, his words far more polite than his tone. He'd been listening patiently up to now, but he'd had enough. He stepped forward and loomed over Zehron. "We did not fake the *death* of Kenji Mishima. He was a member of our crew, part of our family, and we have to grieve for him. Our captain is going to have to write a letter to his mother and his kid sisters back on Alpha Centauri, explaining why he's never coming home again. Now, I know you aren't thrilled about the idea of joining the Federation. But that's no excuse to use a good man's death as fodder for playing politics."

The Jelna's red eyes met his unflinchingly for some

moments . . . and then the director's expression softened marginally. "You are correct, Commander. It was inappropriate. I apologize."

"On behalf of Crewman Mishima," Mayweather told him, "I accept your apology."

The room was quiet for a moment. But then Mayweather began to pace before the directors, meeting their eyes one by one. "Now. We've got a time-sensitive situation here. If there's anything you know that might help us get a handle on where to look, now's the time to speak up."

Sajithen rumbled in her throat. "What concerns me most is the use of hypnoids," the Chelon said. "They are rare creatures—for obvious reasons, difficult to capture. And not easy to train, either. Only certain isolated tribes in the inland forests are adept at finding and taming the beasts." She hesitated. "Tribes that . . . have ties to a radical nationalist faction on Three. Chelons who believe we are still treated as a backward minority, imposed upon by those who consider themselves our betters."

"Oh, imagine that," Zehron muttered. "Leading a primitive existence in the wilds, and they complain that we consider them backward."

Sajithen made an effort to ignore him. "What they wish most, Commander, is to eliminate what they see as offworld domination. Their militant leanings have been kept in check by . . . certain sympathizers in official positions, who are able to offer peaceful alternatives for advancing their agendas."

Okay, Travis thought. The look on Zehron's face

reinforced the first officer's suspicion that those sympathizers included Sajithen herself, though Zehron could not be considered the most trustworthy observer. "So if they don't like offworld interference, why would they work with the Families and whoever provided the transporters? I assume the Families couldn't have just stolen the hypnoids—they would've needed help to train them."

"Exactly. What I fear is that they may have made a deal with the most radical nationalists. If the archives' secrets are revealed, those officials' ties to the radicals will be exposed, nullifying their appearance of legitimacy and their ability to keep the radicals in check. The result could be open revolt."

Mayweather frowned. "But what would the Families get out of that?"

"It could weaken the Commission if our members were fighting among themselves," Zehron replied. "Or divert our effort and resources to Three while they pursued goals elsewhere."

"Like Two," Tenott said, "where we know they crave more overt control."

"Or the Colonies," Zehron shot back, "where they collude with out-system syndicates or governments seeking an illicit edge."

Are they always like this? Mayweather wondered. Were they rehashing what were clearly old arguments in hopes of convincing him to take their sides, or was it a habit they'd carry on even without a spectator?

"We can figure that out later," Mayweather told the directors. "If we know where the kidnappers got the hypnoids, then that's our lead. We need to track those people down and find out what they know."

"They will not listen to you," Sajithen said. "Only to another Chelon. One they know and trust."

"Can you suggest anybody?" he asked as innocently as he could manage.

She emitted a series of rapid-fire clicks that seemed equivalent to a resigned sigh. "I am from those parts. It would be best if I accompanied you myself."

"I really appreciate it, Director. It'd be fastest if we took *Pioneer* . . ."

"Ahh, perhaps your vessel would be more useful elsewhere," Tenott said. "Our search for the ship that traveled to the colonies around Six has hit a snag. Our scans lost their trail in a shipyard facility. While your drives would be trivially faster than ours over interplanetary distances, your sensor systems may be better able to search than ours."

"You are welcome to accompany me in one of our ships," Sajithen said, "while *Pioneer* tends to that matter. That is, if you agree, Commander."

"Sounds reasonable," Mayweather said. "I'll clear it with the captain." He glanced toward Zehron. "I don't suppose you have anything helpful to suggest."

"Only that you not raise your hopes," the paleskinned director said. "The abductors have gone to great effort to impede your ability to track down your crewmen. Wherever you go, you will likely face deceptions, traps, and other dangers. If you and your crew come through them alive, it may well be too late to stop the exposure of our secret files."

The commander met his spiel with an irritated glare. "Do you have a better idea?"

Zehron smirked. "Not at all. I enjoy a good gamble. I'm simply reminding you, Commander . . . that the odds always favor the house."

7

DEVNA'S HOPES WERE RAISED when she was told she would be servicing a human.

The last human male she had encountered, last year on Rigel V, had been a member of Starfleet's most secret, off-book intelligence agency, sent to stymie the Three Sisters' plan to manipulate the Federation into a potentially crippling war. He had interrogated Devna's handler, learning that she was no mere sex worker but, in fact, an Orion Syndicate agent using her seductive arts to goad a Federation commissioner into embracing a more aggressive policy. The fair-haired Starfleet operative had confiscated her knife before confronting her and was somehow immune to her pheromonal allure. She had been at his mercy, and he could have easily arrested or assassinated her. And yet, instead, he had spoken to her kindly, reasoned with her in a way no male ever had. He had shown her his vulnerabilities and extended his trust, prompting her to respond in kind. In exchange for being allowed to go free, she had alerted him to a planned raid in the Deneb system. It had not been the Sisters' true endgame by a long shot, but it had been enough to appease Starfleet and make them feel they had scored a victory. More important to her, though, it had been a gift—a gesture of gratitude to the one man who'd ever earned it from her. She still did not know that man's name—though she had her suspicions. She had searched for his face in computer records and discovered that he bore a strong resemblance to the deceased Commander Charles Tucker of the Earth vessel *Enterprise*—the very man who had defeated the Three Sisters' attempt to capture that ship years ago. If he truly were the same man, having been bested by him would be something of an honor. Yet she had kept this suspicion to herself, as another gift.

Devna had paid for it, of course. She had been spared physical punishment, for her master Parrec-Sut knew she had been conditioned to derive pleasure from pain; but she had been stripped of her privileges as an agent and infiltrator and reduced to the lowest level of sex slave, existing only to service the whims and fetishes of any who would have her. Devna had accepted this fate philosophically, aware that it could have been far worse. Devna had gambled that Parrec-Sut and his own superiors, the Sisters, would understand the strategic calculus behind her choice. Giving up Deneb had let her escape and preserve a valuable intelligence asset for the Syndicate with minimal consequences to their long-term objectives. The short-term loss of revenue had been offset by the gain of making Starfleet complacent. It had been a risky move on her part, but one that had shown initiative. She knew that Navaar appreciated such qualities in her agents. That was surely why Devna was still alive.

Yet Devna still had to serve out her punishment before she could earn her way back into the intelligence service. She had been properly submissive for all of it, retreating into a mental zone of self-abnegation, so that what was done to her body would have minimal impact on her mind or spirit. Yet she still welcomed those occasions when a customer showed some hint of treating her as a person rather than a tool for sexual release. So she had allowed herself some hope when told of her new assignment. The Sisters' ally Jofirek had invited one of his own business associates to join Navaar's alliance and had brought him to Orion to meet with Parrec-Sut, who was filling in for the Sisters' chief overseer Harrad-Sar while the latter was offworld. His name was Charlemagne Hua, and he was a human who controlled the narcotics trade on many of Earth's fringe colonies, worlds without the pervasive law and order of Earth and its Federation partners. Sut had assigned Devna to see to Hua's needs for the duration of his stay. She had let herself hope that this human male would have some trace of the same kindness the agent had shown her.

Sadly, this had not been the case. Charlemagne Hua was a boisterous drunkard, a tall, lean, flamboyantly but messily dressed man with a pencil-sketch mustache and long black hair in a ponytail that appeared perpetually on the verge of coming undone. He seemed cheerful and gregarious, but in an aggressive, imperious way that told Devna he would have little tolerance for any who defied his will. Apparently he had a fondness for young females, which was why the pale-skinned, daintily built Devna was assigned to him rather than one of her more curvaceous slave-sisters. He had pulled her onto his lap with pleasure and wasted no time tearing off her minimal adornments and pawing at her while he sat and drank with Parrec-Sut, Jofirek, and the Mazarite syndicate head Eldi Zankor.

"This," Hua said, laughing and hugging her painfully tight, "this is the stuff, my friends."

Jofirek laughed. "Didn't I tell you?" he wheezed. "We could make a fortune if we got in on the slave franchising."

"Alas, most humans don't look kindly on slavery. There are a few who would appreciate such an . . . exotic luxury item to possess for their very own, but keeping one would require a degree of, um, privacy that can be hard to achieve in a small colonial community. And really, what's the point of owning one of these verdant vixens if you can't parade her around, am I right?" The men laughed, and even Zankor joined in, for the Mazarite had two male slaves in attendance on her.

"But consider this," Hua went on. He grabbed Devna's shoulders and turned her around on his lap, putting her on display. "Look at this. *Feel* this." Jofirek took him up on his invitation, his gnarled hand reaching out to grope her leg. "No, that's not what I mean—though you're welcome." Hua laughed. "Feel the aura she gives off. The overwhelming allure. The irres-irresistible heat. That's power. We want to own Orions so we can tame that power, harness it to our will." He smacked Devna's rump. "But what would people want even more? What would get them to pay through the nose?"

"Just tell us, you bag of wind," Zankor said.

"No, you tell me, my dear. I see the envy in your eyes when you look at creatures like this. You don't just want to own this. You want to *be* this. The Orion physique is a fantasy made real. We purchase it because we want to be close to it, but what we really want is to have it for ourselves!"

Devna braced herself. She could guess where this was going, and it probably wouldn't go well.

Indeed, Parrec-Sut rose from his seat, displacing two of Devna's slave-sisters to do so, and took a step toward Hua. Sut was less burly than a lot of Orion males, tall but comparatively lean, and with a face that Devna found boyishly handsome. But she knew from long experience how intimidating he could be when he so chose. "What are you suggesting, human?" he asked, an ominous undertone in his smooth baritone.

"Well, think about it," Hua went on, oblivious to the raised tension. "Sex is all about hormones. Hormones give us our male and female traits. They regulate our sex drives and mediate our sexual intra— interactions. As pheromones, they promote attraction and arousal." He laughed. "Come on, if there's one thing Orions know about, it's pheromones.

"So this, this irresistible magic you have—at the risk of taking the poetry out of it—it's all chemicals. Hormones can be replicated, synthesized. And most humanoids have basically the same bio, um, biochem-emistry—the same drugs and medicines affect them the same way." The Saurian brandy he'd been guzzling was certainly starting to affect him more now. "Your hormones aren't so different from human hormones or Vulcan hormones or horse hormones—horsemones—hah!—just . . . with a little something extra in the mix. They're written in the same chemical language, and another humanoid body could process them just as well as yours could—otherwise they'd have no effect on other humanoids in the first place.

"Really, Sut, I can't believe this has never occurred to you Orions. You could package your sex hormones, market them as, as a drug. Imagine what people would pay for the chance to make themselves as manly as your men, as wom—well, feminine as your women. To be irresistible to the opposite sex, just by taking a pill!" He spread his arms and laughed, failing to recognize how much deeper a hole he was digging for himself.

But Zankor took pity on him. "Stop, Hua, just stop. Don't you see? That's the last thing the Orions would want. If everyone could be that irresistible, their slaves would lose their unique value, and then where would their business be?"

"Hmp." Hua tilted his head, then tilted it again, as if trying to help the idea trickle down through the whorls of his brain until it reached some part with sufficiently low alcohol saturation to be able to process it. "I suppose I hadn't considered that angle," he conceded. "Yes, certainly it's not something to be rushed into, not without considering the rami— uh, ramica—rafimications," he finished with a firm nod. "But there are other reasons for people to enslave slaves, slaves—to own slaves. It's worth thinking about, at least."

Parrec-Sut was rapidly losing patience. Devna hastened to grab the brandy that sat next to her on the bar and pour—no, on second thought, she just handed Hua the horn-shaped bottle, which the human accepted gladly in the middle of a sentence that trailed off once the bottle reached his lips. Soon enough he lost his train of thought, and soon after that he lost consciousness as well, sparing Devna from having to tend to his appetites any further for the night.

Sut's gaze went unfocused for a moment, suggesting that he was listening to a prompt in his earpiece from one of the Three Sisters. Naturally, Devna knew, they had been watching the exchange from concealment in order to assess Hua's worth as a potential ally. Once he had received their instructions, he patted Devna's shoulder. "Good move, Dev. You may have just saved this partnership—assuming he's forgotten all about this conversation by the morning."

"I'll make sure it stays forgotten, Master." She smiled up at him, appreciating his sincere praise.

He smiled back, then slapped her cheek just hard

enough to serve as a reminder of his authority. "You'd better."

Under Parrec-Sut's watchful eye, Devna summoned a junior male slave who helped her carry Hua to his bedchamber, where she undressed him and lay alongside him, on call for him if he should wake in the night and desire her services. But he was solidly unconscious, and she was left with plenty of time to think.

What if Orion hormones could be made more widely available? What if there were no longer anything special about her—or about the elites who ruled the Syndicate and, by extension, the Orion race as a whole? What would happen to their authority if they were robbed of that monopoly on erotic power? If the playing field were leveled, might their control be broken, their subjects freed from domination?

The thought intrigued her, until she began to consider it from a different angle. What would happen to the rest of the galaxy if other humanoids gained the power of irresistible seduction? Would not all humanoids then be just as enslaved as she was?

Devna remembered what she had said to the Starfleet agent last year: that freedom was an illusion, that any perception of a free state of existence was just another dimension of entrapment. It seemed the principle still held.

Still, every once in a while, it was nice to hope.

Thamnos estate, Rigel IV

"I hope the accommodations are to your liking, Garos."

Dular Garos looked around the suite that Retifel Thamnos had proudly shown off to him. It was indeed even more lush and impressive than the hotel suite in Kefvenek that he had recently vacated (lest the RTC or Starfleet trace certain compromising communications back there—and since he expected Rigel II to become a rather dangerous place in the near future). The technologies the suite offered, however, were less advanced than what he was accustomed to on his own ship, *Rivgor*—which only threw the pervasive air of decadent excess into sharper relief. As did the presence of several cowering serfs—all female and underdressed—whom Retifel had shown off as if they were part of the suite's furnishings. Perhaps the Thamnos eschewed higher technology for it would render serfs redundant, leaving them fewer people to dominate and bully.

Still, for all her willing complicity in her family's abuses, Retifel was at least an agreeable conversationalist, so Garos put a smile on the Zami mask he still wore (albeit with some cosmetic alterations made since leaving Rigel II). "They will serve me quite well. I appreciate the gesture."

The ginger-wigged Zami smiled knowingly, taking a puff on her narcotic stick as she leered toward the servant females, misunderstanding his comment. "Oh, yes—they will submit to whatever services you may demand of them. However, ah, exotic those demands might be." The females fidgeted, avoiding his eyes.

Garos concealed his distaste for seeing females diminished in this way. At least Orion females, even the nominal slaves, had their pheromones to give them an advantage. "That will not be necessary, Retifel. I seek no companionship besides your own."

Her eyes widened, and he could see she was controlling her own reactions just as tightly. "Oh! Well. I'm very flattered, Dular, but—well, I am married, and . . ."

He shook his head, laughing. "Please don't misunderstand. I am irrevocably bonded myself, and incapable of sexual interest in anyone but my mate."

"Oh." She looked quite relieved.

He took a step closer. "What I mean is simply that I appreciate your company on an intellectual level. Living in exile is . . . lonely. I rarely have the opportunity to spend time with a female of intelligence and dignity." Navaar may have possessed a certain cunning and strategic insight Garos could respect, but he found no dignity in the way she and her sisters carried on.

Retifel studied him. "I am more genuinely flattered now. Here I had the feeling that you disapproved of the Families."

He replied with care. "I must live my life among alien cultures, dealing with those whose customs and practices differ from my own. I accept this. Which is why I appreciate admirable traits in my allies where I can find them."

She chuckled. "A smooth and practiced answer. You wear your masks well. I only hope the deceits you have prepared for Starfleet are as deft."

He respected Retifel enough to respond honestly on that point, at least. "I have learned from my past mistakes. Starfleet officers are skilled at penetrating deceptions, it is true. So the key is to employ enough deceptions to keep them busy—until it is too late for them to stop us."

U.S.S. *Pioneer*, orbiting Rigel VI

According to the information Director Tenott and his staff had provided, the Ryneh Shipyard was one of the most disreputable shipbuilding and repair facilities in the Rigel Colonies, a place where smugglers, raiders, and pirates could get repairs with no questions asked or sell off stolen ships for parts. As such, Malcolm Reed had not expected it to look so impressive. The Coridanite-built facility occupied the cored-out center of one of Rigel VI's smallest asteroidal moons, a wide cylindrical shaft running clear through the potato-shaped moonlet's long axis from end to end. The near mouth, and presumably the far one as well, was ringed with shield generators, tractor emitters, and slips for small tugs and repair pods. Through the opening, Reed could see hundreds of docking berths arrayed all around the inner cylinder's walls. The suspect ship that had come here from Rigel V had been tracked this far and had not left.

Naturally there was no chance that Grev, Kirk, and the stolen archives were still aboard, if they ever had been in the first place; the ship had stopped at Colony Two en route and had plenty of opportunity to transfer them to a different ship. But at least a forensic scan of the ship's interior and its database would reveal if they had been aboard and, if so, where they had disembarked.

However, getting past the entryway force field was proving difficult. The shipyard's operator—unexpectedly, a human colonist, a brown-complexioned man named Kuldip—had been putting forth whatever bureaucratic obstructions he could come up with to refuse them entry. But *Pioneer* had come prepared. En route, they had stopped at Colony One, the largest of the Neptune-class giant's three terrestrial moons, to pick up Teixh Veurk, an official for the Colonial Port Authority. "We have the full power of the Trade Commission and the Port Authority behind this order," the stocky Coridanite woman told Kuldip, her stern expression enhancing the natural frown created by the subtly inhuman bone structure between her eyebrows. "If you do not cooperate, I will have to review your operating license pending a full inspection of your facility."

As Veurk harangued him, Reed could see it sinking in for Kuldip that this was not the typical situation where the authorities would look the other way. For her part, Veurk seemed to relish the opportunity to take some real enforcement action for a change, and Kuldip evidently had good reason to fear her wrath.

"*Of course, of course,*" he finally conceded with a stammer. "*I, I simply did not understand the situation. Certainly, you are cleared to enter.*"

Suddenly Veurk became gracious and put on a wide, saccharine smile. "Thank you for your cooperation."

Pioneer was a larger ship than this facility normally handled, but Ensign Tallarico had no trouble navigating the *Intrepid*-class vessel through the asteroid's entrance or the scaffolding and robotic arms that filled much of the interior. Regina Tallarico was a more experienced pilot than her rank would suggest. After her first ship, *Discovery,* had been shot out from under her at Berengaria VII in the first year of the Earth-Romulan War, she had been honorably discharged due to her injuries, and upon her recovery had enlisted as a pilot in the Alpha Centauri merchant marine. After the Federation had been founded, Tallarico had rejoined Starfleet with her old rank reinstated and with years of civilian experience under her belt.

Unfortunately, that didn't help them pick the ship they wanted out of the hundreds of small craft filling the asteroid's berths. "We need you to show us where we can find the ship that entered your facility at, ah, thirty-one eighty local time," Reed told Kuldip. "A type of vessel called a Grennex G-Seven."

"*Ah, yes, the Grennex section.*" Kuldip worked his console. "*I am sending the coordinates to your helm now.*"

Tallarico turned to look over her shoulder at the captain, her blond ponytail swinging. "Got it, sir."

"Proceed."

Reed noticed that Veurk was frowning. "Something wrong?" he asked her.

"Well, Captain . . . Grennex ships are a common make in the Colonies and beyond, and the G-Seven was a popular model for a number of years. I'm concerned that . . . oh. Well, see for yourself."

By now they had reached the coordinates, and the viewscreen revealed what Veurk had feared. The block of twenty-four berths before them currently contained some nineteen ships of various different configurations—but more than half of them were identical. Reed turned to Veurk. "Are those . . ."

The Coridanite Rigelian nodded. "G-Sevens."

Reed faced Kuldip's inset image on the viewer. "Mister Kuldip, you're going to have to give us a little more help than that."

"I do apologize, Captain. But I'm afraid our record-keeping system can be rather erratic. Unless you can give me the registration number of the ship in question . . ."

"The ship didn't broadcast its registry."

"Then I'm afraid I can't help you. I suggest you try contacting the owners or previous renters of the various ships."

"If we knew how to find them—" Reed broke off. It was obvious enough that Kuldip was on the take; trying to reason with him was a wasted effort. "Never mind. We'll manage it ourselves. Reed out." He closed the channel, then turned to his right, addressing Valeria Williams at tactical. "Val, scan the ships. Look for any distinguishing features."

"Aye, sir." The auburn-haired lieutenant spent some moments coordinating with Yasmin Achrati, the ensign filling in at sciences while Sangupta was away on Rigel III with Commander Mayweather. Finally, Williams shook her head. "I should've known, sir. None of the ships shows any significant differences from the others in its displacement, engine specifications, signs of recent usage, anything. In fact, I'd say they're suspiciously identical."

"We do have the authority to search them all," Veurk said. "The right ship won't elude us forever."

"But it only has to elude us long enough," Reed told her. "We need a way to identify that ship as soon as possible."

At the engineering station, just forward of tactical, Tobin Dax raised a hand, index finger extended. "Ah, Captain, I think I might have an idea about that. If I could ask Mister Kuldip a question?"

Reed nodded to Crewman Konicek at communications, who reopened the channel. "We have a question, Mister Kuldip. Go ahead, Doctor Dax."

"Uh, Mister Kuldip, hello. My name is—"

"Just ask the question, Doctor."

"Sorry, sir. Um, could you tell me just what type of hull coating the G-Sevens use? Is it an ablative ceramic, or a carbon-fiber composite, or—"

"*Carbon-reinforced thermopolymer,*" Kuldip replied, "*sandwiching layers of silica-based aerogel foam.*"

"Ah, very good, very good," Dax said.

"How does that help us?" asked Reed.

"Well, normally it wouldn't," the Trill chief engineer told him. "But Rigel V is nearly twice as close to the primary star as we are here, so the UV intensity would be nearly four times as great. As you may know, UV exposure can cause degradation in the matrix of a carbon composite."

Williams shook her head. "Good thought, Tobin, but with this kind of material, the degradation is far too gradual, and it happens over multiple repeated exposures. The amount of time this ship would've spent around Five wouldn't be enough to make any measurable difference in its skin integrity."

"Ah," Tobin said, "but that's under UV exposure alone. It's a little-known fact that if that type of composite is simultaneously subjected to a particle beam in a state of subspace phase transition, it can leave a characteristic degradation signature in the composite matrix."

The armory officer frowned. "A transporter beam, you mean."

"That is what I mean."

"Doctor, I've never heard of anything like that."

Dax turned away from the visual pickup and gave her a pleading look. "I'm sure we've discussed it before, Lieutenant . . . over one of our games of *Xiangqi*?"

Williams blinked a few times. "Oh. Maybe we have at that."

"Right. Now, this isn't a signature you can detect with a normal scan, but if we run it through a subspace phase discrimination filter, then any ship that's been hit by a transporter beam in the past week should light up clear as day."

Kuldip had grown increasingly agitated as Dax spoke, and Reed spotted him working a control on his console while trying to appear nonchalant. The captain was about to challenge the shipyard operator when he noted movement on the main screen image. "Sir!" Achrati cried. "One of the ships is launching."

Williams pumped her fist in triumph. "Good going, Tobin, you spooked them!"

"Val, Regina," Reed said, "don't let that ship get away." He turned to Dax. "There is no transporter signature, is there?"

The Trill gave a bashful smile. "Now there doesn't have to be."

The Grennex was making a break for the exit, but before *Pioneer* could follow, a pair of the shipyard's large manipulator arms moved into the Starfleet cruiser's path, reaching toward it with grippers deployed. Williams was able to keep the arms from grabbing hold by raising *Pioneer*'s deflectors, and a couple of quick phase-cannon shots were enough to blast them out of the way. Almost immediately, though, the ship rocked from what Reed recognized as particle fire. "Three fighters have launched," Williams announced. "And sir, the Grennex is clear and the yard's shields have just gone up. They're not letting us out."

"Niyilar Seventeens," Veurk observed as one of the fighters took up station to the fore. "Small but powerful. Highly maneuverable."

"Which we're not, sir," Tallarico said, "as long as we're stuck in here."

The fighter on the screen shot forward and strafed the dorsal surface of *Pioneer*'s fan-shaped hull, rocking the bridge. Reed clung to his seat arms. Veurk stumbled and caught herself on the side railing. "Mister Kuldip, you may consider your operating license revoked!" The only answer was another fighter strafing the bridge.

Williams tried returning fire, with no effect. "Damn! They're too maneuverable. The targeting sensors aren't designed for point-blank range. Sir, we need to get into open space."

"Can you lock onto their shield generators?"

"I've been scanning, Captain. They must be buried inside the asteroidal shell."

Tobin Dax grinned. "Um, not everything is. I think I've spotted a vulnerability." He stepped over to the tactical console, pointing at her targeting display. "Val, could you target, ah, these two conduits over here? Just enough to put holes in the casings—a few meters wide should do."

Williams looked puzzled, but at this point she trusted the engineer implicitly despite his unsure diction. She had to divert one phase cannon from defense against the fighters, but it was doing little good in that regard anyway. The cannon fired two short pulses, causing faint flashes of light near the edge of the exit portal, amid a cluster of equipment barely visible at this range. But Williams and Dax seemed satisfied by the result. "Now," Dax went on, "just a pinpoint rupture of this tank over here."

"Magnify that," Reed told Konicek. The screen zoomed in on the equipment cluster just in time to see a third bolt penetrate a tank adjacent to one of the two damaged conduits. The tank burst and a cloud of vapor erupted into the vacuum, engulfing the two conduits.

A split second later, a blinding electric arc jumped between the conduits, dancing and twisting for nearly half a second before it faded out. But all the interior lights of the shipyard, plus the outer shield and every active robot arm, shut down moments later.

"Oh, it worked," Tobin said, relieved. "I was afraid the gas would dissipate too quickly to allow a current path to form."

"Regina, pursue the Grennex," Reed ordered, but Tallarico was already engaging thrusters.

Williams, still staring at Dax, let out a laugh. "All that high-tech handwaving for your fake solution . . . and now you save our hides with a lousy short circuit?"

Dax shrugged. "Patter should be confusing. Engineering should be simple." He went back to his station. "Oh, and the power surge should've shut down any external weapons, too. That might help."

Tallarico fired the impulse engines as soon as *Pioneer* was clear, not worrying much about how radiation backwash might affect Mr. Kuldip's precious shipyard. Reed couldn't disapprove. But the fighters were close on the starship's heels. Getting some distance and room to maneuver made it easier for Tallarico to evade their fire and Williams to target her own, and soon two of the fighters were adrift and the third in retreat.

But their quarry had a significant head start, and

Rigel VI's orbital space was an obstacle course of moons, moonlets, and space stations. "Don't worry, Captain," Veurk told Reed. "I have three scout ships en route. We'll be able to corner them."

"That's what concerns me," Reed told her, loud enough for the bridge crew to hear. "These people are going to great lengths to keep us from searching that ship. Its pilot may well be under orders to blow up the ship if it comes to that. If we make them feel cornered, we may lose them."

Still, the Rigelian scouts proved useful, herding the *Grennex* away from several potential evasion routes and limiting its options. *Pioneer* caught up to it as it neared a medium-sized moonlet riddled with mine pits. "Target their engines," Reed said. "Maybe we can disrupt them enough to prevent self-destruct."

"Or, ah, trigger the engines to explode ourselves," Dax added.

"That's a chance we'll have to take."

Veurk shook her curly-haired head. "The G-Seven's engines are well-shielded."

"Just get me close enough," Williams said.

A minute later, Tallarico got *Pioneer* into firing range and Williams took her shots. The pilot's evasions and, indeed, the solid cowling around the inboard nacelles kept her from striking a decisive blow. She kept trying, but then a navigational alarm sounded on Tallarico's console. "Incoming ore transport! Collision course!"

"Veer off!" Reed ordered. Tallarico angled the ship away. Williams managed to get off one more shot, grazing the side of the Grennex before it pulled out of range.

As soon as they were clear of the moonlet, Tallarico did her best to catch up, pouring on the impulse power—tricky to do in orbital space, since thrusting forward faster would take the ship outward into a wider, paradoxically slower orbit. Normally, to catch up with an orbiting craft, one would decelerate to sink into a tighter orbit, overtake it, and thrust outward again. But there was no time to wait for that, so the only option was to blast forward and inward to cancel out the centrifugal effect. It was hardly efficient, but *Pioneer* was powerful enough to make it work.

And so were the Rigelian scouts. Soon, all four pursuers were closing on the Grennex in a pincer movement. Veurk signaled the small ship and ordered its pilot to surrender and submit to inspection.

Moments later, Dax reported, "Oh, no. Energy building up in the engine core. I think they're going to blow it."

"Have your ships pull back," Reed said to Veurk.

"Hold on, please, sir," Williams said. "That may not be necessary."

Indeed, after a few moments, Dax reported, "The sequence is reversing. The engines are shutting down."

A moment after that, the pilot hailed. *"Don't fire! I surrender."*

Reed turned to Williams. "Lieutenant?"

She replied with a rakish tilt to her head. "I have a trick or two of my own. Just before they got away last time? I fused their escape-pod hatch." She shrugged. "These are crooks, not fanatics. I figured the pilot wouldn't be willing to die with the ship."

The captain was impressed, but also a bit annoyed. "You could've told me that was what you were doing."

Her expression grew more sheepish. "I . . . wasn't sure it would work."

U.S.S. Pioneer, **orbiting Rigel Colony One**

"Our people were never aboard that ship," Valeria Williams told Captain Reed as they stood before the windows of *Pioneer*'s conference lounge. Outside, the view was dominated by the cratered globe of Rigel Colony One, lit on one side by the diminished but vivid light from Raij and on the other by the soft blue glow from Rigel VI. Both colors and qualities of light glinted off the domes that covered many of the moon's craters, encasing lush, terraformed biomes centered on large, ornate cities. One of those cities held a detention center that in turn held the captive pilot along with Mr. Kuldip. "It was one of the decoys, ordered to wait in orbit, get a quantity of rock beamed up to them by the relay, and then follow a preset course. This one was sent to Ryneh because it already had a number of identical G-Sevens, and because Kuldip was on the take."

"I see," Reed said, studying the exotic moonscape beyond. As much as security work still felt natural to him, Reed regretted that he had to visit this intriguing locale as an inquisitor rather than an explorer. "Did either of them know anything useful?"

"Afraid not, sir," Williams said. "We questioned them for hours. Veurk offered them some pretty generous incentives for cooperation—Rigelians have a knack for making deals. They would've been happy to play along, but they didn't have anything much to offer in exchange. Kuldip was just a tourist who got deep in debt to a Family-run casino on Two and had to start doing jobs for them if he wanted to keep all his body parts. Strictly menial stuff—the shipyard's the closest thing to authority he's ever had."

"And the pilot?"

"Turns out she's a Suliban."

Reed stared. "Not a leftover Cabal member?" he asked, though it seemed unlikely.

"Actually she wanted to be, but she was too young. Ran some errands for them back in the day, but the Cabal fell apart before she was old enough for the genetic augmentations. Still, she was a fellow traveler, which means the Tandarans came after her, so she ran away, went underground, and ended up on Rigel X, doing menial work for whatever syndicate had a use for her." Williams shook her head. "Same as Kuldip, too low on the totem pole to know anything we can use."

"That's not unexpected," Reed replied. "Whoever's planned this operation is meticulous. We wouldn't even have gotten this far if not for some ingenious improvisation by you and Doctor Dax."

The armory officer smiled, lifting her chin. "Thank you, sir."

Reed sighed. "Well, at least that's one wild goose we've cooked. That improves our odds a bit." He directed his gaze sunward, toward the inner system. "I just hope Travis and Rey are having better luck."

8

Janxor, Rigel III

THE WRECKAGE OF THE SHIP was spread out over half
the mountainside. Travis Mayweather and Reynaldo
Sangupta gazed up at the debris field from the base
of the low, scree-covered slope, with Director Sajithen
towering over them from behind. An even bigger
Chelon, one of her security escorts, flanked the group,
while the other escort, a Jelna exomale, worked his
way gingerly up the slope, scanning the debris. "How
awful," the director rumbled. "I pray that your crewmates were not aboard this ship."

That was a possibility Mayweather refused to
contemplate. He had lost far too many crewmates
over the years, first to the Xindi while aboard *Enterprise,* later aboard the multiple ships he'd had shot out
from under him in the Romulan War. Now he had the
added burden of being their superior officer. He had
given Grev and Kirk the okay to visit the archive—and
he had assigned Kenji Mishima to protect them. For
the first time, Mayweather had to live with the knowledge that he'd ordered someone to his death. For now,
he was coping with it by reminding himself that the
First Families were the ones truly responsible, the
rightful targets for his anger. But he knew it wouldn't
be that simple to live with his own responsibility in the

long term. The one thing that could make it easier was to help bring Grev and Kirk back alive. The thought that some random malfunction or pilot error had precluded any chance of their rescue was unacceptable.

Fortunately, Mayweather had good reason not to believe it. "I'm not sure anyone was aboard that ship," he told the director.

"I do not understand."

The first officer spread his arms to indicate the territory around them, a largely barren volcanic island about the size of Greenland but much hotter. "Why would they have come here? The Chelons who provided the hypnoids live in the Hainali rainforest, clear on the other side of the planet."

"There is a major spaceport at the eastern tip of the island, in the direction the ship was headed. It draws in traders from all over the system, even Rigel IV."

"Yes, and that makes it a plausible destination—*if* we didn't know about the rainforest connection. And we weren't supposed to, because the evidence was supposed to be destroyed in the explosion. If they were going anywhere on Rigel III, they would've gone to Hainali."

"Except they wouldn't have gone there," Sangupta said, "because that would've tipped us off to the very connection they were trying to hide."

"That's right. But if they'd avoided sending a ship to Three at all, that would've looked suspicious in itself," Mayweather went on. "They had to make Three one of the shells in the game—but they sent us here, to the far side of the planet."

"Yeah," the science officer answered, nodding as he filled in the rest in his own mind. "And a crashed ship in a place like this—spread out over square kilometers of an unstable rock face—we could spend days trying to find organic remains or a surviving data module before we ruled this out as a decoy." He grinned. "But since we know they had a connection in the rainforest, that gives us an edge they don't know about."

Mayweather grimaced. "Well, if the nationalists even respond to the message Sajithen sent."

"They will respond," the director insisted. "But indirect channels of communication take time, particularly in that part of the world."

"Let's just hope it doesn't eat up all our head start," Sangupta grumbled.

The Chelon administrator tilted her head. Her features were fairly rigid, but her uncertainty came through in her body language and voice. "So do you propose we abandon searching the wreckage and travel to the Hainali Basin?"

The first officer thought it over. "We've got to check every possibility, just to be safe. But I'm going to gamble that the rainforest should be our first priority. We'll let the local officials search the wreckage."

Sangupta looked over the massive pile of stone fragments that created the tenuous slope. "They're probably better qualified to search here without starting a rockslide."

"Right," Mayweather replied. "We've got enough coming down on our heads as it is."

Undisclosed location

"We're getting impatient!" Rehlen Vons cried, as if the knife his henchman Damreg held against Samuel Kirk's throat were insufficient to make that point. "It's been two days and you've hardly made any progress!"

"Well, what do you expect?" Bodor chim Grev replied, trying to keep his voice firm. "You're forcing me to work without Starfleet equipment, with this inferior public-domain translation software—an artist is only as good as his tools, you know!"

"Oh, a skilled artist can bring out the best in any tool," Vons said. "Perhaps you'd like Mister Damreg to offer a demonstration?"

"You need to understand," Grev went on in a more conciliatory tone. "Languages are made to be comprehensible. You just need to find the right way in, and they help you go the rest of the way. Encryptions are designed to impede you from getting in. It's a lot harder!"

"Well, if you can't do it," Damreg interposed with a flourish of the knife, "we don't need—"

"I know, I know. You could at least try putting some variety in your threats every now and then!" Kirk stared at him with alarm. "Sorry," Grev said, half to him and half to their captors. "I get all Tellarite when I'm nervous."

After a moment, Vons chuckled and nodded to Damreg to release Kirk from the immediate threat. Once the blond Zami had complied, the historian retreated to Grev's side, rubbing his throat. "At this point, Mister Grev, I think I'm keeping you alive mainly for the entertainment value. But bore me . . ." Vons made a show of taking the knife from Damreg and inspecting the edge. ". . . and I'll entertain myself another way."

Oh, a born performer, this one, Grev thought. *Just the kind to say too much, with the right prompt.* As Vons turned and started to leave, Grev called, "Just tell me one thing, Mister Vons. How can you betray your people this way?"

Vons turned back to him and gave a knowing chuckle. "Oh, I always serve my people, Mister Grev."

Once Vons and Damreg were gone, Grev smiled. "That's what I wanted to know."

Kirk stared. "What?"

"Something's been off about him this whole time."

"I know . . . that he was trying to act like he wasn't trying to act suspicious, or something." Kirk coughed. "But he's not exactly hiding it now."

"That's just it, Sam. I thought that was why he seemed off before, but now he *still* seems off, and I've been trying to figure out why. Something about his body language, and the way he enunciates just a bit too perfectly. Everything about that man is a façade."

The historian frowned. "You think he's not really Vons?"

"I think he's not really Rigelian. You catch how he subtly emphasized 'my' when he said 'I always serve my people'?"

"But . . . we saw him use the biometric sensors to enter the vault."

"Exactly," Grev replied. "So either he's Vons . . . or he's using a form of disguise more advanced than Rigelian technology can recognize."

Kirk considered. "Suliban Cabal, maybe? There can't be many left, but . . ."

Grev was skeptical. "They were active at Rigel over a dozen years ago. The RTC would probably have countermeasures for their shapeshifting by now. Besides, what would they have to gain? No, I think we're dealing with a group that's currently active, has a mastery of disguise, uses transporters, and has an agenda to undermine the Federation."

The human had figured out where he was going before he'd finished. "The Malurians."

"The Malurians," the Tellarite affirmed.

Kirk's gentle features grew solemn. "These people have already tried to start a war once. They don't care who they hurt." He went on with resolution. "Grev, we can't let them get the data in those servers. We have to destroy the files if we get a chance."

Grev stared in shock. "But, Sam—what about the loss to history? That information . . ."

"I know," Kirk replied, looking pained. "But . . . the future is more important."

The communications officer took his point, albeit with little pleasure. "What about *our* future? With those files gone, they won't have much use for us anymore."

"Yeah," said Kirk. "That's the other downside."

June 20, 2164
Babel Station

Commissioner Soval was surprised when an aide informed him that Anlenthoris ch'Vhendreni had arrived on Babel. He could not see why a presidential candidate in the midst of a campaign tour would involve himself in a diplomatic conference. Surely a former diplomat as seasoned as Thoris would appreciate the political delicacy of such a venue, particularly in the midst of the ongoing Rigelian crisis.

Thus, Soval found it difficult to control his shock when he arrived in Babel's reception hall to find Thoris addressing the pool of reporters accompanying him on his campaign. "While I have the utmost respect for my diplomatic colleagues . . . particularly my former deputy and esteemed advisor, Avaranthi sh'Rothress," the candidate added, gesturing toward the tall, regal *shen*, who acknowledged the praise stiffly, "the recent events in the Rigel system simply intensify my concern that President Vanderbilt has forced the issue of Rigelian admission. Moreover, they underline the recklessness of the Federalist doctrine espoused by the likes of President Vanderbilt and Councilor al-Rashid—their inexplicable haste to enlarge and consolidate the Federation without regard for the unique needs and heritage of each society.

"In particular, I question the role of the Federation Starfleet in these events. Not only why they were unable to protect the victims of this assault or prevent two of their own officers from being abducted, but why their assailants opted to target Starfleet personnel in the first place. Now, I do not join with those voices who suggest that Starfleet might have somehow provoked this act, that it was some sort of defensive strike against perceived cultural imposition. But I think we need to explore why many Federation citizens might have cause to feel that way."

Soval looked on with dismay. Being seen to exploit a tragedy for the sake of political advantage must surely backfire against Thoris, yet here he was doing it anyway. And indeed, Soval saw similar consternation on the faces of other spectators, particularly Admiral Archer and Ambassador Selina Rosen of Earth. Ambassador Solkar looked on with admirable stoicism, but his aide T'Rama bore a look that a human might approximate to their emotion of pity. Ambassador Baur, an avowed Federalist, looked on with positive glee at the misstep by the leading Planetarist candidate. Yet Avaranthi sh'Rothress struggled to hide her distress at her former mentor's behavior.

On the other hand, the more dedicated Planetarists, Ysanne Fell and Mikhail Kamenev, seemed entirely drawn in by Thoris's words—so persuaded of the truth of his critiques against the Federation that they were untroubled by the manner in which they were delivered. No doubt there were others in the Federation public who felt the same. But did Thoris truly calculate that their numbers would be sufficient to make this speech politically advantageous?

Indeed, the reporters raised that very question when he finished. "My friends," he replied, "I understand the media's incentive to focus on the political calculus of every act. I was advised that many would misunderstand my intentions here today, or would attempt to twist this against my campaign. But in the face of events such as these, we must put political considerations aside and speak from our hearts. Babel simply happened to be the nearest available venue for my campaign caravan to reach when the incident occurred. As you know, it was chosen as a diplomatic site specifically for its isolation. Stopping here also gives me the opportunity to consult privately with high-ranking officials such as Admiral Archer of Starfleet and my good friend Commissioner Soval. I have always prided myself on remaining fully informed on all matters that affect the security of the worlds I represent."

It proved impossible for Soval to approach Thoris afterward without the candidate attempting to create the appearance that the commissioner endorsed his statements. But Soval had long experience managing the press and was able to avoid responding to the questions they called out as a group. Soval had long wondered why human, Tellarite, and Andorian reporters believed that ganging up on reluctant interview subjects and shouting questions at them would somehow make them more receptive to cooperating rather than less.

In any event, Soval finally persuaded Thoris to give him a few moments to speak privately in a small, currently empty conference room. "I know what you're going to say, Soval," the thin-faced Andorian told him. "I know that many will see my words today as a shameful, mercenary act. I was fully aware of that risk when I came here."

Soval studied his old colleague closely, seeing something beneath the surface. "You disagreed with that decision."

Thoris's antennae drooped. "I needed to be convinced, yes. It is a rather . . . unconventional gesture."

"Your entire campaign seems unconventional in light of your past record," Soval told him. "I have always known you for your ability to compromise. You fight fiercely for what you believe in, but treat opposing viewpoints fairly. And in the past, you were one of the strongest supporters of interworld cooperation. Together, we helped create the Coalition of Planets. We both resisted its dissolution."

"I know, Soval, I know. I haven't gone senile, however it may appear."

"Then your endorsement of the extreme Planetarist position is puzzling."

Thoris tilted his head, his antennae twisting sardonically. "I'm well aware there are some rather . . . irrational voices on the Planetarist side. But don't you see? That's a symptom of the real problem. The Federation formed too fast, centralized too swiftly. That was bound to anger and alienate the more extreme nationalists and . . . well . . . those who have not yet learned how to trust other species. And that has provoked a backlash that could have been avoided had we proceeded more carefully."

"Then why do you encourage such groups now? All you do is intensify their radicalism."

The Andorian spread his wrinkled hands. "What's the alternative, Soval? Let someone like Professor T'Nol or Governor Lecheb carry the Planetarist flag? The Federation would never survive if they were elected."

"Their odds of being elected at all would be minimal. Yours are not."

"Exactly. Many Planetarists are not against the Federation's existence, but recognize its hasty formation has left many questions unresolved. There are still too few checks on central power, too little institutionalized protection of planetary rights. A moderate president motivated to solve those problems can make the Federation better, healthier."

"But you do not campaign on a moderate platform."

"Because my constituents wouldn't let me. This is about emotion, Soval, not logic. It's anger and fear of government domination, fear of the change that's come with this new era, that's firing up our base. I'd have no chance of winning if I didn't speak to those fears. But once I'm in office, once those fears are mollified, I can lead the Planetarists in a better direction. I can compromise with the Federation Council in ways I can't be seen doing as a candidate."

Soval responded with a skeptical gaze. "Are you sure you will be able to do so? In hopes of winning this election, you have compromised your own beliefs, succumbed to your advisors' judgment over your own, and pandered to the wishes of an extreme and vocal few who disproportionately dominate political discourse. Do you really believe that those who are working to place you in office will tolerate your abandonment of those practices should you be victorious? Will they not instead feel betrayed and pressure you to remain in line? And how far will the other factions trust your integrity if it becomes evident that your campaign strategy was based on calculated deception?"

Thoris studied Soval silently for a time, his antennae tensing and curving forward, then sagging. "I'm sorry you perceive my campaign in that way, Soval. But this is the strategy I've chosen. It's too late for me to change course now." He strode toward the exit.

"Yes," Soval told him, halting him in the doorway. "That is exactly what I fear: that it is too late."

Jonathan Archer hastened to track down Ambassador Jahlet and Director Hemnask after Thoris's inflammatory speech. He caught up with them in a widely curved hallway near the outer edge of the habitat dome. "I really have to apologize for what happened back there," he told the Rigelian women. "Here we go to such lengths to make you feel welcome, and then he has to come along and . . . Well, I want you to know that this is not how we usually do things in the Federation. I'm very sorry you had to go through that."

"Your apology is appreciated, Admiral," Jahlet said. She retained her usual easygoing manner, in contrast to the stern, pinched appearance her craggy features lent her. "We know that you do not share the candidate's views—or his tactless manner of expressing them."

"Still," Hemnask said, "in his defense, he did seem

to be speaking out of concern for our people's rights and free choice."

"I wish I could believe he really meant that," Archer said. "But he was trying to use your tragedy to score political points. To pander to those factions that are afraid of opening up to new races, new ideas. I want to assure you that most people in the Federation aren't really like that."

Hemnask smiled. "You don't need to explain plurality of viewpoints to a Rigelian, Admiral. No formal apology is necessary." She took a step closer, softening her voice. "But your personal apology is most gracious, and most appreciated. It is gratifying to feel . . . welcomed."

Her big green eyes held his, and he smiled back. "You are certainly welcome, Director." After a moment, he caught himself and turned to Jahlet. "Both of you."

She gave the other two a knowing look. "I thank you, Admiral. But if you will excuse me, I must consult with our government. You and Director Hemnask will have to carry on your dialogue without me, if that is all right with you."

"It is, Boda," Hemnask told her. "I'm sure the admiral can keep me entertained."

Hoping to live up to that expectation, Archer took Hemnask for a walk on Babel's esplanade, a public area beneath a transparent dome affording a view of the stars above. The esplanade was home to a variety of shops whose vendors had come from many worlds to cater to the diplomats and reporters attending the conference. "This Babel is quite a place," Hemnask told him as they strolled among the shops, casually looking over their exotic wares and inhaling the eclectic aromas of their foodstuffs. "So many different peoples . . . it reminds me of the Colonies back home. Yet so few are in your Federation."

"Well, not yet, anyway," Archer replied. "Maybe someday."

"Hmp." She gave him a teasing look. "Councilor Thoris would accuse you of cultural imperialism."

"We're only seeking partnership."

Hemnask smiled. "Aren't we all?"

She stopped at a clothing kiosk run by a middle-aged Mazarite man, who gushed about the privilege of being visited by Jonathan Archer himself. Archer resisted his offer of a free suit, but Hemnask laughingly prodded him to play along and let himself be measured, if only to see holograms of various options. He found them all uniformly garish and embarrassing, but he didn't have the heart to tell Hemnask, who seemed quite impressed by them. She put in an order for a pair of dresses herself.

But once they left the shop, she grew pensive. "Are you all right?" he asked.

She sighed. "I'm . . . concerned. I wonder if Thoris may have been right."

"That the Federation's bad for Rigel?"

"That Rigel's bad for the Federation. That we aren't ready for it. It can't be a coincidence that this raid on the archive happened now. We have our own factions who fear new races and new ideas. Perhaps this attack shows that we are not as united as the image we project to the galaxy."

Archer touched her shoulder lightly. "But the First Families aren't part of your community."

"And maybe that's symptomatic of something—that we haven't been able to make peace with those who are right in our midst." She shook her head, causing her hair to tumble appealingly. "They're Zami, just as I am. We have a kinship—and kinship is paramount to our people." A bitter scoff followed. "But we are so far from being able to build common ground. Not with the likes of the First Families."

Archer clasped her shoulder more firmly, sensing her need for comfort. "Sedra . . . there's something personal between you and the Families, isn't there?"

She gave him a grateful look, calming under his touch. "Yes, Jonathan, there is. My own . . . shameful secret that's in those archives along with everyone else's. A secret I keep not to protect myself, but to protect my mother," she continued softly, for his ears only. "Who, before she came to Five and married Gorvel Hemnask . . . was the kept woman of a minor scion of the Thamnos clan, one of the leading First Families. Who, when she fled . . . was already pregnant with me, and not by choice."

"My God," Archer breathed. "Sedra, I'm so sorry."

She stared and gave a confused chuckle. "That's sweet, but . . . why do you apologize? You bear no culpability."

"Uh . . . well, it doesn't just mean 'I apologize.' It means . . . I feel sorrow. I sympathize."

"Ah. I understand. Thank you. But I long ago accepted that how I was conceived did not diminish who I am, or who my mother is. It only diminishes the man who did it to her." She sighed. "Yet not everyone would agree, so I keep it private, for her sake."

"You're certainly entitled to."

Hemnask reached out and snagged an elaborate necklace hanging in another kiosk, letting its multicolored beads slide between her fingers. "We're so proud of this community we've built on trade. But it's really about enlightened self-interest, held together only by a mutual craving for profit and a tenuous balance of secrets and extortion." Hemnask turned back to him. "Maybe you're asking too much from Rigel, expecting us to be like you. You have your holdouts, but you formed a union with no commercial incentive, no threats. You came together out of trust and mutual friendship. And perhaps that makes you overly ready to trust us, when you should not."

"I don't understand," he said, clasping both her shoulders now. "I thought you wanted Rigel to join the Federation."

"Because I feel it would help us change. Force us to crack down on the crime and the piracy, give us the will and the means to break the Families' power once and for all. I'm just not so sure now that it would be good for you. And I . . ." She stepped closer into his embrace, gazing up at him. "I know that as a politician I should be selfish, should place the good of my Commission, my world, my constituents first. But . . . I can't think only of myself when I'm with you."

Archer learned moments later that a Zami's lips were just as soft as a human's, and maybe a few degrees warmer. Although he couldn't be sure, for it had been a while since he had last felt a woman's kiss. So he proceeded to repeat the experiment, to gather more data for the comparison.

Although by the time Sedra got him back to her room, he had long since forgotten about any other woman.

9

"HAIL *PIONEER*," Captain T'Pol ordered once *Endeavour* dropped to impulse within Rigelian space.

Hoshi Sato moved to comply. "That's odd," she said after a few moments. "They're responding . . . but from a position behind Rigel IV's moon, and on an encrypted channel."

"Onscreen. Encrypt our reply."

The bearded visage of T'Pol's erstwhile first officer appeared on the main viewer. *"Welcome to Rigel, Captain T'Pol,"* said Malcolm Reed. *"You made good time."*

"I shall relay your compliments to Chief Engineer Romaine. What is your current status, Captain?"

Reed did not comment on her preference to get straight to business; he was habitually much the same. *"We're providing support for an infiltration down on Four. One of the target ships was tracked to a spaceport in the territory of the Corthoc Family. Lieutenant Williams is checking it out."*

T'Pol's brows raised. "How did you arrange access to First Family airspace?" Even if Reed had deemed the situation extreme enough to warrant the risk of transporter use, the Families would still have detected the beam.

"Fortunately, the Families are far from a united front. The

Commission was able to bribe one of the lesser Families, the Kanyors, who have a fierce rivalry with the neighboring Corthocs. They granted our team access to their airspace and transport onto Corthoc lands." He gave a tight smile. "*Nothing like a little dissension in the enemy ranks.*"

"Indeed. May I join you aboard *Pioneer?* I would appreciate a fuller briefing while we await word from your armory officer."

Reed frowned, contemplating. "*Actually,* Endeavour *could be more useful elsewhere. One of the target ships went to Rigel VII, but the Commission is reluctant to send a ship of its own there, even in an emergency.*" He grimaced. "*Apparently, while the Kalar shun most modern technology, they make an exception when it comes to defending their territory. They have weaponry that can shoot down atmospheric craft.*"

"Then the ship that traveled there was most likely a decoy and may have already been destroyed."

"*Possibly, but we must follow every lead.*"

"Understood," T'Pol said. "I would still like to meet with you, Captain. With your permission, I shall come aboard in a shuttlepod while *Endeavour* proceeds to Rigel VII."

Reed hesitated for a moment. "*Very well. Less risk of detection that way, I suppose. We'll send you the safe approach vector.*"

"Thank you, Captain." She offered an appreciative nod, softening her expression slightly. "It will be agreeable to see you again, Malcolm."

He paused before replying more stiffly. "*And you, Captain.*"

Babel Station

Archer awoke to find Sedra Hemnask sitting up in bed beside him, her knees pulled up against her bare chest, arms wrapped around her legs. She seemed lost in thought. "Hi," he said.

She started and looked at him, relaxing her pose in a way that considerably improved his view. "Welcome back to waking," she said.

"It's been a long time since I've woken up to such a beautiful sight."

"Always the deft-tongued diplomat," she teased.

But before he could reach for her, she sighed and eased herself out of bed, moving to gaze out the window of her suite, which looked out on the hangar dome and the cratered landscape beyond. "Penny for your thoughts," he ventured.

She turned to stare. "Excuse me?"

"It's an old Earth expression. It means, what are you thinking?"

Her brow furrowed endearingly. "Why does it mean that?"

Archer sat up in bed. He was coming to enjoy this game. "Well, a . . . penny is a kind of old coin."

"A coin. So you're offering to bribe me into telling you my thoughts?"

He got out of bed and slipped on a bathrobe, not as accustomed to the cool air as a Rigel V native like Hemnask. "It was a very small coin. The lowest denomination. So it's—"

"So you're saying my thoughts are of minimal value."

He stepped closer to her. "I was going to say, it's a token gesture. And you're avoiding the question." He put his arms on her bare shoulders. "Something's on your mind, Sedra. I'd like to know what it is."

"Jonathan, I . . ." She pulled away, moving closer to the window. "I'm wondering if this was a mistake."

His face fell. "Oh. I'm . . . sorry, I thought . . ."

"Oh, no, not because of you!" Her hand rested on his chest. "No, what we shared was . . . special. That's why I fear it was selfish of me to seek it from you."

He stroked Sedra's cheek. "The last thing I would call you after last night is selfish."

"But I was." She moved away and finally donned her own robe, not from the chill. "I didn't think about how it would look. Politically, I mean."

Archer frowned, shaking his head. "But we're both already known for supporting membership. I don't see a conflict of interest."

"That's just it. They could claim our relationship existed earlier, back on Rigel. Accuse you of seducing me into supporting the Federation."

"That's ridiculous."

She spread her arms. "Welcome to politics! All it takes is the appearance of scandal to poison a deal. And our chances of winning over both Rigel and the Federation are tenuous enough already. It wouldn't take much to ruin them."

Hemnask smiled wistfully, coming up to Archer

and tenderly stroking his cheek. "It's sweet and romantic of you to speak up for what we did. But can you truly tell me you never contemplated that it might be unwise?"

Archer pondered her words. The truth was, he had recognized last night that his behavior was a little out of character. Maybe that was why he'd done it. Ever since his talk with Dani, he'd been aware of how solitary he'd let himself become. After all, he wasn't getting any younger. If he ever wanted to pass the Archer legacy forward to another generation . . . or even just have someone to keep him company once he finally retired . . . he had to change his way of doing things. Maybe his yearning for a companion had made him reckless in giving in to his attraction to Hemnask.

After a moment, he shook his head, rejecting the thought. "You are not just someone I slept with because you were convenient. I may have been feeling a little lonely lately, but not that needy. There's something real between us. Something worth pursuing."

She came up to him again. "I'm not saying there isn't. This does mean something to me. But . . . it was ill-timed. We should probably defer exploring it further until after the conference, when there's no longer a potential conflict of interest." She gave a lopsided grin and moved in against him. "Or at least we should keep this as private as we can." She kissed him slowly. "We Rigelians value our secrets."

He kissed her back, and it was a while before they parted. "All right. For now, this is just between us."

"Agreed." She self-consciously grasped his hand and shook it in the human manner.

But he took her hand in both of his, smiling. "You know . . . it's still a few hours until local morning."

She tilted her head. "I believe you're right." She pulled his head down to hers again.

Archer had barely gotten her robe open again when his communicator beeped. He let it sound a few times before they both sighed, pulled apart, and rolled their eyes in mutual understanding. Retying his robe, he fished the palm-sized instrument out of his uniform pocket and flipped open the grille. "Archer here."

"Admiral, this is Captain Williams. You'd better get down to the esplanade, sir."

Sensing the intensity in his aide's voice, Archer frowned. "What's wrong, Marcus?"

"Sir, someone just took a shot at Councilor Thoris."

Many of the ambassadors and their aides had gathered near the center of the esplanade by the time Archer arrived, and a fair number of the Andorian Starfleet troops handling security for the conference were there as well, keeping the crowd back and questioning witnesses. Archer spotted Marcus Williams easily: his aide was a tall, strongly built man, a former wide receiver for Starfleet Academy's gridiron football team back in the '30s. Once Williams spotted Archer, that background assisted him in negotiating the crowd to rendezvous with the admiral. "Where's the councilor?" Archer asked.

"Back aboard his ship," Williams replied in his Iowa drawl. "Babel security's taking his statement there."

Archer furrowed his brow. "What was he even still doing here? He should've headed off for his next campaign stop hours ago."

Williams worked his lantern jaw. "Seems like they had some engine trouble. Had to lay over for repairs."

"That seems oddly convenient for whoever wanted to take a shot at Thoris."

"The thought occurred to me as well." Archer turned at the new voice, seeing the serene Vulcan visage of T'Rama, Solkar's aide and daughter-in-law. "I trust Babel security will investigate the matter."

"I'll make sure they do," Archer said. Over T'Rama's shoulder, he noticed Hemnask's arrival, arranged to come a comfortable interval after his own and from a separate direction. Their eyes met briefly without overt acknowledgment.

He caught a snatch of conversation from the nearby cluster of Planetarist-leaning ambassadors. As usual, Mikhail Kamenev was raising a fuss to make a Tellarite proud. "Mark my words, this has Federalist fingerprints all over it," the Martian exclaimed.

Avaranthi sh'Rothress tilted her antennae skeptically. "You aren't seriously proposing they attempted to kill him."

"Scare him off, maybe. Intimidate him, intimidate us into backing down."

"Al-Rashid himself wouldn't dare try it," Ysanne

Fell put in. "But perhaps some deranged supporter. You know how fanatical some of their followers are. Or maybe some Rigelian gangster trying to guarantee admission."

Archer tried to tune them out. "I take it the shooter hasn't been found yet?" he asked Williams.

The captain shook his head. "The station's been locked down. No ships are allowed to leave, and shields went up automatically as soon as the station's sensors detected the weapons fire."

"So the assailant is still present," T'Rama said. She quirked an eyebrow. "Not a reassuring insight."

Archer's gaze went to her belly. "Maybe you should hang back."

"Your concern for my embryo is appreciated, Admiral, but I judge the risk to be minimal," T'Rama said, striding toward the security contingent. "The sniper targeted Councilor Thoris specifically," she went on as Archer followed, "and he, she, or other would not risk capture by firing at another target with security already on the scene. Not to mention that if there were an active shooter, this crowd would not have been allowed to assemble."

"You make a good argument," Archer conceded.

"I *am* a Vulcan," she replied, though he caught the same kind of deadpan teasing in her voice that he'd learned from long experience to recognize in T'Pol's. "Additionally, I had eleven Vulcan years of experience as an investigator in ShiKahr prior to joining Administrator T'Pau's security detail."

"I imagine such crimes were more common before the *Kir'Shara* reforms."

"Not particularly; it was mostly the High Command that was prone to aggression for what were deemed logical reasons. But violent crimes did occur among immigrants or visitors. And on occasion, the policies of the High Command provoked political assassination attempts by Andorians, Mazarites, and the like."

They reached the security contingent as she spoke, and its head, a gray-uniformed lieutenant commander named Astellet ch'Terren, turned to them, holding a scanner he'd just been handed by a subordinate. Looking up from it with a solemn expression, the young Andorian gazed at Archer for a moment before turning to T'Rama. "Ma'am, you say you have investigatory experience?"

"That is correct."

"We could use your assistance, then," he said, eyes still darting to Archer. "It may have now become a rather sensitive matter, and it might be preferable to have a non-Starfleet investigator involved to avoid a conflict of interest."

T'Rama studied him. "What have you found, Commander?"

Ch'Terren hesitated. "My people identified the rooftop from which the shots were fired. The ledge around it shows radiation traces consistent with a Starfleet phase pistol, matching the burns on the street below. And . . . well, see for yourself."

The Vulcan diplomat took the scanner he offered and studied its readings. Raising her brows, she turned to Archer. "Admiral. This says that hair and skin cells found at the shooter's position are consistent with your DNA."

Archer did a double take. "What?! That's ridiculous!"

"Then I trust you can provide an alibi for the time in question."

"Of course. I—"

He realized that Sedra Hemnask was standing close by in the crowd. No doubt she had heard everything. He met her eyes, prompting her to come forward. Surely this changed things.

But Hemnask returned his gaze with apology . . . then turned and walked away without a word.

Corthoc estate, Rigel IV

The guard slumped, unconscious, and Valeria Williams released her grip from around his neck. She'd employed a Vulcan *Suus Mahna* sleeper hold that left no mark; with luck, when the Zami guard recovered, he'd simply assume he'd fallen asleep on watch and gotten a crick in his neck. But she had to act quickly to be in and out of the hangar before that happened.

Getting into Corthoc territory had been relatively easy with help from the rival Kanyor clan, a well-bribed operative of whose had brought her across the border in the garb of a servant. Her light skin and auburn hair let her blend in well with the Zami, and those who lived in the Kanyor lands often had rounder pinnae than the species norm, so Doctor Liao hadn't even needed to give her prosthetic ears (which was almost a shame; she was somewhat curious to see how she'd look with points added). After that, she'd been transferred into the care of the local resistance, though indirectly. The Kanyors were happy to abet anyone who wished to undermine the Corthocs, but they were still feudal lords who oppressed their own commoners just as harshly (according to the resistance, though the Kanyors insisted they treated their serfs better, like beloved pets), so any cooperation between the two groups was strained at best.

The downside of the stealth approach was having to leave her phase pistol and communicator behind. The Corthocs, like most of the First Families, hoarded higher technology to themselves and constantly scanned the peasant districts for contraband. The districts that Williams had passed through on her way here had been an odd mix of technological levels. The most advanced contrivances the peasants were allowed were the 2D viewscreens that broadcast an endless barrage of propaganda and pabulum to lull them into complacency. The screens seemed out of place in dwellings that, in some districts, were virtually medieval. The farming and construction vehicles were cumbersome, rusty things on rubber wheels, powered by hazardous and unreliable internal-combustion engines. Many farmers and merchants made do with carts pulled by four-horned, orange-furred Rigelian yaks, which were arguably better suited for the rough, cobbled roads than the combustion-powered trucks were, at least when they didn't find one of those trucks broken down in their path.

Yet Family-owned facilities such as this hangar, or the fortresses where the feudal lords dwelt, were full of the modern technologies and comforts that the Families denied their serfs. Which included security sensors to supplement the live guards, so Williams had to be careful from this point. Luckily her scanner could operate at low enough power to avoid tripping the contraband sensors, unlike the power pack in a phase pistol or the subspace transceiver in a communicator. Plus, she had intelligence from the local resistance about the best places to subvert the security system. Williams was thus able to locate the sensor fields, tap into their control circuits, and do to them essentially what she'd just done to the guard.

The resistance, sadly, was still weakened from a series of recent purges, biding its time and rebuilding its strength. So it hadn't been able to spare anyone beyond a single junior recruit who still hadn't overcome his fear of the Corthocs enough to risk entry into one of their facilities. Williams supposed that someone whose only exposure to high technology was the lash of the oppressor's whip could be forgiven a certain technophobia. So she had the youth stand watch outside while she infiltrated the facility.

An emergency ladder, a couple of picked locks, and a maintenance-catwalk crawl later, the lieutenant stood above the target vessel, a Grennex RK6 light freighter. After ensuring its own systems, security included, were powered down, Williams lowered herself onto its bridge tower by rope, then made her way down and back to the vessel's dorsal spine. She found a maintenance port and hooked her scanner to its computer interface. Two minutes later, she'd verified that Grev and Sam had never been aboard this ship—which frustrated but hardly surprised her. It had always been unlikely that the Corthocs would have brought the abductees to their own estate. But the RTC's intelligence reports suggested that the Corthocs were not known for having much intelligence of their own, due to extreme decadence and a degree of good old-fashioned inbreeding, so it had been worth checking the possibility.

But even after she successfully exfiltrated the hangar, the mission was only half finished. Her friends—and the vital secret files—may not have been here, but the Corthoc estate's computers probably had information on their location. So now she simply had to break into one of the most heavily secured and technologically advanced facilities on the planet, hack its computers, and get out again, with no useful assistance from her resistance escort. *Why did I have to go and convince Captain Reed that a sole infiltrator had the best chance?*

Fortunately, for all the Corthoc fortress's technology, it still had live guards, and guards could be bribed. Well, one had been, though he proved unwilling to provide any assistance beyond what he'd been paid for. Once past the gate, she was on her own again. But so long as she maintained the meek, downcast manner appropriate to her servant's attire, she could hopefully manage to avoid attention.

"You there! Girl!" Williams had made it all the way into the central complex before she got noticed. Not wishing to draw more attention, she froze and tried to act properly deferential as she turned. The bearded, potbellied, ornate-wigged dandy who looked her over matched the resistance's descriptions of Fetrin Corthoc, the second son of the current patriarch and a man known for his cruelty and licentious appetites. Indeed, his eyes were roving over her in a way that made her feel unclean. "My, my, I haven't seen that ass in here before. Ohh, fine sleek curves from the front, too. Mm, where have you been hiding, my dear?"

A fat hand pawed her chest roughly, and she restrained herself from breaking his wrist, reminding herself of the mission. There were limits to what she would tolerate, though, and she began planning her options in case his invasive attentions continued.

His other hand came up to her chin and lifted her face, forcing her to meet his eyes. Once he got a good look at her, though, his face fell. "Oh. You're older than this body makes you look." He pulled away with the manner of a customer displeased by the merchandise. "Get away, then. Go."

Williams hastened to comply, suppressing a shudder. If twenty-seven was too old for him . . . she didn't want to think about it.

"Here," came a hushed female voice. Seeing a plain, fortyish servant beckoning her toward a side corridor, Williams made her way over. "Aww, you're a new one, aren't you, poor dear?"

"That's right," she said, not wanting to give much away.

"Well, you were lucky. Fetrin may lose interest once you're full-grown, but other Corthocs aren't so choosy." The maid lowered her eyes. "We learn soon enough to keep to the back passages, avoid attention as we can. At least it betters our chances, most of the time." Looking more closely, Williams realized the woman had once been striking, before life in the lords' service had worn her down. "What's your name, pet?"

"I'm . . . Valeria." Who here would recognize it as an Earth name?

"Denuri. Come, I'll show you the way of things."

Being found by Denuri proved a godsend. She wasn't getting any closer to a computer terminal, but the invisibility that came from blending in with the servants, following their expected schedules and routes, and being perceived as little more than a household appliance gave her the opportunity to overhear a good deal of the gossip that the Corthocs engaged in as a favorite activity. Much of it was about gambling and drinking, the laughable ill fortunes of rival Family members, or the kind of sexual conquests that made it hard for Val to restrain herself from unleashing some *Suus Mahna* on the Corthoc men's nether regions. But here and there she caught snippets of important information that even the house computers might not contain:

"I tell you, we haven't even needed the code broken! Some people's secrets are easy enough to guess. We're making headway through bluffs alone. . . ."

". . . Federation or no Federation, the Commission is still the root of the problem. They wouldn't have considered bringing those aliens in if they weren't already getting ideas about another 'intervention' on behalf of our poor, oppressed peasants. And the last thing we need is real support for these revolts . . ."

". . . That fool outworlder thinks Two is the prize! These criminals, they have so little imagination. To think our ambitions could be as limited as theirs."

"Filthy outworld creatures. I'll be glad once we've put them all in their place—or in the ground."

And what she couldn't overhear directly from the Corthocs, the servants themselves had picked up, and they enjoyed gossip no less than their masters (plus Williams got groped less in the process):

"Well, my mistress said, 'Why settle for one new ship? The whole company will soon be worth less than one of their ships is now. . . .'"

". . . Then Master Vemrim threatened to send me out to die in the war. I was fool enough to talk back, ask what war. Thought I was in for a flogging, but he just laughed and said I could take my pick soon enough. . . ."

". . . Lizards? Did he mean the tortoises?"

"*I* wasn't going to ask Master Dectof, you can bet on that! 'We'll make the lizards dance, too,' is what he said."

It all suggested some very interesting things, and Williams made sure to record notes on her scanner when she got the chance. She'd need more information to piece the whole picture together.

To that end, she finally managed to convince Denuri to help her get a few minutes' access to the house mainframe. The senior maid was able to arrange a minor kitchen disaster to draw the Corthocs' attention for a while, and Val followed her directions to an appropriate terminal.

She was halfway into hacking through its user lockout with her scanner when she heard a slap and a cry—the cry of a fairly young girl. After that came a voice whose aggressive yet covetous tone she recognized.

Despite herself, Williams jogged out to the hall and peered around the corner. Fetrin Corthoc stood there, holding an adolescent blond girl by the arm. Val recognized her as one of the younger servants, though she blanked on the girl's name, having disciplined her memory to focus on mission-relevant data. But Fetrin was determined not to let her go. He was stroking her hair, pulling at her clothes, laughing with twisted affection as she wept and pleaded.

Williams seethed, but duty held her back. *This is everyday life here. I can't change that. I can save the most people by getting that data, retrieving the archives. The greater good.* She forced herself to turn away and start back for the computer room.

Behind her, fabric ripped and the girl wailed.

Twenty seconds after that, Fetrin Corthoc lay dazed and aching on the floor, struggling to right his bulk and screaming for the guards as Williams and the serving girl fled hand in hand. Val had resisted the temptation to hurt him as badly as she'd wanted; all that would have achieved was to make him more vengeful toward whatever other girls he got his hands on next.

No, I can't save everybody. But I can help someone right in front of me—and what would I be if I didn't? She squeezed her eyes shut briefly. *Grev and Sam would understand.*

With the guards alerted, there was no chance of getting to a terminal now. All she could do was help the girl elude pursuit—after donating her outer blouse so the poor child could cover up again. But once her initial adrenaline rush wore off, the girl hesitated. "Please . . . if I escape, my family will be punished."

Val looked her over. "What's your name?"

"Mindlen."

"Well, Mindlen, I have contacts in the resistance. If we can get to your family, I can take them and you to safety."

"The resistance?" Mindlen's eyes lit up. "I thought they'd been crushed."

"That's what the Corthocs want people to think.

But there's always hope, Mindlen. The more that people like Fetrin try to crush it, the stronger it grows. Remember that."

The girl set her jaw and nodded, a bitterly determined smile on her bruised face. "I will. Let's go."

Inspired by hope, Mindlen sure-footedly led Williams through the servants' corridors. Once informed of the situation, Denuri ran interference to get them out the rear of the building and back to the gate where the bribed guard awaited. But he warned them that the guards had been called out to search and he could grant little in the way of a head start before he'd need to join the pursuit.

Indeed, Williams and Mindlen nearly ran afoul of the guards' hovering skimmers a couple of times before they reached the girl's home. En route, Williams told the girl where to meet her resistance contact in case they got separated.

Mindlen's parents were initially reluctant to abandon their home, but learning that the resistance survived—and seeing their daughter's torn dress and bruised face—was all they needed to motivate them, even without the knowledge that the guards would surely be pounding on their door before long.

The family was just about to follow her outside when she raised a hand, stopping them in the doorway. A guard skimmer was turning onto the street and slowing down. "They're here," the lieutenant said.

Thinking quickly, she pulled the scanner from her pocket and handed it to Mindlen. "Make sure the resistance gets this—tell them it needs to get back to my ship, or to the Trade Commission. There's urgent information in there."

"But what will you—"

"I'll lead them away. Once I have them occupied, you run. Fast as you can, no looking back. You understand? You have to get away."

Mindlen nodded bravely, her lip quivering, and clutched the scanner to her chest. "I understand. Your box must be protected."

Val reached out and stroked her cheek. "Yeah . . . that, too."

She came out the door, knelt, and pulled a pair of fist-sized paving stones from the front walk. She jogged toward the skiff, crossing the street away from Mindlen's family. "Hey!" she called, hurling one of the stones. It hit the side door of the skiff, its arc just too low to strike the driver. Williams cursed under her breath; she still hadn't fully adjusted to the local gravity. But she'd gotten their attention. "Yeah, I'm talking to you! I have an urgent message from the United Federation of Planets!" She hurled the other stone, but the guards ducked this time. Still, she struck one on the shoulder.

That did it. Identifying herself as a Federation operative made her a high-value target, enough that the guards forgot about Mindlen and pursued Williams en masse as she ran down a side street. She dodged and weaved through the narrow streets, taking advantage of her much leaner cross-section and tighter turning radius to stay ahead of the skiff.

But then a second skiff descended in her path, the

guards bringing their weapons to bear. She dodged as energy bolts tore past her, but the first skiff was blocking her retreat.

Williams took solace in that as stun bolts hit her from both sides and her consciousness faded. At least it meant that Mindlen had a chance.

10

Babel Station

"I'M SORRY, ADMIRAL, but it doesn't look good," Astellet ch'Terren told Archer. They were in Babel's austere security section, Archer seated in front of ch'Terren's desk while T'Rama stood alongside the lieutenant commander. A pair of Andorian guards hovered behind Archer's shoulders. "Witnesses have confirmed seeing a figure in a Starfleet Command uniform and cap heading into that building before the shots were fired. Your backup uniform and cap are missing from your quarters, and we found a phase pistol power pack compatible with the model used to fire the shots."

"That's ridiculous," Archer said. "I didn't bring a phase pistol—this is a diplomatic conference! Obviously someone broke into my room last night, took my uniform, and planted the power pack."

"Access logs show no unauthorized entry to your room—and one entry conforming to your voice key."

"That must have been faked. I wasn't even in . . ." He broke off.

T'Rama leaned forward. "Admiral, if you have an alibi, why not simply tell us?"

Archer was sorely tempted. But he had to believe that Hemnask wouldn't hang him out to dry like this unless the consequences of revealing their relationship really would be as politically dire as she'd asserted. Not to mention that it simply seemed wrong to violate her privacy without her consent.

So the admiral chose another tack. "Do I really need an alibi? Think about it. Why would I wear my own uniform to sneak up to a rooftop and shoot at a presidential candidate?"

"It could be argued," T'Rama countered, "that a Starfleet uniform would allow you to go anywhere without being questioned."

"The esplanade isn't exactly a high-security area. Besides, don't you think a Starfleet admiral would have enough phase pistol practice to be able to hit his target?"

"Unless that admiral suffered from nerve damage that limited his manual dexterity."

"Then that admiral would have the sense not to take the shot himself."

T'Rama contemplated. "These are logical counterarguments. Yet your reluctance to provide an alibi remains an outstanding concern. It suggests you are protecting someone who has something to conceal."

He rolled his eyes. "If I were, then I wouldn't have let them go out on the esplanade in my uniform and use a Starfleet phase pistol." Archer took a breath. "Look, there's gotta be some other line of evidence you can pursue. Something that'll clear me."

"It is for us to determine the direction of this investigation, Admiral."

Archer sighed, but said nothing more. After a

moment, ch'Terren said, "I take it you have no further statement, sir?"

"You may take it and—yes, that's correct."

"Then I'm sorry," the young Andorian told him, "but I have no choice but to confine you for the time being. We will continue to investigate, of course. But procedure must be followed."

"I understand," Archer told him.

Indeed, he could understand everyone's actions—ch'Terren's, T'Rama's, even the shooter's. The staged assassination attempt had clearly been meant to hurt the Federalists' standing and undermine Rigel's chances of admission, and possibly to worsen the existing divisions within the Federation.

The one person whose actions he couldn't understand—the one whose actions hurt the most—was Sedra Hemnask.

June 22, 2164
U.S.S. Endeavour, **orbiting Rigel VII**

"I've located the ship," Elizabeth Cutler reported from the science station. Thanien rotated the command chair to face her. "It's in a mountainous region north of the main settled territories."

"How far north?" Takashi Kimura asked.

"Not far. A few hours' march from the nearest city."

"Still," Hoshi Sato observed, "that's a strange place to set down. We know the Kalar shoot down intruders.

Could they have crashed?" Thanien heard the concern in her tone: what if the abducted *Pioneer* crewmen had been on that ship?

The lieutenant shook her head uncertainly. "I can't tell at this range. I'm only getting a partial read on the ship . . . it's in a narrow cleft under an overhang, and there are refractory minerals around it that confuse my scans. Plus all the volcanic dust in the air reduces visibility."

Thanien narrowed his eyes. "That seems conveniently well-hidden for a crashed ship. They may have evaded the Kalar's artillery and landed there to avoid detection."

The first officer stood and addressed Ortega at the helm. "Ensign, adjust our orbit for optimal line-of-sight on the vessel on our next pass. Altitude, two hundred fifty kilometers." He turned to the tactical station. "Commander Kimura, prepare a team. Unless Lieutenant Cutler can offer a more definitive scan on our next orbit, I want you to proceed to the target ship in shuttlepod one to determine its status and occupancy."

Sato leaned forward, frowning. "Sir, if the Kalar detect the shuttlepod—"

"A fast, low approach from the north may elude detection."

"There are still other options we haven't tried. We could send a sensor probe."

Thanien feared the communications officer was letting her romantic relationship with Kimura compromise her judgment. He strove to appeal to her reason. "I'm concerned with the risk of tipping off the craft's occupants, if any. If they are down there, and if they have our people, I don't want to give them a chance to bolt, or worse. I want the team ready to strike as soon as possible."

"Understood, sir. But maybe if we hail the Kalar, explain that we're going after other intruders into their territory, we might convince them not to fire."

He threw Sato an impatient look. "Do you really think that's likely, Commander?"

"It's worth a try."

"And it might alert our quarry if they're monitoring our communications." Thanien was growing weary of this. He'd tried to be patient with Sato, but her constant second-guessing was becoming excessive. He turned back to Kimura. "Commander, ready your team."

The armory officer glanced briefly at Sato. Thanien recognized it as concern for his lover's feelings rather than a challenge to his authority, but it was still reassuring when Kimura looked back to him and acknowledged, "Aye, sir."

He left the bridge, and Sato gazed after him with concern and displeasure. Thanien kept an eye on her, hoping she would offer no further disruptions.

Veranith, Sauria

Four days ago, a riot had broken out before the Veranith Parliament Building, instigated by protestors condemning the government for allowing its people to die by the thousands in the name of a historical grudge against M'Tezir. Three days ago, with the riots threatening to escalate, the Parliament announced that it had formally requested medical aid from Basileus Maltuvis and severed its ties with the Saurian Global League. Two days ago, the Veranith Defense Force, aided by the M'Tezir troops that had arrived overnight, had begun evicting all non-Saurian residents from the country, officially to protect them from the unruly populace. The claim was not without merit; on the night of the riots, a Tellarite couple had been beaten nearly to death on their way to the Federation embassy.

Today, the evacuation had been declared complete, with all offworlders successfully and safely expelled from Veranith territory. However, if anyone were to check the records, they would show that a human named Albert Sims had conveniently left under his own power four days earlier, just before he would have been compelled to leave. Further records would show that he had applied for residency and employment in Lyaksti, the central state of the Global League. If the captain and first mate of the sea shuttle on which Sims had been registered as a passenger were questioned afterward, they would both confirm that he had indeed been aboard—though the captain might be hard to find, having suddenly come into an inheritance, retired, and turned over ownership of the sea shuttle to the first mate, fulfilling both their longtime ambitions.

Charles "Trip" Tucker, on the other hand, was currently lurking in the undergrowth behind the medical clinic where he—or rather, Albert Sims—had been volunteering until just days before. Said clinic was now under the control of the M'Tezir Expeditionary Medical Corps, who had turned it into an armed and guarded camp, nominally to protect the vital plague treatments within from theft or offworlder sabotage.

Tucker wondered if that included offworlder theft as well. The only way to find out, he supposed, was to get past the guards and alarms so he could try it for himself. With his training, that was unlikely to be too difficult.

But then he caught a glimpse of movement near the rear entrance. Setting his night-vision visor to magnify, Tucker grimaced when he realized that Antonio Ruiz was attempting the same thing he was. And likely to get both of them caught and expelled, at best, for he seemed oblivious to the guard turning the corner and heading his way.

Tucker moved toward Ruiz as quickly as he could without rustling the undergrowth too noticeably. Finding a suitable rock, he hurled it into the deeper growth. Once the guard moved to investigate the sound, Trip broke cover, grabbed Ruiz from behind, and dragged him back into concealment with a hand over his mouth. The wiry young Cuban struggled and swung, his fists flying with little technique but considerable force, so Tucker hissed in his ear. "Calm down, Antonio! It's me! Albert!"

Ruiz settled down and tried to turn his head.

Tucker let him, and flipped up the night visor so Ruiz could see both his eyes. "Al!"

"Shh!"

"Al," Ruiz went on in a whisper. "It is you. What are you doing here, man?"

"I was gonna ask you the same question. Why weren't you evacuated?"

Ruiz gave him a knowing look. "I wouldn't be much of a mining engineer if I didn't know my geology. I know a couple of good hidey-holes up in the hills."

"Okay, next question. Why did you hide? Why are you trying to break into the clinic?"

"Same reason you are, I reckon. Those lavender *ladrones* are hoarding medicine that could help Saurians in other countries. Using it as a bribe for—"

"Yeah, I know. We had this conversation."

"Right, and I know you're as angry about it as I am. So you couldn't pass up a chance to get your hands on an actual dose of that medicine any more than I could."

Tucker conceded with a tilt of his head. "Great minds think alike. And so do ours, apparently."

"Hey, watch it."

"So how were you planning on getting inside?"

"I have the security code."

"Which they would've reprogrammed the moment they took over the building."

Ruiz stared for a moment. "Oh. 'Great minds' . . ." He rolled his eyes in self-deprecation. "So I take it you have a better idea?"

"I'm pretty good with machines," Tucker said.

"I await a demonstration with bated breath."

Tucker looked at him sidelong, holding the engineer back until the returned guard went past. They must have been undermanned, since the disruption to the patrol pattern left a gap of a full thirty-two seconds for the humans to get to the rear entrance and crack the code. No surprise that a force supposedly on hand to guard the medicine seemed to be devoting the lion's share of its attention to other things—probably solidifying their control over Veranith.

"So how'd you learn to do things like this?" Ruiz whispered as they made their way through the clinic's corridors to the lab.

"I told you, I've trained in engineering."

"Not just that. The way you manhandled me back there. The way you sneak around without a sound and know how to avoid armed guards. And you have been asking a lot of questions since we met, y'know."

"I'm just naturally inquisitive. Which sometimes gets me into trouble, so I need to keep a low profile."

"Right. Like that trouble with the freighter captain's wife?"

"It was the first mate." He caught Ruiz's eye for a moment. "Nice try."

"Fine. Forget it. Just tell me, Mister Bond, how we find the medicine."

"First, we find a computer. We can get an inventory listing from there."

"Now, that I can do."

Ruiz led him to an office whose lock Tucker overcame almost unthinkingly. Telling Ruiz to keep watch at the door, he accessed the computer and hacked his way into the recently installed M'Tezir database. While tracking down the medicine was on his agenda, he also searched for data that might reveal something about what the M'Tezir were really doing and how—and with whose help—they were pulling it off. Yet the search was futile, as he had expected; such sensitive information was unlikely to be stored in a place like this. He had to settle for the location of the medicine. "I got it," he told Ruiz. "Let's go."

The storage room containing the medicine was guarded, but Tucker had scouted out the maintenance passages in the clinic's drop ceilings days before, so he was able to get himself and Ruiz inside without the guard noticing. Moments later, they pried a container open and beheld the hundreds of vials arrayed before them. "And there we are," Ruiz breathed. He reached in and pulled out a vial—then hesitated.

"What is it?" Tucker asked.

"Any medicine we take out of here," the other man said slowly, "is a dose one of the Veranith patients won't be getting. What if someone dies because we took this?"

"Think of how many people will die if M'Tezir keeps hoarding this treatment. You need to get this to Doctor Lucas and his team so they can reproduce it, get it out planetwide with no strings attached."

"I know, but . . . the big picture's still made up of little pictures. How do we have the right to choose one life over another?"

"It's Maltuvis that's forced that choice, not you, Tony. He's the one to blame for this mess." As Ruiz continued to think it over, Tucker added, "Look at it this way. Taking too long to act could cost lives, too." *Including ours.*

Ruiz sighed. "You're right. Let's get out of here." He pocketed the vial.

Tucker took a second one. "Just in case," he explained. "If there's trouble, we split up. One of us has to get back to Doctor Lucas."

As they worked their way out of the building, Tucker resolved that if only one of them could get away, it had to be Ruiz. This wasn't just selflessness; Tucker had met Doctor Lucas before, following the Augment attack on Cold Station 12. It had been a decade since then, and he had changed somewhat, but an observant physician like Lucas could probably recognize him if given a good look. Besides, if Tucker got the M'Tezir troops to chase him, he'd have a better chance of eluding them—or surviving interrogation if captured—than Ruiz.

Reaching the rear exit, they bided their time until the next gap in the patrol. "You know," Ruiz observed in a whisper, "if I were, oh, the troublesomely inquisitive sort, I think my next move would be to get into one of the countries M'Tezir's been occupying for a while, so I could discover how they were treating their people, bring back evidence to the League. If people could see what Maltuvis was really doing, then maybe that whole 'angel of mercy' image might get tarnished."

Tucker pursed his lips, nodding. "Maybe."

"So if I were that kind of person, I'd need some

connections to get me into such a country without being noticed. Which I imagine would be harder than just lying low in the country you were already in."

"I imagine so." Tucker studied him. "You have a suggestion?"

Ruiz grinned. "I have a connection. An old friend who's been smuggling Narpran rum out of the country since the occupation. He knows where to go to avoid notice, and who'll look the other way if they do spot his boat. He could get us inside."

Tucker turned his head sharply. "'Us'?"

"Well, he won't trust just anyone. Now, I'd be happy to let you go alone if it were up to me." He rubbed his neck. "Rocks are amazing things, but pillows they're not, so I'd be happy to go catch up on my sleep. But my contact probably wouldn't be willing to help if I didn't come along to vouch for you."

Tucker nodded sarcastically. "Right. Of course."

Still, he admired the man's resourcefulness and determination. And in his own way, Ruiz was good company. That was something Tucker appreciated right now more than he cared to admit. He hadn't achieved a telepathic link with T'Pol in weeks, and he wasn't sure if it was simply because they were on opposite sides of explored space or because they still hadn't worked their way past their dispute. Either way, it had gotten lonelier in his head, and he could use some companionship, a friend he had common ground with, even if he couldn't admit how common.

He wondered if Narpran rum was as good as Saurian brandy. . . .

Hainali Basin, Rigel III

"Are we lost?" Rey Sangupta peered out the windscreen of the hoverskiff, searching in vain for any sign of the Hainali River's coastline. They had arrived during the flood season, and portions of the river were so wide at this time of year that to an observer in midriver, both shores could be below the horizon. Aside from the occasional tussocks of floating vegetation, there was nothing in Sangupta's field of view but water. "It's conceivable we could be lost."

"We're not lost, Rey," Commander Mayweather replied with studied patience. "This thing has satellite navigation." The first officer chuckled. "I thought you colonials were supposed to be hardy frontier types."

"Frontiers of science, sure. My parents teach at the University of Alpha Centauri. I grew up in the heart of civilization. Not very close to the ocean."

"It's a river, not an ocean."

"It's a river doing a damn good impression of an ocean." He glanced left, then did a double take. "I think I saw something move down there."

Director Sajithen, who sat beside Sangupta in the rear seat while her two escorts sat up front with Mayweather, threw the science officer an irritated look. "The river contains much life. Many things move down there."

"Thanks, that's a comforting thought."

"What you *should* be watching out for," Mayweather told him, "are First Family agents. Someone could be waiting for us besides Director Sajithen's contacts."

The director had finally received a response from the Chelon nationalists, a group that resided deep within the rainforest that covered much of Rigel III's northern continent. As Chelons were adapted for a semi-aquatic existence, the majority lived along the planet's many rocky coastlines or on smaller land masses like Janxor, readily accessible to the Jelna traders who had started coming to their world more than six centuries ago and introduced them to metallurgy, writing, and other technologies that the bulk of the Chelon populace had taken to readily. But the tribes of the Hainali had remained more isolated and traditionalist, resisting the efforts of civilized Chelons and offworld traders to "develop" their lands and harvest their natural resources. It was no surprise that the nationalist movement had its heart here.

But while Sangupta had enough doubts about getting the Hainalians to cooperate, he dismissed Mayweather's concern. "How would they even know we're here? You said it yourself, sir, they have no idea we know about the Rigel III connection."

"They *had* no idea," Sajithen replied. "But as I have noted, they had one agent inside the Commission, so they could still have another. By now they may know we discovered the hypnoids' involvement and are coming here."

"Oh. Wonderful." Sangupta resumed scanning the horizon. "Then the sooner we can find these old friends of yours, the better."

Fortunately, it was not much longer before the shoreline started to emerge on the horizon. Initially it appeared overgrown with lush rainforest vegetation, but the skiff drew nearer swiftly enough that he soon began to discern settlements along the shore. As the Chelon escort slowed the skiff and turned it to enter a tributary, Rey got a closer look at one of the villages: no mere cluster of huts, but a large community containing hundreds of single-story dwellings atop sturdily built earthen mounds connected by causeways. The earthworks were high enough that now, at the peak of the flood season, the dwellings and causeways remained a couple of meters above the waterline, making things easy for the villagers who dove into the water with empty nets and climbed out later with hauls of fish. There were a few signs of outside technology—thermoconcrete reinforcements for some of the mounds and causeways, solar panels atop many of the dwellings—but they were integrated smoothly into the Hainalians' traditional designs and construction materials. Rey reflected that some of his distant maternal ancestors in the Amazon Basin had probably lived much the same way half a millennium before. Francisco de Orellana, a member of the first group of Spanish explorers to travel that way, had described riverbanks densely populated with hundreds of such communities—communities that had all but disappeared by the time later explorers returned, their populations devastated by the imported diseases that had raced ahead of European colonization. Here, mercifully, the Chelons had been spared that fate, their exotic biology leaving them immune to the plagues that had ravaged their humanoid neighbors in the past.

Soon they left the villages behind, though the forests along the bank were clearly well-cultivated. In these rainy climes, clearing the forest would wash away the soil, leaving traditional agriculture untenable. So like the native Amazonians, the Hainalians had turned the forest around them into a vast orchard, its trees and smaller plants bred over centuries into forms useful to the Chelons for food, textiles, dyes, building materials, medicines, and so forth.

Still, as one got farther from the villages, the forest grew thicker and less populated. Eventually the Chelon escort settled the skiff in the water in one of these backwoods areas and retracted the canopy. Sajithen herself emitted a loud ululating cry punctuated by a rapid clicking of her beak. No doubt it was the signal to let her contacts know they'd arrived. Sangupta hoped the nationalists were prompt—if only so that his ears hadn't suffered for nothing. Not to mention the rest of him. The heat and humidity here were stifling, a shock after the climate-controlled environment of the enclosed skiff. Even diffused by the mists that hung overhead, the radiance of Raij at this proximity was intense.

After waiting a few moments, Sajithen made the call a second time, but then seemed content to wait. Several minutes passed, and Rey's attempt to scan the river's edge for any sight or sound of Chelon movement faded into a borderline fugue state of sweltering discomfort and boredom . . . only to be interrupted by a surge in the water and the emergence of an enormous head not ten meters from the skiff. Startled, Rey stumbled backward into his seat. The creature that rose from the river had a leathery, bright green head with owlish dark eyes and an elongated beak tapering to a sharp point. Its plesiosaurian neck was nearly as long as the skiff and attached to an even longer body whose scaled back barely breached the surface.

"Do not be alarmed," Sajithen said while Sangupta was still fumbling for his phase pistol. "The *kreeyitch* is harmless, an eater of plants, insects, and small fish. It was only curious." Indeed, the creature was already darting away, if any movement by such a ponderous animal could be called "darting." The escorts both made sounds of amusement.

Mayweather grinned as he watched the *kreeyitch* undulate away, the wide paddle at the end of its meters-long tail propelling it with a sinuous up-and-down motion. "It's like a river dolphin," he observed.

"That's one big river dolphin," Sangupta replied.

"It's one big river."

"Many of the larger villages keep tame *kreeyitch* to assist in fishing and warding off river predators," the pilot-escort told them.

That brought a double take from the science officer. "I hope that means the predators are smaller than that."

"The ones that travel in packs are, yes." The escort's Chelon features were the perfect deadpan; Rey could only hope he was teasing.

The director scanned the forest. "They should have come by now. Let us move onto the ground, let them see us more clearly."

At her nod, the pilot moved the skiff in toward the bank. But then something huge erupted out of the water before them—a scale-armored head even larger than the *kreeyitch*'s, with a gaping mouth filled with sharp serrated teeth. The pilot veered off as it roared and lunged toward them.

"You weren't kidding about those predators, were you?" Sangupta cried.

The Jelna escort had drawn his sidearm, but Sajithen clacked her beak thoughtfully and said, "Wait. Bring the skiff to a halt." The escorts complied.

"Don't tell me that's harmless, too," Mayweather said to her as it roared in their direction.

"A *tukhanthik* is far from harmless," Sajithen told him. "But the *kreeyitch* know that. If one had been anywhere near here, the *kreeyitch* would be elsewhere." She turned to the pilot. "It is a hypnoid illusion. Take us toward it." As the Chelon complied, Sajithen turned her head back toward the humans. "The nationalists are here, but they try to deter us. Perhaps a test to ensure it was truly I who came."

"I really hope you're right," Sangupta murmured as the skiff drove right toward the *tukhanthik*'s gaping maw . . .

. . . which flickered and faded from his view as the vehicle passed right through where he'd believed it to be. Rey blinked, impressed with the level of detail the hypnoids had been able to conjure.

Moments later, the skiff settled onto the bank and its occupants debarked. Sajithen repeated her ululating, clacking call. "You see it is Sajithen who comes to you!" she called. "Despite my high obligations elsewhere, my purpose is urgent enough to come in my own flesh to meet with you! Let us play no more games!" She moved forward. Mayweather kept pace with her, and Sangupta followed, but he could see no one. "I have seen through one hypnoid trick! If you stand before us, then let us see the truth of it so we may parley!" Startled, Rey looked around, narrowing his gaze, trying to will himself to see through the illusion or spot some motion in the corner of his eye.

And he did. Specifically, he spotted Travis Mayweather's hand jerking up to grab at his neck, where a slender dart protruded. Just as the first officer started to wobble and lose balance, Sangupta saw the Jelna escort struck as well, then felt a sharp sting in his own neck. He fell to the ground just after his superior officer, and as his vision started to blur, he finally saw the illusion of emptiness give way, revealing a fair number of well-armed Chelons with hypnoids at their heels.

As Rey's consciousness faded, he prayed that those darts had not been coated in the Chelons' own, quite lethal venom.

Shuttlepod one, over Rigel VII

"Incoming!"

Ensign Pedro Ortega veered the shuttlepod to port, evading the exploding shell that left a smoky black smudge against the purple and magenta hues of Rigel VII's sky. "Damn," Takashi Kimura said. "Their planetary defenses are more comprehensive than we thought. Can you still get us down?"

"Watch me!" the cocky young pilot replied.

With warning from the shuttlepod's sensors, Ortega was able to evade the incoming fire while still maintaining course toward the mountains. The next few minutes were a harrowing ride through a sky made hazy by a mix of volcanic dust and artillery smoke, and even the highly disciplined members of Kimura's security team—Crewmen Ian Legatt, Sascha Money, and Marie Chiang—were looking a bit airsick by the time they finally closed in on their target.

The tricky part was holding position long enough to gather useful sensor data from the target vessel's landing site without getting blown out of the sky. Ortega brought the shuttlepod in low through the craggy peaks, navigating them like an obstacle course, taking advantage of their refractory minerals to obscure the shuttlepod from the Kalar's sensors. The barrage continued, but fewer of the explosions came near enough to rattle the shuttlepod. The philosopher in Kimura appreciated seeing a disadvantage thus turned to their advantage.

Finally, they closed in on the cleft where the Rigelian skiff was ensconced. "Scan for biosigns," Kimura ordered.

In the seat behind Ortega's right shoulder, Crewman Legatt worked the sensor controls on the swing-out console before him. But Ortega had to veer to starboard to evade another artillery shell; with the pod holding station, the Kalar were starting to find their range again. "I need you to hold it steady, sir," Legatt said.

"Tell *them* that!" Ortega told the grayshirt.

Kimura had years of experience and discipline, first as a MACO and now as Starfleet Security, and was well accustomed to facing danger calmly and accepting the reality that there were some risks he could do nothing to prevent. Still, deliberately sitting still in the middle of a shooting gallery was not particularly conducive to his peace of mind.

"Sir," Legatt reported, "confirming the ship is not intact. Underside's caved in, multiple hull breaches, debris. No way this was a controlled landing." The red-haired Scot looked up at him. "Best guess, they were aiming for the cleft to give them cover, but their luck ran out a few moments too soon."

Let's hope history doesn't repeat itself, Kimura thought. "Any biosigns?"

Legatt shook his head. "None, sir, either in the ship or nearby. But I'm reading organic decay markers from within, and penetrating radar gives a density profile consistent—"

Ortega veered to avoid another shell. "High points, please?"

"Two bodies. Vulcanoid biochemistry."

"That means Zami," Kimura said. Another explosion rattled the hull. "Our people aren't here."

"But they could've been before," Legatt said. "We should try to recover their data banks."

"If we try landing," Money countered, "I doubt the Kalar would let us take off again."

"She's right," Kimura said. "And this planet's too far off the beaten track—they wouldn't have had a chance to transfer them off. This was a decoy." He turned to Ortega. "So get us out of here, best speed."

Ortega was pulling back on the joystick before Kimura finished the sentence. "Just what I've been waiting to—"

Just then, an alarm sounded. "What is it?" Kimura asked.

"We've lost sensors!" said Ortega.

Legatt worked his controls. "Some kind of jamming field, sir! Must be from the Kalar."

Kimura's eyes lifted to the pod's domed windshield, beyond which the artillery barrage continued unabated. "That means . . ."

"That means no more warnings," Ortega said. "Everybody, eyes out the windows! Call out any incoming you spot!"

Money and Chiang promptly directed their gaze out the side ports. But Kimura said, "You just point this thing up and floor it. The sooner we get out of here—" He broke off before he jinxed it.

Too late; it seemed cosmic perversity was in abundant supply on Rigel VII as much as anywhere else in the universe. No sooner had the words left Kimura's mouth than the shuttlepod rocked from an impact. The pod swerved downward, rocky crags filling the viewport. Ortega struggled with the controls. "They hit our wing!"

"Try to aim for someplace flat."

"Do you have a suggestion?" Ortega replied. "Because I'm not seeing a lot of options, sir."

"Legatt, hail *Endeavour*. Try to punch through the jamming, get that data to them." At least then the mission would be a success, technically. If they didn't survive the crash, at least it would mean something.

The crewman tried, but shook his head. "The jamming's too strong!"

So much for that idea. Even if Ortega could bring them down in one piece, Kimura knew it wouldn't be long before a band of hulking, murderously xenophobic Kalar came hunting for them.

This is what I get for not listening to Hoshi was Kimura's final thought before the shuttlepod went down.

11

MALCOLM REED PACED in the tight confines of his ready room, intermittently pausing to stare at the data on his desk monitor, data transmitted by the Kanyors just minutes ago. "Another decoy ship," he said to *Endeavour's* captain, who stood by the door, calm and motionless. "Another dead end. And another member of my crew gets captured." Mayweather and Sangupta were hours overdue for contact, and the Rigel III satellite grid was unable to detect the navigational beacon from their skiff. Reed feared the worst. "They're picking us off, T'Pol! They sent us off on this, this interplanetary scavenger hunt to split us up, to divide and conquer. And I let them. I played right into their hands."

T'Pol replied with reassuring calm. "Given the situation, it was a reasonable allocation of resources."

"Superficially, yes. But that's what they wanted us to decide. I should've seen it. Should've . . ." He trailed off, studying the reflection of his bearded, gray-fringed visage in the ready room's small viewport. His mind contrasted it with an image of the crisp, clean-shaven face that had stared back from the mirror in his prime. "Back when I was an armory officer, I would've questioned it. That was my job: to be suspicious of

everything. Now . . . all I could think about was protecting my crew, getting justice for Mishima."

"You thought like a captain."

"I believed I did. But . . ." He couldn't voice it.
What if he wasn't ready for this responsibility? Was
that why Archer had sent T'Pol to backstop him when
things had grown tense? At first Reed had felt a twinge
of resentment about his former captain being assigned
to look over his shoulder. Now, though, he was grateful for her check on his judgment. "What would you
have done, T'Pol?"

The Vulcan contemplated the question. "I cannot
judge what my state of mind would have been in that
hypothetical situation, for I now have information I
would not have had then, and thus my perception of
the situation differs. As does yours."

T'Pol stepped closer. "Malcolm . . . the important thing is not to reconsider our past decisions, but
to focus on the decisions we must make now. And
to make them with a clear mind and a focus on our
goals."

Reed met her dark eyes gratefully, imploringly.
"Do you have any suggestions?"

Her reply was gentle, pointed, and understanding.
"Trust your officers."

Babel Station

". . . All I have been saying is that there is no need for
haste." Avaranthi sh'Rothress's gaze moved to meet the

eyes of the other ambassadors at the conference table. "How can we legitimately and fairly decide what standards we should use to judge a world's readiness for Federation membership when we haven't even reached a full consensus on what we want the Federation to be? Is it fair to ask Rigel, or even Vega, to join us when we offer them mixed messages about what we expect?"

T'Rama observed the Andorian ambassador's delivery carefully. If she sought to pursue a diplomatic career herself, she could pick a worse role model than this poised, charismatic statesperson. Though sh'Rothress's views on Rigelian admission put her at odds with Solkar, her reasons struck T'Rama as considerably more rational than Mikhail Kamenev's thinly veiled xenophobia or Ysanne Fell's preoccupation with political standing. T'Rama was of the opinion, which her husband's-father shared, that sh'Rothress was the one opposing ambassador who was likely to be swayed in favor of admission if her concerns could be adequately assuaged through reasoned argument.

Kamenev, however, was as stubborn as ever. "This is ridiculous," the dark-mustached Martian exclaimed. "Why are we even still here, pretending to have a civil debate with these pawns of the state, when their poster boy Jonathan Archer has tried to assassinate a presidential candidate?"

"Allegedly tried," T'Rama corrected. As Solkar's assistant, it was not normally her place to participate in the negotiations without the ambassador's invitation;

but Kamenev's allegation was not part of the diplomatic debate, and it involved a matter on which she was the one most qualified to comment among those present. "The investigation is still under way."

"Of course it is. An investigation by Starfleet and a Federalist diplomat! It's sure to be decided in the Federalists' favor."

"Come on, Mikhail, think it over." That was Selina Rosen, the olive-skinned woman who served as Earth's ambassador. As she and Kamenev came from neighboring planets, they had a familiar, if contentious, relationship. "How could an attempt like this have done anything other than make the Federalist side—if you accept the premise that there is one—look bad?"

"That's right," Ambassador Baur put in, shaking a pudgy finger. "If anything, this attempt was probably staged to do just that!"

"What are you accusing us of?" Kamenev demanded.

The Tellarite ambassador gestured in triumph. "How revealing that you immediately conclude you are the ones to be accused!"

"Baur, stop it," Rosen said, putting a calming hand on the ambassador's wrist and casting a glance toward the petitioners—Jahlet and Hemnask of Rigel and Tamara Ann Arouet of Vega Colony—who sat uneasily along one side of the conference table. "Nobody's accusing anyone of anything. That's not what we're here for. Now, Ambassador sh'Rothress has raised an interesting point about the standards for admission, and I'd like to hear the petitioners' thoughts on—"

Kamenev spoke over her. "Nobody's being accused? What about Jonathan Archer, whose DNA was on the scene?"

Sh'Rothress emitted a hissing sigh, her antennae pulling back in irritation. "Mikhail. Take a breath. Calm down." The *shen* caught the Martian's gaze and held it firmly, her force of will compelling him to listen. "Consider what you're proposing. Whatever our disputes with his position, this is Jonathan Archer we're talking about. The one being who is most responsible for convincing our separate empires and nations to look past our differences and work together in peace. The man who was sent on a mission of war against the Xindi and single-handedly persuaded them to cancel their annihilation of the human race. The man who assured victory over the Romulans at Cheron, not by weapons alone, but through the years he spent building alliances and restoring the frayed trust among Earth and its allies. The man who prevented the Malurians from dragging us into manufactured wars with the Tandarans and the Vertians."

Ambassador Fell sniffed. "She has a point," the gaunt, middle-aged Centaurian acknowledged. "Not that I have any great trust toward Starfleet . . . but Archer has managed to rein in some of the military's excesses. I must admit, it is hard to believe he would attempt crude violence against a political rival."

Kamenev appeared reluctant to let his accusation drop, but the lack of support from his own faction had robbed him of impetus. "Well . . . then . . . if it wasn't Archer, then who? Who would benefit from Thoris's death?"

"Perhaps Thoris was not the target," T'Rama said. "The type of weapon employed is precise, and the Councilor was not in rapid motion when the shot was fired."

"That's right," Rosen said. "This could've been staged to implicate Archer, to turn public opinion toward Thoris. If he were elected—or even if our recriminations caused this conference to fall apart—it would prevent Rigel's admission."

"If I may." It was Director Hemnask. The cinnamon-haired Zami Rigelian leaned forward, taking a moment to choose her words. "I would not put it past the First Families to attempt something like this. We know they have taken Starfleet personnel hostage, along with sensitive state secrets that they could use to undermine the Trade Commission."

"Indeed," Ambassador Jahlet affirmed. "As we've agreed, applying Federation law throughout the system would cripple their illicit activities."

"Yes, but there's more to it than that," Hemnask went on. T'Rama noted that the Jelna ambassador found her words unexpected, but merely listened curiously. "We have seen the sheer brazenness of the Families' recent acts. And our intelligence suggests that they may have garnered the support of some extra-Rigelian hostile power seeking to gain a firmer foothold in our system. It is conceivable that the Families are gearing up for war against the member worlds of the Commission. If those worlds became members of the Federation as well, then any attempt to conquer the system would be met by the full force of Starfleet, and their victory would not be as easy as they would wish."

"Wait, wait," Kamenev said. "Are you suggesting that if Rigel joins, the Federation could find itself dragged into another war?"

"Oh, I would hope not," Hemnask replied. "With luck, merely the threat of Starfleet's wrath would be enough to deter the Families. And I have no doubt that if any other power abetted the Families, then the combined power of Starfleet and the Rigelian Defense Forces would make short work of them."

Hemnask's words were poorly received by the Planetarists. Kamenev made his distaste for being drawn into a foreign war clear with his usual verbosity, with Fell chiming in to profess support for each world's right to fight its own battles. Sh'Rothress said nothing, but her expression was concerned.

But none of this affected their existing stances on membership. What might make a difference, thought T'Rama, was Solkar's reaction. Though her husband's-father had excellent emotional control, she was familiar enough with him to deduce his thinking from subtle somatic and facial cues. Moreover, she shared much of his knowledge and views, and took her

responsibility for representing the consensus of the
Vulcan people as seriously as he did. Thus she could
anticipate his reasoning. The recovery of Surak's true
writings and the dissolution of the warmongering
High Command a decade ago had led the Vulcans
to recognize how far they had strayed from Surak's
founding principles—and to be reminded of the danger if they ever reverted to their ancient savagery. Vulcan needed to commit itself to peace more than ever
now, at least until it had purged the remnants of the
High Command's values from its thought and custom.
And for Vulcan to be at peace, the Federation must be
at peace.

True, at some point, a new enemy would surely
emerge or an old one would strike anew. But one could
not concern oneself unduly with possibilities outside
of one's control. Yet what if one had foreknowledge
that admitting a new member risked embroiling the
Federation in a conflict already under way? Solkar
would have to rethink his position on Rigelian membership in light of this new information.

And that was what puzzled T'Rama. Throughout
this conference, Sedra Hemnask had struck her as an
intelligent, capable negotiator. The Zami woman had
reached her position of authority through her career
in business, no doubt gaining much experience at per-
suading others to take positions or actions that she
favored. Thus, it seemed an amateurish mistake for
her to put forth an argument that would not only
solidify the positions of the faction opposing Rigel's

admission, but potentially flip a pro-admission vote to the other side. T'Rama could find no answer in her diplomatic training for why Hemnask would have made such a move.

But her security training made her very, very interested in investigating further.

U.S.S. Endeavour, orbiting Rigel VII

"We managed to image the impact site," Lieutenant Cutler said, displaying the overhead shot on the situation table as Thanien and Sato looked on. "Looks like all our people are alive, but at least two are injured. They aren't mobile, and as you can see, the shuttlepod is even less mobile." Ortega had somehow managed to bring it to a skidding stop on a reasonably flat peak, coming up just a few meters short of a cliff edge. "There's a relatively easy slope down from where they are," Cutler went on, indicating it, "but that means it's also an easy climb for these guys." She shifted the image several kilometers to the southwest, where a group of some twenty massive figures marched in close formation. "Kalar warriors," she said, "and making good time. They'll reach the shuttlepod in just under two hours at their current pace."

Thanien's antennae curled inward in displeasure. He looked at Cutler. "Is there any chance of punching a transporter beam through their jamming?"

The lieutenant shook her head. "Even without the

jamming field, the minerals in the area could scatter the beams."

The first officer contemplated for a moment. "Very well. Continue monitoring the area. Look for options."

"Aye, sir." Cutler returned to her station.

Taking a deep breath, Thanien turned to Sato. "Commander, with me."

He led her into the captain's ready room. Rather than offer her a seat, he simply faced her. He felt he should do this on his feet. "Commander Sato . . . I find I must apologize to you."

The human woman frowned. "Sir? For what?"

"My . . . judgment has been compromised by an unfair assumption. I should have heeded your advice, pursued other options before sending the shuttlepod down. But I was . . . biased against your suggestions."

Sato still looked puzzled, merely confirming the conclusion he'd finally reached about her. "Why, Commander?" she asked very softly.

"Because I believed . . . that you were competing with me. You have been Captain T'Pol's colleague and confidante for many years. I am a far more recent arrival. In my insecurity, I felt that you were presuming a more central place in this vessel's decision-making process than my own. When you offered suggestions and advice, I interpreted it as a challenge to my authority."

Her eyes were wide. "Honestly, Commander, I had no idea you felt that way. Why haven't you talked to me about this before?"

He smirked. "Because I thought I was being the bigger man. That it would be petty for me to succumb to such feelings of rivalry and that I should simply do my duty. The implication I did not admit was that I assumed you were the smaller one. I did not dispel my belief that you were deliberately competing with me; I simply persuaded myself that I was not lowering myself to the same level."

The Andorian shook his head, letting out a sharp breath. "And that arrogance has led to this. As long as I hold the conn, you are one of my most senior advisors. My obligation is to heed your counsel. To rely on you as I wish the captain to rely on me. And I have not done so, and for petty reasons I have endangered my officers—and your partner. For that, I must apologize, both to you and to myself."

Sato took in a shuddering breath as she absorbed his words. "Commander . . . I swear I had no idea. If I've been intruding on your authority in any way, if I've been taking advantage of my friendship with the captain . . . I'm truly sorry."

Thanien smiled. "And there is the surest proof I was wrong about you, Hoshi. You have every right to be angry at me for placing your lover at unnecessary risk due to my foolish pride. And yet your concern is for my hurt feelings. I am shamed by your good nature."

She reached out to him, clasping his arm. "No. I understand. I just . . . you should've just talked to me. And I should've listened more to you."

He clasped her forearm in return, a soldierly

gesture of solidarity. "Now," Thanien said, "let us work together and find a way to bring our people home."

Vinaula Mountains, Rigel VII

If the promontory where Ortega had set down hadn't been the only survivable landing site in the area, Takashi Kimura would have called it the worst position he and his crewmates could be in. While they had used their phase pistols to blast craters and cut fissures into the promontory's climbable slopes, the damage they had been able to inflict without draining the weapons' power packs had been limited. It had slowed the Kalar soldiers somewhat, but the burly, hirsute humanoids had shown surprising sure-footedness in clambering around or through the roughened terrain, not appreciably slowed by their heavy animal-skin vests, high-crowned helmets, bladed weapons, and shields. Kimura had tried calling to them, attempting to persuade them that the shuttlepod's occupants wished nothing more than to leave the planet and trouble the Kalar no more; but whatever language they spoke didn't seem to be in the translator's database of Rigelian tongues. Then again, they didn't seem particularly verbal, mainly just grunting and hurling spears at him. He had returned fire but had managed to stun only two of the twenty warriors before needing to retreat. Tactically, it might have been wiser to shoot to kill, for the stun effect would likely wear off in minutes. But Kimura couldn't forget that his people were the trespassers here. He'd escalate his response if he had to, but only if he were backed against a wall.

Or a cliff, as it turned out a few minutes later. With Legatt and Money both injured in the crash, that had left only Kimura, Chiang, and the one unbroken arm of Pedro Ortega to defend against twenty bearded berserkers. Their only defense against the Kalar's spears and crossbows had been to drag the injured back into the shuttlepod (hoping the toxic fumes released in the crash had cleared by now) while the other three stayed between it and the cliff edge, firing at the Kalar from cover. The indigenes bellowed with rage as they charged, using *"Kalarrrr!"* itself as their battle cry (or maybe the other Rigelians called them that *after* their battle cry), and a number of them fell stunned, their triangular shields offering only limited protection. But they quickly proved they were no mere savages; they ceased charging into the line of fire and advanced within the shadow of the shuttlepod itself, with several flanking Kalar arraying their shields to maximize resistance to sniping shots from around the pod's edges.

From his vantage leaning against the rear engine, Kimura couldn't quite see what they did next, but he heard running feet and clanking metal beneath the roar of *"Kalarrrrr!"*—and then was almost knocked off his feet when the shuttlepod rocked from a massive impact. The whole pod slid a good half-meter closer to the cliff face. "Uh-oh."

He jogged over to peer through the pod's side window and out the other one, and he saw the warriors backing up to prepare for a second charge. Money was dragging herself toward the aft ladder, no doubt hoping to get to the top hatch to lay down suppression fire. But before she could get more than halfway up, the mass of Kalar flesh closed in on the pod and Kimura had to jump back as the compact craft was knocked another thirty-some centimeters edgeward. Their only defense had just become a weapon against them.

He stole a glance through the side port again. Money was down, moaning and semiconscious. Legatt had been knocked to the deck, showing no signs of motion.

Chiang and Ortega looked to Kimura for guidance. "Get ready," he said. "Our only chance is a full assault, continuous fire." He made a decision, adjusting the setting on his pistol. "Shoot to kill. Take down as many as you can before—" Another roar warned them to jump back just before the pod was pushed sideways again. This time, it teetered forward, and for an alarming moment it seemed it might tip over onto them. He met the others' eyes intently. "Our priority is to protect the wounded. Got it?" he asked with meaning.

Chiang nodded gamely, but Ortega gave a weak laugh. "I don't suppose that includes me?" Kimura just glared. "Got it."

"All right. On my count. One, two—"

"Wait!" Chiang called. "Look!"

Kimura had not fully registered the rumbling sound over the roaring of the Kalar. But it was rapidly growing louder. He looked up for the source of the sound, the blue-white gibbous face of Rigel VIII dominating his view. Against that cratered expanse, he saw a glint of light that swiftly resolved into a gleaming silver shape: a wide disk trailing two narrow cylinders and a third, lower ellipsoid.

Endeavour!

Kimura laughed as the ship closed in on their position. "The mountain comes to Muhammad!" he cried.

The Kalar air defense forces were doing their best to cope with this latest intrusion, but their artillery shells exploded against the vessel's shield envelope. Her flight looked a little rocky, but still stable.

As for the living battering rams down here, they had halted their attacks. Peering through the side ports again, he saw them backing away in alarm, though their leader gestured for them to hold their ground.

And then the first phase cannon beam hit between the warriors and the shuttlepod. Kimura could feel the heat even from behind the pod, and under the fierce warble of the beam and the crackling of ionized air he could hear rocky shrapnel clattering against the pod's hull. The Kalar broke into retreat, and the phase cannon fire herded them away down the slope.

Endeavour's course took it beyond the promontory

moments later, but it banked into a circle, continuing to lay down defensive fire. "Nice flying," Ortega said. He cradled his broken arm. "I wish I could take credit for it."

On the next pass, Kimura saw the shields drop just long enough for shuttlepod two to emerge from the ship's port launch bay and descend toward the promontory. The artillery fire continued, but *Endeavour's* hull plating was strong enough to weather it until the shuttle was clear. The ship was low enough that the pod reached them in under thirty seconds, hovering along the cliff edge. The door opened . . . and Hoshi Sato beckoned to Kimura, crying, "Come on!"

Kimura and Chiang pulled open shuttlepod one's side hatch to retrieve their injured, and Crewmen Abnett and Zircher climbed out of the second pod to help them make the transfer with due haste. Within a minute, the rescue was done, and Kimura was the last man into the crowded shuttlepod. He gave Hoshi an efficient but heartfelt hug and kiss. "Nice rescue."

"You looked like you needed it. Seriously, the edge of a cliff? You're so melodramatic."

"Hey, I like to keep our relationship exciting."

As the pod drew near to *Endeavour's* drop bay, he saw that the tractor beam was already drawing the damaged pod up toward the other bay. "I see we're not leaving any nasty high technology behind."

"Least we could do to make up for the intrusion." Sato looked around at the rescued personnel. "I take it the ship was empty?"

"Two dead, both Zami." Her face fell. "At least we're narrowing it down."

"But we're still playing by their rules. The odds favor the house."

He stroked her chin. "That's when you find a way to change the game."

12

Hainali Basin, Rigel III

ONCE TRAVIS MAYWEATHER'S SENSES fully returned (along with a splitting headache that made him regret a couple of said senses), he found himself, Rey Sangupta, Sajithen, and her escorts in a wooden boat with their hands bound behind them. Their captors, burly Chelons in homespun loincloths and burnoose-like hooded cloaks, paddled the boat upstream through an unfamiliar tributary. When Mayweather asked where they were being taken, Sajithen advised him that they would be at their destination soon. Although the Hainalians treated her the same as the other prisoners, she retained the confident bearing of one who belonged exactly where she was.

Eventually they reached a massive earthwork deep in the forest, made of a dark, tightly packed soil like the kind the Hainalian villages were built upon. "*Terra preta*," Sangupta said. "Incredibly rich soil, mixed with charcoal, pottery shards, food waste, and, um, organic residue from the villages. It's the secret to sustainable rainforest agriculture, fertile as hell and resistant to nutrient leaching. Slash-and-burn agriculture almost destroyed the Amazon rainforest until twenty-first-century humans relearned how the native Amazonians used to make the stuff."

This earthwork was agricultural, topped by a dense grove of plants with bulbous, pear-shaped trunks and wide canopies of fern-like leaves spread out in an umbrella formation that Mayweather realized would make good camouflage from overhead.

Soon they reached a region where the trees were spaced marginally wider and had narrower trunks, leaving room for a number of large huts, more than one of which had antenna arrays on their roofs. One of their captors called out, and moments later the largest hut's door was pushed aside from within. There emerged a wide-bodied Chelon in an ornate toque worn over a loose, colorful keffiyeh, with similarly bright fabric draped around the body. This Chelon was somewhat shorter than the rest, though significantly taller than Mayweather. He, or she, was accompanied by a pair of attendants who stayed two paces behind at all times.

"Ganaiar," exclaimed Sajithen. "Why do you breach the etiquette of parley by taking us captive? I came to you in good faith!"

"So you claim," the rebel chieftain intoned. "As you have claimed to aid us in the past, while holding us back from pursuing our real goals. But we have new allies now, and they have warned us about these new outsiders your great Trade Commission has sold out to."

"What allies? The First Families?" A scornful rattle emerged from her beak. "They have sought to exploit our homeland as much as any others, or even more. And they stand outside the Commission, refusing any checks on their exploitation."

"Not that the Commission imposes many such checks of its own."

"We maintain the balance with a subtle hand. You know how the game is played."

"Yes," Ganaiar grated. "You give us license, and give the same license to those who would harm us—acting only to ensure neither goes far enough for any real change to occur. Or so it was. Now you let this Federation come in to subjugate us all."

"Excuse me." Mayweather thought it was about time he got in on the conversation. "Hi. I'm Commander Travis Mayweather of the Federation vessel *Pioneer*. This is my science officer, Lieutenant Sangupta."

"We know who you are."

"With all due respect, sir, it doesn't sound like you do." The "sir" was pure guesswork.

The chieftain growled. Sajithen turned to Mayweather. "Many Hainalian traditionalists do not adopt a permanent gender role. Call Ganaiar by the title *Velom*."

"Of course, my apologies," Mayweather said to the chieftain. "*Velom* Ganaiar, whatever the First Families have told you about the Federation, it's not true. We're not here to subjugate anyone. We want the Rigel worlds to join us as partners."

"You know how the Families lie, Ganaiar," Sajithen added. "Why would you follow them now?"

"We do not," the chieftain growled back. "Our cause aligns with their goals at the moment, that is all.

Like them, we have no wish to be ground under by the Federation or any others. Now that your Commission has sold out, we will no longer wait for your *peaceful* methods to work. It is time that we rise up openly and free ourselves from your control."

"This is madness, Ganaiar. The Families have used your hypnoids to steal our most sensitive secrets. We believe they will use them to attempt a seizure of Rigel II. Do you really believe they will grant this world its liberty?"

"Their agendas are their own. As are ours. Once we take control of our world, once we capture and nationalize the offworld ships on and around it, we can defend it ourselves."

"Oh, no," Mayweather moaned. "Don't you see? You're playing right into their hands. They're using you to get the Commission fighting on two fronts so they won't have enough strength to hold Rigel II. And that'll just make the Families stronger and you weaker. *Velom*, there's nothing to gain by this.

"But there's a better way. If Rigel joins the Federation, you'll all be protected by our laws. The exploitation will have to stop, and your right to live the way you want and control your own lands will be guaranteed."

"Do not lead me astray with Federation lies."

"It's the Families who are lying to you!" Sangupta insisted.

"We do not do this at their request," Ganaiar shot back. "We heed the truth that has been brought to us—the same truth that has come to the Families. The truth that your Federation has hidden about the secret crimes of its members. The biological warfare Earth waged against the Klingons. The Vulcans' support of the corrupt rulers of Coridan. Your vaunted Admiral Archer's abandonment of the Valakian race to extinction."

"Oh, for the—seriously?" Sangupta asked. "Where are you getting this 'truth' from, the Alrond Newsfeed?"

"Rey," Mayweather cautioned. He turned back to the chieftain. "So you're saying you've been contacted by some other power? Someone from outside the Rigel system?" He set his jaw. "If they have accusations to make against us, let them do it to our faces."

"They will not grant the likes of you the privilege of gazing upon them, mammal."

Sangupta seized on that. "So they're not mammals? Maybe something more like yourselves, more reptilian?"

Ganaiar hesitated, casting a glance back toward the large hut. Mayweather nodded, a small smile forming. "I'll take that as a yes. And at least one of them is here right now. Let me guess: shaped like us, but with gray scales and no hair?"

"Of course you know of them," the chieftain spat. "How else would they know of your abuses?"

"Malurians," Mayweather and Sangupta said almost simultaneously. The first officer went on. "*Velom,* we have dealt with them before, and, well, they're not exactly known for their honesty. At least, not the ones you usually find outside their home system."

"Of course they try to slander us," came a new voice. The humanoid who emerged from the tent was just what Mayweather had expected: a Malurian, his gray-scaled head adorned by a series of low, parallel ridges across his cheeks and scalp. "Don't listen to them, *Velom*. Now that they know I'm here, we can't take any chances. You should kill them at once."

Ganaiar glanced sidelong at the Malurian and replied with controlled patience. "Had I wished to kill them, they would be dead already. Sajithen may have been an impediment to our goals, but her death would backfire. And killing Federation officers could bring down a *tukhanthik* on all our heads."

"Then what is it you have planned?" Sajithen asked.

"You must answer for the crimes of the Federation and its Commission puppets. We will put you on trial before all Rigel, and prove that our grievances are just."

The Malurian came forward. "No, you mustn't! They'll give away our presence."

"If you join with us in a just cause, you should not fear to step forward."

I can work with this, Mayweather thought. "*We* do not fear to step forward!" he declared. "If you want to put us on trial, fine. I will stand trial and answer whatever charges you have to make."

"He lies," the Malurian said.

"I have no reason to lie, because I'm not afraid

of the truth. Have we made mistakes?" He nodded. "Sure. Some of us have made some questionable calls. Or done things that seemed right at the time but turned out badly. Every society has. But it's only by facing those mistakes that we can try to make ourselves better. That's why the Federation wants people in it who hold a wide range of different viewpoints—even people like you. Because having people who disagree with us keeps us honest, forces us to question ourselves and recognize our mistakes."

"He's right," Rey Sangupta said. "Listen, I'm from a former colony world myself, and sometimes we feel like we're an afterthought, like our point of view gets drowned out by the big voices. But the fact is, we get to express that point of view, and nobody tries to stop us. And that's what the Federation is about."

"Propaganda," the Malurian said. "Surely you aren't blinded by this."

"Do not question my vision, Rinor," Ganaïar barked. "I will hear and assess all arguments. You will not dictate to me which one I believe."

"Fine, that's fine," Mayweather said. "Put me on trial if you have to. But let the others go."

Rinor sneered. "How noble."

"It's more than that. *Velom*, this Malurian's allies have kidnapped two of my crewmates. We think they're still alive, but we don't know how long that'll last. Please, we're just trying to rescue our people. We came to you to see if you could help." He looked at the chieftain imploringly. "If I agree to stand trial for you, will you let the others go and tell them what you know about where our people are being held?"

Ganaiar studied him for some moments. "*Velom*, you aren't considering this?" the Malurian protested.

"Please, *Velom*," Travis went on, holding the chieftain's gaze steadily. "We don't have a lot of time."

Rinor sighed. "No," he said, pulling out a disk-shaped communicator. "You don't." He hit a switch, and a moment later, three swirls of energy resolved into armed Malurians surrounding the Chelons in the camp.

"This is outrageous!" Ganaiar boomed. "You agreed to come unarmed into my camp as a sign of allegiance. You swore to abide by my will."

"And now you will abide by mine. Kill these three, or my people will kill you and them."

"You need our cooperation."

"We need a revolt on Rigel III. And the fact is, your martyrdom will achieve that just as well as your leadership. Our weapons are set to mimic Starfleet phase pistol signatures."

The chieftain faced him with arms crossed. "Is that so, Rinor? Our weapons are more straightforward."

A number of armed Chelons rose out of the surrounding undergrowth, drawing back on heavy longbows. The bolts flew true and impaled the Malurian ambush party. Mayweather winced and looked away, in time to see Rinor grappling with one of the humans' captors over the latter's crossbow. The

Malurian was stronger than he looked, able to resist the massive Chelon's grip and force the weapon toward his opponent's head. But the guard clung to him firmly, and soon Rinor began to weaken and tremble. His eyes rolled back, and when the guard released him, he fell to the ground with a heavy thud and lay there twitching.

"Oh, my God," Sangupta said. "Their contact venom. It's lethal stuff. He's got hours at most."

Mayweather stepped forward, arms still bound behind him, and looked pleadingly at the chieftain. "Do you have an antitoxin? We need to find out what he knows about our people."

Ganaiar studied him. "I am sorry, no. We have not yet devised one for his kind." The *Velom* surveyed the other bodies. "As for the rest . . . were they Chelon, they would have simply been wounded. As it is . . . unfortunate, but they left us no choice."

Mayweather gazed down at Rinor, who was trembling harder and starting to moan. Sajithen came up alongside him. "It is taking effect quickly," the director said. "He received quite a dose. The agony will be extreme."

Travis faced the *Velom*. "Can you at least give him something to ease the pain?"

"He will not be coherent enough to tell you what you seek, even given an incentive."

"You think that's what I care about?" Mayweather shouted. "Just ease his pain, please! Nobody deserves to suffer like that."

The chieftain studied him for a long moment . . . then gestured to an attendant. The attendant's heavy staff lifted into the air . . . and came down with great force on Rinor's neck. Travis closed his eyes, wincing.

When he looked up again, he saw Ganaiar examining him with surprise and approval. "Release them," the *Velom* ordered. As the attendants complied, Ganaiar went on. "I regret that I know nothing about where they hold your people, Commander Mayweather. And I regret that I was unable to deliver them to you alive for interrogation.

"Most of all, I regret that I allowed Rinor to mislead me about your Federation. If it appoints people like you as its military officers, that reveals much about its true intentions."

Mayweather accepted the apology with a grave nod. "You thought you were doing what was necessary to protect your people. Believe me, I understand that."

"Yes." Ganaiar gave him the Chelon equivalent of a smile. "But while I cannot help you locate your people . . . I do have some knowledge regarding the First Families' operative inside the Trade Commission."

"If you mean Rehlen Vons," replied Sajithen, rubbing her unbound wrists, "we know of him."

"Rehlen Vons is dead, and a Malurian wears his face. But perhaps I can direct you toward the source of the information they needed to replace him."

June 24, 2164
Babel Station

Sedra Hemnask answered the door of her suite, attired in casual evening wear. Her eyes widened when she saw Jonathan Archer standing there. "You've been released!"

"And you've been avoiding me," he told her, perhaps redundantly.

Eyes darting furtively, she summoned him inside. Once the door shut behind him, she said, "I felt you faced enough scandal without me complicating things."

"You could've given me an alibi for the shooting."

"Clearly you didn't need one. I knew you were innocent. And whoever attempted to frame you must have been a fool to think anyone would believe it."

He stepped closer. "Still . . . they didn't have to prove me guilty. Just create enough anger and suspicion to scuttle the talks."

She smiled. "And that hasn't happened. Your reputation carries much weight, it seems."

"And you were just . . . protecting that reputation," he added in slow, skeptical tones, "when you refused to come forward."

Hemnask came up to him and stroked his cheek. "I'm sorry, Jonathan. It was selfish of me. But please believe me . . . there are . . . family obligations that keep me from admitting the truth. Obligations I can't explain in terms you would understand. But it's not a problem anymore. There's no reason it should—"

She had begun moving in to kiss him, but he stopped her with his hands on her shoulders, then stepped away. "I don't think you give me enough credit for understanding, Sedra."

Archer moved to the door and opened it, watching Hemnask's face as she saw who stood beyond it now. "You know T'Rama," he said as he showed the new guests in. "And I believe you're acquainted with Lieutenant Commander ch'Terren, the head of security here."

Hemnask nodded at them, her response wary but tightly controlled. "Madam. Commander. To what do I owe this visit?"

Archer fielded the question. "I thought you'd like to know that they've captured the shooter."

After a brief moment of surprise, she smiled. "That is excellent news. Who was it? What was their purpose?"

Commander ch'Terren moved forward and held up his scanner, whose screen displayed an image of a humanoid with skin flaps on his cheeks and white hair along his temples. "Director, do you recognize this man?"

Hemnask studied the image. "I believe he is a Mazarite, but beyond that I do not know him."

"He registered with Babel Security under the name Rihat Diraf," ch'Terren told her. "He was posing as the proprietor of a clothing shop on the esplanade."

"Posing?"

"Since his arrest," ch'Terren replied, "we have determined that he is in fact Ibed Tarzah, an assassin for the Zankor syndicate, a prominent Mazarite criminal organization."

"Of course," Hemnask said, almost to herself. She gave a small laugh and shook her head. "Another syndicate threatened by the Federation's rise." Her large eyes focused on the investigators again. "How did you find him? What led to his arrest?"

T'Rama stepped closer. "When we interviewed neighboring proprietors, they remembered seeing you and Admiral Archer visiting his shop on the evening before the shooting. He scanned the admiral to measure him for a suit. We determined he used the biometrics thus gathered to gain entry to the admiral's quarters and steal the uniform used to impersonate him."

She scoffed. "A careless frame."

"Don't sell yourself short, Sedra."

The director stared at him. "Jonathan, what do you mean?"

"Don't you remember? You were the one who got me to stop at that kiosk. You talked me into getting scanned. You talked with that man for twenty minutes—the man you just said you didn't recognize." His expression hardened. "I would've thought you'd have a more vivid memory of the night we first kissed."

She froze, staring. After a moment, she lowered her gaze, thinking, and finally sighed. "I see where this is leading," she said, turning away. "You've investigated me now."

"That's right," Archer said. "We got some information last night from *Pioneer*'s first officer—a lead on the abduction and replacement of your assistant Rehlen Vons with a Malurian operative. Now, Malurian mask technology is good enough to fake the biometrics they needed to get into the vault, but someone had to give them Vons's code phrases and teach them enough about him that they could carry off the impersonation. T'Rama had a hunch—sorry, a logical hypothesis—that you might be involved. So she and Commander ch'Terren asked my people at Rigel to help them look into your past. The Trade Commission was very cooperative as well, in light of recent events there."

She turned back to him, pleading and fear in her eyes. "But you already know my secret. You know I am the *last* person that would have anything to do with the First Families."

"That's the secret you shared with the Commission. But a secret isn't much use to you if you tell the whole thing. My people dug a little deeper. They found that your mother—and you—have had periodic contact with your birth father, Voctel Thamnos." She winced at the name. "Clandestine contacts, but fairly regular—and initiated on your end. Not something you'd do with a man who violated your mother.

"That was a convenient story, wasn't it?" he asked

her. "The only kind of family tie that a Zami Rigelian would be expected to renounce totally—the kind that was forced. But it wasn't forced, was it?" He shook his head in disgust. "The very same First Families you've been telling me for months how much you hated and wanted to bring down—and you've been in their pocket the whole time."

"You don't understand!" Hemnask cried. "I *do* hate them. I do want them broken . . . because of the hold they have over me. Because they can force me to do their bidding when it's the last thing I want."

"I know how much the Zami value family ties," he said, "but this . . ."

"You don't know all the facts." She was weeping now. "You're right . . . Voctel didn't rape my mother. He chose to claim he did because it gave him prestige within his twisted clan—and let him hide the fact that he had fallen in love with a commoner. My conception was accidental, but hardly coerced. Voctel was too young to handle the responsibility for raising me, especially knowing how I would be treated within the clan as a half-common bastard. So he helped my mother flee to Five, where she and I would face no stigma, and convinced her to go along with the lie that she had fled his cruelty, for his own protection as well as mine.

"But once he matured enough, he married—and he had more children. I have half-brothers and half-sisters . . . and some of them have children. This is why we stay in touch. Voctel sought us out so I could know my blood kin. But though he meant well, his actions entrapped me." She shook her head, loose waves of hair tumbling around her face. "The First Families are corrupt and cruel. They elevate family, but not through love and protection. Rather, they demand loyalty and obedience at all costs. Failure, betrayal . . . these are severely punished. And as a child of the Thamnos, even illegitimately, my actions reflect on my father and my kin. If I fail in what they expect of me . . ." She sank to the bed. "My siblings, my nephews and nieces could suffer."

Archer hesitated to trust her now, but her fear and distress seemed sincere. "Then . . . why this convoluted plan? Seduce me, then frame me?"

She looked up at him, almost amused. "Give me some credit, Jonathan. I wouldn't be so sloppy. Whoever sent that Mazarite to frame you, they've exposed me and doomed my efforts to failure. I don't know what might happen to my family now because of their stupidity."

"But you and Tarzah—"

"There's the terrible irony of it. I was honestly just having fun. He offered to fit you for a suit and I was genuinely curious. I didn't even remember his face because I was busy admiring his wares!" She gave a bitter laugh. "Think about it. If the shooting hadn't happened, no one here would have investigated me, and my secrets might never have been exposed. Far from being my accomplice, Mister Tarzah has ruined my plans entirely." She sighed. "For which I'd be extremely grateful . . . if not for the cost to my kin."

"Then if you weren't involved with the shooting . . ."

Hemnask stood, moving close to him. "Jonathan . . . my instructions were to seduce you to create a scandal. To convince the Rigelians that you had in fact seduced *me* into supporting membership, and then to retract that support once the scandal broke." She sighed. "I did as I was ordered . . . and I know this sounds like something from a cheap melodrama, but I found afterward that I couldn't go through with it. You were too . . . kind." She reached out as if to stroke his hair, but stopped, lowering her hand a moment later. "Too lonely. I could tell that what we shared . . . it meant something to you. It was something you had needed for a long time. I couldn't bring myself to ruin it for you."

She turned to T'Rama. "Instead, I kept my silence about that night, and carried on with the other part of my instructions: to persuade the ambassadors that joining with Rigel could drag the Federation into the very war that the First Families seek to provoke. To make us undesirable to you as members." Hemnask released a bitter sigh, squeezing her eyes shut. "The damn Thamnos, they take joy in forcing me to protect the very status quo I hate. I would give anything to see the Federation bring its law to Rigel and crush the Families once and for all. But I am a prisoner of my blood, and my blood kin are hostages to my obedience."

Hemnask wrapped her arms around herself. "And

poor Vons . . . I had no idea they would kill him. I didn't realize how ruthless the Malurians were. I almost confessed when I found out, but the threat to my family held me back. I didn't know what else to do."

She trembled, looking lost, and Archer chose to believe her. He placed a tentative hand on her shoulder, feeling the palpable relief in her body when he did so. "Sedra . . . maybe there's something we can do, with the Rigelians' help, to protect your family on Rigel IV. But we'd need something from you in exchange. The First Families still have your archives, and two of my officers. Anything you can tell us that will help us find them . . . would go a long way toward proving your sincerity."

She gazed up at him with gratitude. "I'll help you any way I can. I may never fully cleanse the stain from my conscience . . . but I welcome the opportunity to try."

Thamnos estate, Rigel IV

"What were you thinking?" Garos demanded, leaning forward in his seat. "I had my own plan in motion on Babel! And now your ham-fisted assassination ploy has ruined it!"

On the large monitor in his suite's overly ornate, not especially functional workspace, D'Nesh glared, no doubt resenting being spoken to in such a way by a male. *"Remember, Garos, you are the one who answers to us, not the other way around!"* Next to her, Navaar looked on in concern, while Maras hovered behind her looking bored. The youngest sister seemed to participate in these conference calls only to provide the visual of the Three Sisters as a united front—an image Garos was beginning to have his doubts about.

"So you take responsibility for allowing that incompetent Zankor to proceed with this?"

The fact that Eldi Zankor was right next to the Sisters had not deterred Garos's insult in the least. *"It was a good plan!"* the Mazarite crime boss insisted. *"We were trying to tear down Archer, the same way you were!"*

"You imbecile. Making the Rigelians question Archer's integrity is one thing. Getting the Federation to believe their great peacemaker would attempt murder is another. Don't you understand the first thing about a con? You want to convince the marks of what they're already inclined to believe! Push too hard against their preconceptions and they'll sense they're being fooled."

"He does have a point, sister," Navaar said. *"It was a little unsubtle."*

"As opposed to Garos's plan? His is so subtle I can hardly tell how it was supposed to work!" Navaar just stared, arms folded over her otherwise mostly uncovered chest. D'Nesh sighed. *"We had an opportunity,"* she insisted. *"Zankor could get a man in place on Babel. We have hooks into Thoris's advisors, so they could divert him to Babel to make a high-profile speech, then sabotage the ship so it'd be stuck there for repairs."* She spread her arms. *"Even if we failed to discredit*

Archer, think of the sympathy we gained for Thoris! It was worth the risk to get our puppet closer to the presidency."

D'Nesh's choice of epithets underlined her over-confidence. The Syndicate may have infiltrated Thoris's campaign team, but Garos knew that the Andorian himself was a *chan* of integrity who had to be handled delicately lest he suspect how he was being used. Indeed, Garos was surprised he'd been so easily maneuvered to Babel in the first place. "But think of the sympathy he lost by exploiting the Rigel crisis for political points!" he told D'Nesh. "You Orions may see such crass opportunism as a matter of routine, maybe even admire it, but the Federation's peoples look poorly upon it." He sighed. "If you'd consulted me, I could have—"

Zankor scoffed. *"Don't be coy. You would've been happy to see me fail."*

"Yes, I would have—if you were the only one affected. What I was about to say is that I could have warned the Sisters that your plan endangered mine. That after Jofirek brought in Hua and his network, you were so pathetically desperate to prove your worth that you overreached, just as you always do, and didn't consider the consequences." He shifted his gaze within the Zami mask he still wore. "I would've thought you, at least, would have had the good judgment to consult your sister first, D'Nesh."

Navaar pouted. *"Sorry, dear, but I have to agree with Garos on this one. You should've kept me apprised of the specifics of your plan, so we could've coordinated with Garos."*

The middle sister stared, looking confused and

betrayed. "*I thought Rigel didn't matter to you. That's why you left it to Garos.*"

"*I never said it didn't matter. Working in concert with our partners is what matters. The Malurians have the most at stake if Rigel is lost, so Garos was the one most motivated to solve that problem. But I always meant him to have our support if it was needed, because that's how this partnership is supposed to work. We shouldn't be undermining or obstructing our own allies.*"

D'Nesh was still sullen, but her expression grew chastened. "*You're right, sister. I'm sorry. It won't happen again.*"

Navaar's eyes shifted to Zankor. "*No. It won't.*" She gestured to an Orion male whom Garos recognized as Parrec-Sut. The tall, wiry Orion came up to Zankor and seized her from behind.

"*What? What are you doing?*" Zankor cried.

"*I'm so sorry, Eldi,*" Navaar said, reaching out and stroking her shoulder. "*I do believe you sincerely meant to prove your worth to us, and I cherish your devotion. Unfortunately,*" she went on with a coquettish frown, "*the Federation now knows your syndicate was behind the shooting at Babel. That will lead back to you, Eldi. And it's very important that we make sure the trail ends with you.*"

"*No.*" Zankor gasped as she realized what was about to happen. She screamed and struggled as Parrec-Sut bodily removed her from the suite. Navaar gazed on with a mix of sympathy and grave disappointment. D'Nesh looked away, her features bitter and embarrassed. Maras giggled and clapped; she tended to find violence funny.

In this case, at least, Garos could agree. He smiled

broadly as he contemplated what state Zankor's remains would be found in—if they were ever found at all.

"*That is such a shame,*" Navaar sighed once the screams subsided. "*This alliance was going so well, and now we have to sacrifice one of our major players, along with her entire network. Those resources and connections will be hard to replace.*" She ran a hand through her hair. "*And all because that gisjacheh Mazarite wanted to show up Jofirek. We're supposed to be working together, not bickering and challenging each other.*"

"You're right," D'Nesh conceded. She reached out a hand and brushed Navaar's wrist. "*I guess . . . this means we have to work all the harder to hold on to Rigel. Help Garos . . . so we all win.*"

Navaar's expression slowly warmed into a smile, and she clasped her sister's hand gratefully. "*Thank you, love. Yes. That's exactly what we need.*" Her piercing dark eyes turned back toward the visual pickup. "*Garos, you have our full support from now on. You remain our most important ally.*"

Garos granted her a courtly nod. "Thank you, Navaar. I appreciate it. Now, if you'll excuse me . . . I have some damage control of my own to handle."

"*Of course.*"

The screen went dark . . . and Garos growled under his breath, praying for the time when Raldul would be strong enough that he no longer needed to indulge those ludicrous green females and their childish seduction games.

He had to search the console for the intercom

control. He really should remember its location by now, but the design was that confusing. "Bring in the prisoner, please."

Garos rose to meet the human female as a pair of the Thamnos' guards led her in, her wrists bound in front of her. "Welcome, Lieutenant Valeria Williams," he said, spreading his arms graciously. The Starfleet officer didn't seem to be in much of a condition to appreciate the gesture, though. She was bruised from the beatings that the Corthocs had futilely used to attempt to elicit more from her than her name, rank, and serial number, and she had been stripped to the flimsy cotton undergarment of a Zami female servant. He supposed her captors might find this alluring, for her mammalian attributes were not unlike those of the Three Sisters in their curvature and prominence, although the underlying physique was more tautly muscular. "I trust," he said, "that your time in the Corthocs' custody was not . . . excessively invasive."

Her eyes blazed defiantly. "I taught them to keep their hands to themselves."

"An impressive achievement, given the Corthocs' appetites. I guarantee, however, that it would not have lasted. Sexual abuse is one of their favorite forms of domination."

"I've noticed."

"Yes, and nobly attempted to intervene, so I gather. I applaud the effort—oh, rest assured, in case you were wondering, I am entirely indifferent to mammalian charms. Although that does not mean my own interrogation methods will be particularly agreeable."

But Williams's gaze had sharpened at the previous sentence. "The dancing lizard."

"Excuse me?"

"And how are things in the Raldul alignment lately? Do I have the pleasure of addressing Dular Garos himself?"

Garos beamed. "Ahh, how refreshing—another intelligent female to talk to! If, perhaps, somewhat rude." He gestured to one of the guards, who forced the woman into a seat and strapped her to it with a leather band around her waist. "I think you could stand a lesson in humility."

Once the guards had secured her ankles as well, he instructed them to leave, preferring some privacy for what followed. He returned to the console and sent a signal. Within a minute, the screen lit up with the face of Rehlen Vons—or rather, the simulacrum thereof worn by one of Raldul's finest impersonators, chosen for his facial and vocal resemblance to the late assistant director. "Mister Toric," Garos greeted him. "Let me introduce you to Lieutenant Williams of Starfleet. She serves with your Mister Grev and Mister Kirk."

Toric looked her over with a smarmy grin, simulating a prurient appreciation of her state of undress. *"Charmed, young lady."* He was a good man, Garos thought, but fonder of such gratuitously sadistic flourishes than he needed to be. To Williams's credit, she showed no sign of letting it get to her.

"Mister Toric, I'm eager to know—have your guests attempted to enact their plan to destroy the secret archives yet?"

"We overheard them finalizing their plans last night," Toric replied. He then explained for the lady's benefit: *"We let them get this far so that it would have more impact when we punished them for the attempt."*

"Them?" asked Garos.

"Well, technically Mister Damreg only tortured the human prisoner. But the little Tellarite certainly got the message."

Williams gasped, wincing and looking away. "Yes, that must be distressing to learn," Garos told her. "That by choosing to rescue a stranger, you condemned your crewmate to be tortured."

The Starfleet lieutenant glared with fury in her eyes. "The only ones responsible are you people. And I swear I will make you bastards pay."

Garos studied her, intrigued by the passion in her voice. "My, my, could it be that the hapless Mister Kirk is more than merely a crewmate?"

"He's a friend," she replied. "We're all friends. That's something I doubt you'd understand."

Garos sighed. "How little you know me, Lieutenant. I count many friends among the members of my alignment and my crew. It pains me when I must sacrifice them for the sake of our goals. But I know they understand, as I do, that the good of Maluria surpasses all personal considerations."

She peered closely at him for several moments, long enough that Garos decided he'd made his point and turned back to the screen. "I take it, then, that Ensign Grev has responded to this new . . . incentive?"

"Oh, yes. He's broken the first layer of encryptions—enough to give us file headings and partial descriptions. We don't have the secrets yet, but at least we know who and what they're about, and we can make some educated guesses. I've already sent messages to various politicians on Two and Three, implying we know more than we do, and their imaginations have filled in the rest. They'll do as they're told."

"Excellent, Mister Toric. See that the Tellarite proceeds with more alacrity from here on. Our bluffs can only achieve so much; if we're to win Rigel II, we need proof of the secrets we hold."

"I understand, sir."

"That will be all." Garos signed off, and the screen went dark.

After a few moments, he heard a strange sound from Williams. As he stepped toward her, the sound escalated into a tired laugh. "Perhaps the Corthocs did more damage than I thought. I wouldn't expect Rigel's plight to be so amusing to you."

"No, it's not that," Williams said. "See, I just realized I know more about the First Families' plans than you do."

He waited, aware that she was making him ask. Finally he gave in. "What do you believe you know?"

Again that soft, knowing laughter. "You really think this is just about Rigel II and the Federation, don't you? That the Families will blackmail the Trade Commission into rejecting Federation membership and seize control of Two in the process. And maybe if there is a war over Two, even a rebellion on Three, then that might prompt the Vulcans to vote no on membership anyway. Oh, you've figured all the angles."

He retained his aplomb. "I did say I enjoy intelligent company."

"Oh, if only I had some." More chuckling. "They're playing you, Garrie. The master manipulator, and you're being conned by a bunch of feudal hicks."

"Just say what you intend to say. My indulgence has its limits."

She shook her head. "Dectof Corthoc was right. You lack imagination. You're so used to thinking like a criminal that you assume the Families are content to be criminals too. That once they solidify Rigel II as a base for their activities, they'll just go on with their usual piracy, and you can keep your lawless, Federation-free status quo."

"Your deductions are interesting."

"And yours are lacking. Think about it! The Families are absolute rulers on their world. They revel in their domination of everyone around them. Do you really think people who used to being kings would settle for being pirates and gangsters? They don't just want Rigel II, Garos. They want *Rigel*."

Garos controlled his reaction. "An entirely plausible suggestion. But wanting is one thing, achieving another."

Williams's head shook in disappointment. "You're

not thinking it through. You know they already have the means. Think about what *else* they could do with the information in that archive. Don't trust me, reason it out for yourself."

Garos pondered . . . and, despite himself, expressed his thoughts aloud for her consideration. "Of course the secret archives have the potential to ruin businesses across the system. To throw the entire Rigelian economy into chaos."

She nodded. "And destabilize the whole Kandari Sector and beyond. Economically, politically, even militarily."

Including Maluria, he realized. He shook it off. "But how would that benefit them? They depend on that economy as much as the rest of us do. Mining and interstellar tourism are the basis of Rigel II's economy—it would be worth little if that were taken away. Not to mention their shipping concerns."

"It's pronounced 'piracy.'"

"As you will. Without active interstellar commerce, with a depressed economy or even system-wide warfare, their business would be severely undermined."

"And that's the root of your problem, Garos. You think they care about business. You think holding on to offworld trade is important to them. Garos, they *hate* outsiders. They hate it that their civilization's dependent on the Jelna for all its advances since first contact. And they see more exotic species like the Chelons or yourselves as little more than livestock."

"We are allies. Partners." No doubt some of the Zami felt as Williams described, but he could not believe it of Retifel Thamnos, not after the time he'd spent in her company.

"You're using them and you'd throw them out an airlock as soon as it was convenient. They'd do the same to you. In fact, I heard them brag about having dirt they could use to control *you* along with everyone else. 'Make the lizards dance,' they said." He couldn't look away now. "They don't care if they control a healthy economy on an interstellar scale," Williams said. "They don't care if they have to throw away the profits they make from outsystem trade and tourism. They're not that rational. They just want to be in absolute control, like it was in the bad old days. They'll gladly settle for a smaller pond, because that makes it easier to be the biggest fish."

Garos paced the room for several moments, contemplating. But he remained skeptical. "Granted, they could do as you say. But it comes down to your claim about their motives, their priorities. How do I know you speak the truth?"

"I'm sure you still have a mole or two with access to the Trade Commission. The Commission should have a record of the data files I sent back to my ship, the conversations I overheard in the Corthoc estate." She shrugged. "Or find out yourself. I was able to infiltrate as a servant, go unseen and overlooked for a few hours, and find out all I needed about their real plans. You're supposed to be the masters of infiltration—you really haven't tried this already?"

Garos didn't want to believe her. But he was a master of deception, and she would have to be extraordinary to fake such sincerity well enough to fool him. At the very least, he had to look into it.

"What a shame."

He and Williams spun to face the door. There stood Retifel Thamnos sucking on her narcotic stick, flanked by the two guards from before—who had their weapons drawn on him. "Of course you'll have to investigate her claims, Garos," the Zami matriarch said. "It's only prudent. And it's only prudent of us to assume you'll find she's telling the truth. So I'm afraid we have no choice but to skip a few steps and kill you both now. We'll make it look like she killed you and was then killed by our guards, so that your fellow lizards will be none the wiser."

Garos stared at her for a long moment. *Extraordinary indeed*, he thought. Retifel had managed to fool him completely. Or perhaps he'd just been so starved for the company of a worthy female that he'd allowed himself to be fooled. Either way, he realized, it only increased his respect for her.

Though he was not about to concede the game. He chuckled softly, stepping closer to Williams, casually moving one hand out of their view. "And, what, you thought it was courteous to tell me first rather than shooting me in the back?"

"Well, we have to stage the scene properly, you know. But yes—for all that I know you're a hideous reptile thing under that rather fetching mask, I have enjoyed the pretense that you're someone worth treating as a person. Call me sentimental, but I wanted to say good-bye."

Garos took what comfort he could from that as he placed his hand on Valeria Williams's shoulder. "Good-bye," he said, giving Retifel a last respectful nod as he worked the remote control hidden in his clothes. He felt the transporter beam engulfing him and the lieutenant, and he appreciated it greatly that the Zami were too dumbstruck by their disappearance to raise their weapons in time.

Unregistered Malurian shuttle, Poustof Hills, Rigel IV

Valeria Williams tried to get a leg beneath her once she materialized in a seated position aboard Garos's escape craft. She just ended up with her ass landing on her foot rather than the deck, but it was something. She rose to her feet, hands still bound before her, but Garos was moving to the controls, not troubled by having his back to her. She looked around: sure enough, there was a barefaced Malurian underling covering her with a boxy bronze pistol.

But Garos had other concerns. He activated the shuttle's comm system. "Tiroc, respond! Tiroc! The Families have betrayed us! Get out while you can!" There was the sound of a brief scuffle and cry from the speaker, then silence. Garos stared for a moment. "Damn them," he muttered, then turned to the engine controls.

Williams took a careful step forward, minding the guard. "Garos. Why did you take me with you?"

The Zami-masked criminal was busy launching the ship, but once it had shot into the air (at some speed), he deigned to reply. "I seem to be having an epidemic of unreliable allies today. Those who haven't betrayed me have proved fatally incompetent. You, my enemy, are the only one who's actually been helpful. I thought I'd take a gamble that you might be again." He shook his head, turning in his seat to face her. "Disappointing, really. Oh, don't misunderstand, I've sacrificed many allies when there was a need for it, but there should be certain basic standards of professionalism. You should understand that, Lieutenant. You humans have a saying about honor among thieves, don't you?"

Williams grinned. "We do. It goes: 'There *is* no honor among thieves.'"

"A great comfort you are not."

"Which is very comforting to me."

Garos rose and came over to her. "Mind your hostility, Lieutenant Williams. As of now, we have a common enemy in the First Families." He reached down and undid her shackles. "I have information you can use to retrieve the stolen files—oh, and your unfortunate colleagues." She restrained the urge to throttle him at that, aware that he was making a case worth considering. And freeing her was itself a surprising show of good faith, enough to get her attention. "Whereas you have Starfleet and the Rigelian government at your back, and thus are more than capable of recovering them and putting the Families in their place, once I give you the information you need."

She rubbed her wrists. "So that's the deal? You help us out in exchange for immunity?"

Garos smiled. "Oh, I am immune to your justice no matter what. I intend to drop you off at some neutral location with the data your people need to swoop in and save the day like the fine Starfleet officers you are . . . by which point I will be comfortably, and gladly, away from this whole misbegotten star system." He started to turn away, then looked back. "If you ask me, the Federation is welcome to it."

Williams had much the same sentiment toward the being before her right now: that she would gladly never see him again, unless it was in chains or in a courtroom. But in his own way, Garos had displayed an unexpected trace of . . . of something that it would be a reach to call nobility, but that might be the beginning of something. And what was the Federation about if not making allies out of enemies? "Garos," she began. He turned back around, and she chose her words carefully. "I know you're doing what you think is right for Maluria. Just consider . . . there's a better way. If you're willing to work with us today, maybe that means it's worth doing again."

Garos's smile was almost affectionate. "I want you to know I sincerely appreciate the offer, my dear. Such graciousness, after all that's been done to you, is truly touching—if a bit gullible.

"But subsume Maluria's destiny within that of the Federation?" He shook his head. "Let Rigel fall into that trap. Oh, I will gladly exploit the Federation's aid when it works in my world's favor. But if your agendas get in the way of Maluria's again, I will just as gladly tear you apart."

He smiled again. "From a safe distance, of course—and in a way you'll never see coming."

13

SAMUEL KIRK TRIED not to enjoy the sight of Rehlen Vons's death.

He certainly had reason to feel hatred toward the Malurian who had ordered his torture and then watched it like a spectator at a sporting event. But if he gave in to that malice, it would mean that they had won—that they had contaminated him with their own cruelty. So he resisted the sense of satisfaction that welled up in him.

What helped quell any pleasure, certainly, was that the executioner was none other than Damreg, the Zami who'd actually carried out the torture, and thus the one person he hated more than Vons. The Malurian, still in his Jelna disguise, had just gotten a rather harried emergency communication from his superior Garos. But it had come just too late, for Damreg had surely gotten a parallel warning just moments earlier. Vons had barely been able to draw his sidearm before Damreg's beloved knife buried itself in his spine.

Now Grev, who had been slaving over the decryption equipment under Vons's eye, jumped away in shock and stood shoulder-to-shoulder with Kirk, watching Damreg intently. The assassin smirked at the ensign's reaction as he pulled out the knife and wiped its blade on Vons's jacket. "Don't worry, pig, we still need you alive until you break the rest of the code. But you know I don't have Vons's patience, and he's not here to hold me back now." His eyes met Kirk's, and the historian had to force himself not to look away. "You get my meaning?"

Grev moved in front of Kirk protectively. "We understand."

"Good," the assassin said, not embellishing it with a smile as Vons would have. Instead, he drew his plasma pistol. "Now let's go. We're moving out before Vons's people get here. Or anyone else."

Kirk hoped that meant *Pioneer*'s crew was drawing closer to finding them. But with the falling-out between the co-conspirators, the situation had become more volatile. He didn't know what that meant for their chances of being found—or of lasting long enough to be found alive.

June 25, 2164
U.S.S. Pioneer

Malcolm Reed was delighted to have his armory officer back, so soon after his executive and science officers had returned safe and sound from Rigel III. But the way it had occurred was hard to credit. "So Garos just let you go?" he asked once the rest of the bridge crew had welcomed her back.

Valeria Williams shrugged. "Once he found out the First Families' plans would hurt Maluria, he wanted to stop them as much as we do. But he was in no mood to answer to Starfleet for his actions. So he used me to pass along what he knew and let Starfleet fix things while he went slinking back home."

"And he told you where the hostages and the archives are?" Reed turned to the main viewscreen, which was split between feeds of Captain T'Pol aboard *Endeavour* and Admiral Archer at Babel. It was the latter who had spoken.

"According to him, sir, they were being held in one of the asteroid mines around Rigel I's L5 point." Williams frowned. "But with his man getting killed, it's a safe bet they've moved them."

"But at least we can narrow it down to the inner asteroids," Archer said.

"There are thousands of individual mines in the Trojan clusters," T'Pol countered. *"And they would surely be taken to a location of which the Malurians were unaware, so Commander Williams could offer no insight. How can we narrow it down?"*

"There may be a way," Archer said. *"Director Hemnask has been very cooperative. She's shared her knowledge of some of the First Families' secret contact frequencies and encryption protocols."*

"And now that we know where to look," Hoshi Sato added from T'Pol's side, *"we can intercept their communications and scan for keywords."*

"Then what are we waiting for?" Reed asked.

T'Pol looked uncertain. *"We should keep in mind that Dular Garos is a master of deception and manipulation. It is not inconceivable that he has falsified this sequence of events in order to misdirect us."*

"I wouldn't put anything past Garos," Archer agreed. "He's completely ruthless. He wouldn't have let Val go if he didn't have some angle."

Williams shook her head. "With respect, Admiral, I don't think so. It all fits too well with what I learned in the Corthoc estate."

"And if he were more aware of the Families' plans than he led you to believe," T'Pol countered, "he could have constructed his deception accordingly."

"I don't agree, Captain," Reed told her. "Everything fits too neatly. Val's findings on Rigel IV. The Trade Commission's reports about the spate of corporate blackmail attempts, not just on Rigel II but on Five and the Colonies."

He faced his erstwhile captain squarely. "Captain T'Pol, Admiral Archer, I understand you both have good reason to mistrust Garos. Maybe too good. But I have to go by the evidence, and that tells me that what Lieutenant Williams was told is probably true, regardless of the source."

T'Pol studied him. "You are confident of this?"

He looked within himself . . . and nodded firmly. "In my judgment it's the right call." He took in Williams with his gaze, then told T'Pol, "I trust my officers."

She met his eyes approvingly. "Then I concur."

Archer took in the exchange silently, but Reed got the sense that he saw exactly what had passed between them. "Okay, then, Captains. I'm sending Hoshi the comm protocols she needs. Now go bring our people home."

Lyaksti, Sauria

"*They shut down the bar right after the occupation,*" said the Saurian female on the monitor screen. "*They said the saunas were contaminated with alien germs, had them filled in. Tore apart the whole place to decontaminate it. Oh, they rebuilt it, according to state-approved plans, but it hasn't been the same.*" The speaker's face was not in the frame, but her hands kneaded a richly textured cloth. Her voice was disguised, but her story and the calluses on her hands told Jeremy Lucas that this was Bavot, the bartender from Redik's. Antonio Ruiz and his friends had taken Lucas there a few times before the crackdown.

"*Some of the old crowd never came back,*" Bavot went on. "*A few . . . Naralo was arrested for protesting state policy. I . . . don't know what became of him.*"

"*All these arrests,*" came Ruiz's voice. Lucas knew the young engineer had used his connections to sneak into Narpra and reconnect with his old friends—those who would speak to him—although the man he'd gone in with had remained anonymous, keeping silent and out of the imager's view. "*The curfews, the laws against assembly, the soldiers patrolling the streets. Why are the people standing for this?*"

"*You saw how bad it got before Maltuvis came to our aid!*" She sighed. "*Yes, it's been hard, but these austerity measures are necessary while the economy recovers.*"

"*And do you really think Maltuvis will let up once things get better? You must see what's going on here. You've been occupied. He sent the plague to give him a pretext.*"

Her hands kneaded the cloth more ferociously.

"They told us the aliens would claim that. That they'd say anything to hide their own culpability for all the death."

"'The aliens'? This is me you're talking to."

"Yes, and you shouldn't even be here. If I'm caught with you . . ."

"Look at yourself, amiga. *You're afraid of your own leaders. Is that what—"*

He had been reaching for her hands, but she yanked them away. *"I'm more afraid that they might be right. You . . . you should go now."*

After the playback ended, Presider Moxat, the elderly green-bronze female who chaired the Executive Council of the Saurian Global League, blinked her enormous eyes at Lucas. "What does this prove, Doctor? Only that the Narprans accept M'Tezir's presence there."

"You've seen the other evidence," Lucas told her. "The data we obtained from the clinic in Veranith, the samples of their treatment. I can prove that the M'Tezir have deliberately weakened the serum so that it only controls the symptoms. Sobon is already synthesizing a full-strength version that should be a permanent cure. It's not a fraction as expensive as Maltuvis claims, and it should be easy to teach Saurian physicians how to manufacture and administer the cure for themselves. Presider, we can prove that Maltuvis has been lying to the people!"

"You can *assert* it," Moxat replied in a weary tone. "Even back it up with evidence. But many will not trust evidence from offworld sources. You heard that Narpran. Even she, who has felt the bite of Maltuvis's oppression as long as anyone outside M'Tezir itself, believes that aliens would lie to conceal their guilt."

Lucas peered at her through narrowed lids. "Is that what you believe, Presider?"

Her reply was apologetic. "It is what I am concerned the electorate would believe, Jeremy. The opposition is threatening a vote of no confidence against our coalition. They are backed by a growing popular movement that wishes to sever our trade deal with the Federation and expel all aliens from our world."

"But we can prove that belief is based on M'Tezir propaganda! Lies!"

"And do you really think so many would be ready to admit they were so gullible? More likely they would choose to believe you were the liars. It would only inflame matters."

"Then what are you suggesting, Presider? That we just let Maltuvis keep spreading this plague and holding the planet hostage to his half-cure?"

Moxat rose and moved around her desk, speaking more softly to mollify him. "Of course we will distribute the cure—and let its existence and availability reveal the lies in Maltuvis's words. Believe me, there is no one who wants to reclaim our lost territory from that petty tyrant as much as I do. But . . . forgive me, Doctor . . . it is best if we present the cure as a Saurian breakthrough. It will be more readily accepted planetwide if its true origins are not known. And we can wage the rhetorical battle with M'Tezir more effectively if we focus on the issues where we can gain ground without inflaming matters further . . . which means that, for now, it is best if we stay quiet on the issue of alien acceptance."

Lucas seethed, but he held back the caustic reply he had in mind. He reminded himself that, however much contempt he felt for politicians and their self-serving games, he was still a healer first. If Moxat's political maneuvering had impeded the availability of the cure, he would have fought it to his last breath. But as galling as it was, Moxat had a point: this bit of political compromise probably was the best way to get the cure distributed as widely and swiftly as possible. Maltuvis had gotten Sauria so stirred up with xeno-phobia that many would reject the cure if they knew it came from Federation doctors—even if all those doc-tors had done was purify the watered-down medicine the M'Tezir were already using.

"Consider the long game, Jeremy," Moxat said. "With Maltuvis weakened and the plague defeated, in time the fear of offworlders will subside. The League will maintain its trading ties and its current policies toward offworlders for as long as my coalition stands. Eventually matters will normalize again."

Lucas huffed a breath, ruffling his mustache. "I hope you're right, Moxat. But something tells me Maltuvis isn't just going to take defeat lying down."

Basilic Palace, M'Tezir, Sauria

Maltuvis paced slowly around the globe of N'Ragolar—"Sauria," as the offworlders called it—and examined the lay of the land. The color of the lights illuminating Ve-ranith from within the globe had finally changed to solid orange, indicating that the last active opposition had been silenced and the country was now firmly in M'Tezir control. That made fourteen nations, twelve of them former Global League members, that had now fallen under his rule.

Unfortunately, Veranith would be the last nation gained through the plague stratagem. "My spies tell me that the Federation has given the Global League the cure," he told his visitor. "They've begun mass-producing it and will distribute it to affected nations promptly."

Harrad-Sar crossed his muscular green arms. "You don't seem too upset," the Orion merchant prince said.

Maltuvis flicked a hand as though shooing off an insect. "I knew it was only a matter of time before they obtained a sample. You and your mistresses may love your games of deception, Orion, but the truth has a way of coming out eventually, and the successful conqueror plans for the contingency." He gestured to the field of orange-hued states on the globe. "I chose the nations to infect carefully. M'Tezir has now gained a clear advantage in resources and strategic positioning. I have pincers around many of the Global League's key states and a wedge driving between the two largest."

"If you can hold on to the nations you have," the Three Sisters' lackey countered, "now that they'll be told you lied about the cure."

"I've already mobilized my medical troops to begin

releasing the real cure, ahead of the League. I'll tell them it's a new breakthrough, one the League copied from us. Any claims to the contrary can be spun as more alien lies." He directed a snide smile at Harrad-Sar. "No offense."

The Orion simply glared from beneath those ridiculous hunks of metal he had driven through his scalp. "And what if they don't believe you? You said the truth will come out eventually."

"All I have to do is sustain doubt and division long enough to solidify my rule. Before much longer, it'll be too late for them or the Global League to do anything about my conquests."

"Don't get overconfident, Basileus. The Federation knows what you've done."

Maltuvis scoffed. "And what can they do about it? They depend on the resources I now control. Besides, they're preoccupied with their own internal strife, which your Syndicate has helped to exacerbate. The troubles of a world so far from their borders won't be of much concern to them as long as nothing interferes with their precious flow of minerals."

Harrad-Sar tilted his head in acknowledgment. "That's the plan," he agreed. "Just don't get overconfident. The Federation takes its notions of 'freedom' more seriously than you might think. Best if you don't provoke them too far."

"I can bide my time," he said. "I've waited this long for those ships you promised me, haven't I?"

The Orion caught the implied chastisement and replied with some of his own. "Maybe you should concentrate on conquering this planet before you start going after others."

"That is the point, Sar. Your concerns about my ability to hold my territory would be moot if I had a fleet of warships in orbit. N'Ragolar would be mine in days."

"You know we have to proceed carefully with the ships. It has to look like you built them yourselves. We're training your people as fast as we can, but—"

"I know, I know. Your insistence that there be no proof tying back to the Syndicate. A cowardly philosophy. I may use subterfuge to win, but I do not hide my face, my name, as I gain in power." He gave a sharp hiss of disdain. "Where would be the point in that?"

Harrad-Sar, predictably, hid his true feelings behind a forced smile. "Rest assured, Basileus, our commitment to your goals is strong. Soon you will rule all of N'Ragolar. And that will be just the beginning."

Yes, Maltuvis thought, raising his eyes from the globe to the stars in the window beyond. *One world is too small an arena for me, now that I know the galaxy is in reach. Soon the M'Tezir Empire will spread across the heavens.*

His smile widened. *No—make that the Maltuvian Empire.*

14

"You know," Samuel Kirk said to Grev, "I really thought Val would be better at hide-and-seek than this."

Grev patted his shoulder, feeling him tremble despite the heat in their stony cell. "It's a big system."

"You say that like it's supposed to be encouraging."

If nothing else, Grev and Kirk's forced relocation had confirmed to them that they were in space. Their new cell was in extremely low gravity; it took several minutes for anything dropped from arm height to settle to the floor. Thus, the artificial tunnels they and their captors now occupied must be within an asteroid. And judging from the oppressive heat that the tunnels' inadequate environmental systems let through, they must be very close to Beta Rigel itself. Most likely, they were in one of the Trojan asteroid mines, one too new or too small to have gravity plating or effective environmental control. Grev could only hope they were deep enough beneath the asteroid's surface to be adequately shielded from the subgiant star's radiation.

Although he doubted Damreg and their other captors were concerned about their long-term health. As soon as Grev had decrypted the archives, he and Kirk would be ejected into space, or perhaps fed into the mine's waste recycler. Grev hoped it would be the latter. He'd always wanted his remains to be interred in the soil of Tellar or one of its colonies, so that his biomass would sustain new life. This would not be quite the same, but his options were severely restricted at this point.

The problem was, with Damreg's constant threats looming over Sam, Grev had had no choice but to produce results. He'd reached the point where his decryption algorithms were close enough to accurately translate about twenty percent of any file, but sometimes that was enough to give the Zami what they needed to blackmail an official or sabotage a corporation. Damreg had taken pleasure this morning in telling him how the leak of the proprietary engine designs of a major shipbuilding firm in the Colonies, courtesy of Grev's decryptions, had already resulted in half a dozen other firms underbidding their contracts and throwing their stock into a death spiral.

At least Grev now had enough of a feel for the patterns of the encryption that he could attempt to target the files least likely to contain seriously damaging information. But there was simply no way to be sure until they were decoded.

The best he could do was to try to drag things out, to keep himself and Kirk alive until *Pioneer* could find them. Despite their hopes, their move to a new location had offered no opportunities to reach a transmitter or otherwise secure their escape. Damreg had kept them in harsher, more austere conditions than before. Vons had at least understood that mistreating Grev could undermine his memory and cognitive skills, so he had granted the communications officer relatively comfortable working conditions and saved his torture for Kirk. Damreg had been equally rough on them both—plus microgravity made Grev woozy and upset his digestion. Ironically, this was to Grev's benefit, for it slowed his work and kept him and Kirk alive longer.

The question was whether that was really a desirable outcome. "Grev," Kirk asked a while after Damreg had finished gloating and left, "do you think we should . . . find some way to . . . provoke them to kill us?"

"I think that would be a Pyrrhic victory at this point," Grev replied carefully, hoping the historical allusion would go over any listeners' heads. The truth, which he was in no hurry to reveal to Damreg, was that Grev had already laid sufficient groundwork that any competent operator of the decryption equipment could complete the task without him.

Kirk nodded, intuiting Grev's meaning. "Then . . . maybe we should've done it days ago. Maybe if we were braver . . ."

Grev interrupted. "Where there is life, there is hope," he said, adding an affirming nod.

The human stared. "How can you still do that? No matter what, you always try to cheer everyone up."

"Heh. Everyone?" The Tellarite shook his head. "At this point I'm just trying to keep myself going."

After a solemn silence, Kirk spoke again. "You know what? You were right."

"Hm?"

"I should've asked Val out while I had the chance."

"Hm."

"I mean, she would've said no. Probably. But at least I would've asked. Let her know . . . that I think she's worth asking out."

Grev smiled. "Sam?"

"Hm?"

"I think *you're* worth asking out."

Kirk threw him a look. "Grev? Are you asking me out?"

Before the communications officer could answer, he heard a sound from beyond the metal hatch. He listened carefully, and in a moment he distinguished voices raised in alarm—and shots being fired. "I'll get back to you," he said.

The noises got louder, the shots coming closer. Then the hatch burst open and Damreg pulled himself inside just before an energy beam speared the air where he had been. He held on to the frame for leverage as he desperately dragged the hatch closed. He released his drawn weapon to do so, but in the microgravity it stayed too close to his grip for Grev or Kirk to make a grab for it. With the hatch shut, he grabbed the gun once more and waved it at them both. "You're my hostage, Tellarite! You're getting me out of here! And you, human—you're dead weight." He fixed his aim on Kirk.

The hatch blew open behind him, knocking the

Zami assassin forward and sending his shot flying into the asteroidal rock. He tumbled in midair, trying to bring his weapon to bear on Valeria Williams as she surged into the room. But she moved with far more confidence in the negligible gravity, pushing herself off the frame to fly feet-first into his midsection. He spasmed, sending the gun flying, but he recovered and went for her throat. Before his meaty grip could close around her slender neck, she joined her hands into a club and delivered a fierce chop to his carotid. Damreg went limp in midair, sinking toward the floor in a slow spin.

Williams turned to Grev and Kirk, who were staring at her in amazement. "You good?" she asked. They nodded dumbly. "I need words, guys. You functional?"

"We're, we're good," Grev said.

"Yes," Kirk put in, grinning. "We're fine now."

"We're just very glad to see you," Grev gushed.

"Mutual. Where are they keeping the archives?"

"We'll take you there."

"Okay, come on. I'll clear the corridor."

She ducked outside, fearlessly rejoining the firefight that was still going on. As Grev helped Kirk to his feet, he leaned over to whisper in his friend's ear.

"You should *definitely* ask her out."

U.S.S. *Pioneer*

"Williams to Pioneer," came the lieutenant's voice over the bridge speaker. *"I'm back in the shuttle. Sam and Grev are with me, and so's the archive."* Malcolm Reed's heart

lifted, but he permitted himself only a small smile of contentment, though Mayweather and the rest of the bridge crew expressed their gratitude more vocally. *"Grev wiped the outpost's database, but there's no telling what information they managed to send offsite,"* Williams went on.

"Don't worry about that," Reed told her. "Just get our people home."

"Aye, sir, as soon as we finish mopping up." There was a distant sound of phase-pistol fire, then moments later: *"About time, you guys! We secure? . . . Sir, undocking now. We'll be home any minute."*

"We'll keep a light on for you." Fortunately, Williams wasn't exaggerating about the brief travel time. The Rigelian asteroid fields were quite close to the star, so *Pioneer* was waiting in the asteroid's umbra, letting its mass shield them from the heat and radiation. The entire mining facility had been built on the permanent dark side created once the asteroid's rotation had been synched with its orbit. Even so, it was chiefly automated, like most of the mines here—which was no doubt why the First Families had deemed them a good hiding place. Also, the radiation would have made it problematical for a ship to spend too long searching here unless its crew knew where to look—as they had done once Hoshi Sato had decrypted and tracked a signal to the Thamnos estate alerting them to an ongoing fraud investigation whose exposure would endanger a number of undercover investigators on Rigel II. The Trade Commission had warned those investigators even as *Pioneer,* the nearer of the Starfleet ships, had flown to their crew's rescue.

They're not home yet, Reed reminded himself as he watched the shuttle undock from the mining outpost. The asteroid remained in hostile hands. It had no weapons to speak of, but there was still the possibility that—

"Sir!" Rey Sangupta called from the science station. "Energy buildup on the surface." He frowned. "It's a magnetic signature, not a weapon, but . . ."

"Shields," Reed ordered, anticipating. Crewman Detzel at tactical complied just before the ship rocked from a fierce impact. Consoles sparked and flickered, suggesting that the blow was forceful enough to shake some internal connections loose. It certainly felt like it knocked some of Reed's internal connections loose.

"What was that?" Travis Mayweather asked.

"They fired their mass driver at us," Sangupta replied. "Launched a packet of asteroidal ore at high speed."

Ensign Tallarico threw him a quizzical look. "They're throwing rocks at us?"

"Don't knock it, Ensign," Reed said. "Kinetic energy's still as potent as any other kind. So I suggest you move us out of its line of fire."

"Easier said than done, Captain," Sangupta said. "The driver track circles the whole asteroid, so they can launch on various trajectories. And we have to stay in the umbra, for the shuttlepod's sake if not our own."

"Don't worry about us, Rey," came Williams's voice over the open channel from the pod. *"Keep the ship safe."* She left it unsaid that the pod was stuck outside as long as *Pioneer*'s shields stayed up.

"Incoming!" Detzel called. Tallarico's hands raced, but the ship suffered another glancing blow before she could dodge completely. The hull rattled and groaned, and Reed struggled to stay seated.

Mayweather clung to the safety handle on the front of the science station. "Damage report!" he called when the shock subsided.

"Shields at half strength," Detzel replied. "Damage to hull plating and subsurface conduits. And one of the impulse reactors is down."

"Polarize the plating," Reed belatedly instructed.

"These shields aren't designed for a low-tech attack like this," said Mayweather.

"Then let's stop relying on them," Reed replied. "Detzel, target that damned mass driver."

The crewman frowned. "Sir, which part?"

"The part that a projectile would launch from to hit us! Surely you remember tangents from geometry class."

A humbled Detzel hastened to comply, and his phase-cannon blast damaged the track at the appropriate place. The ore packet that had already been accelerating toward launch struck the damaged section and crashed, producing a nice splash of ejecta from the impact site. "Excellent," Reed said. "Shuttlepod, proceed to docking!"

Williams acknowledged, and the pod began to move toward *Pioneer* again. But then Reed saw lights on the asteroid's surface, and Sangupta announced, "Thrusters, sir! They're rotating the asteroid!"

"Detzel, keep firing at the track! Take out as much as you can!"

"Sir, the shuttle's too close to the line of fire!"

"Val, abort approach!"

But it was too late. Another ore packet flew from the surface, missing the shuttlepod by only a few hundred meters, and clubbed *Pioneer* hard and head-on. Reed was knocked halfway out of his chair, Mayweather thrown to the deck. Once the captain recovered from the ringing blow, he saw that the bridge lights had dimmed, making it easier to spot the small fire that had erupted on Detzel's console. Its cooling fan whirred fiercely as the crewman batted the fire out with a gray sleeve.

"Sir," Detzel reported grimly a moment later, "the power grid on F deck is damaged. Our weapons are down."

Reed didn't pause to dwell on the news. "Will shields hold long enough to get them working again?"

"Negative, sir."

Mayweather stepped closer to Reed. "Captain, let's grab the pod in a tractor beam and get out of here, best speed."

"That mass driver has unlimited range, and impulse drive is hobbled."

"Sir, we'll go back in," Williams offered. *"If we can reach the driver controls—"*

"Negative! We can't risk letting that archive fall back into their hands. And I won't risk you again either." He paused. "Make a break for the nearest asteroid, use it for cover. We'll shield you as long as we can. As for the radiation, you'll just have to hope—"

"Sir!" Sangupta interrupted, beaming. "It's *Endeavour*!"

Multiple phase-cannon bolts and spatial torpedoes speared from the black into the mass driver, striking the track in enough places to render it useless. Moments later, the *Columbia*-class starship hove into view on the screen, taking up position in the asteroid's umbra near *Pioneer*. Then the image changed to a sight Malcolm Reed had never found more beautiful: the face of Captain T'Pol. *"Captain Reed. Do you require assistance?"*

Reed decided it would be ungrateful to tell her she had a talent for the obvious.

"Kirk and Grev will both be fine physically in a few days," Doctor Therese Liao told Captain Reed as Valeria Williams stood at his side. "Mentally," the compact, middle-aged physician went on, "it's harder to say. They've both been through rough treatment, and Sam was subjected to several sessions of torture. I'm going to need to have him in for regular psych counseling for a while, and I recommend a reduced duty schedule."

"Of course, Doctor," said Reed. "Whatever he needs."

Williams let the rest of their conversation wash over her, too preoccupied with the thought of what Kirk had endured over the past week. Finally Liao gave her permission to speak to the historian.

Kirk's face brightened when he saw her. "Val!" He

beckoned her forward, clasping her hands when she drew in range. "I . . . I really wanted to thank you for saving us. I, I know that's not adequate to—there are no words—"

She shook her head uneasily. "No, that's okay. Don't worry about it."

"Val, you saved my life. And I want you to know . . . that is, there's something I've been meaning to say to you—"

"Sam, wait." She pulled her hands away. "There's something I need you to know first."

She told him about Rigel IV, about how she'd had the opportunity to discover where he and Grev were being held but had passed it up to rescue a stranger. "That was five days ago. Before you were—Sam, if I'd done my job then, we might have found you before . . ."

He just lay in the medical bed, staring at nothing, absorbing what he'd heard. She spoke again, tentatively. "Sam . . . if you're mad at me, I understand. I'm so sorry."

"Mad." He scoffed gently, and Williams realized what a totally inadequate word it was. But then his eyes met hers, very briefly. "No . . . I understand why you . . . felt you had to do that. I can't blame you for it. What they did—I blame them. It was all them."

She was more relieved than she fully understood. "That's good. I'm glad—I mean, I appreciate—" She broke off. After a moment's silence, she said, "You, um, said there was something you wanted to tell me?"

Kirk looked at her for a long moment. Finally:

"No. No, there's nothing to say. In fact . . . I think I want to be alone right now, if that's okay."

She lowered her head, understanding that it would be a while before things were okay. "Of course. I understand."

He said nothing more to her. There was a tear in her eye as she left.

15

June 27, 2164
Thamnos estate, Rigel IV

"WHAT'S HAPPENING, THAMNOS?" a panicked Vemrim
Corthoc demanded over the viewing screen. Behind
him in the Corthocs' communications parlor, his
senior siblings were undertaking more important
tasks, delegating the panic to the otherwise useless
Vemrim. *"Our people are being arrested all over Two and Five
and the Colonies! Our offworld assets have been seized—the secret
ones nobody was supposed to know about! And our peasants have
risen up! They've taken the armory and they're heading for the
mansion! We tried shooting at them from our ships, but someone
sabotaged the weapon systems!"*

Retifel Thamnos smirked. *That Starfleet woman was
more resourceful than I realized. No wonder the lizard liked her.*
"It's Garos," she told Corthoc. "Apparently he was
playing our own game against us—accumulating data
on our activities and holdings that he could use as
blackmail fodder if we turned on him."

"That's just low. Who would sink to such a thing?" She
didn't deign to answer. *"Retifel, dear, you have to help us."*

"Do you imagine that Garos spared us the same
assault? We're dealing with crises of our own. At this
point, Corthoc, it's every Family for itself." A distant
explosion sounded over the comm, and the ornate

chandeliers behind Vemrim shuddered and chimed. "And it sounds as if you have your hands full, so I'll leave you to it. Sorry, dear."

She shut off the screen before Vemrim could spew more desperate babble, finally letting herself laugh out loud at the Corthocs' misfortune. True, the seizures and arrests of the Thamnos' own offworld assets were no mere jest, and the populist uprisings were undoubtedly just beginning. The Thamnos, and other clans less brazen in their brutality than the Corthocs, were managing to censor the news of their worst atrocities for now, but it would surely reach the masses in time, and Retifel had no illusions about her Family's ability to fend off an insurrection with its offworld assets so severely compromised.

But Retifel had faith in the Thamnos' ability to adapt to change. It had been that adaptability that had enabled them to displace older, more ossified Families and claim their lands and wealth. This latest hardship would simply clear more of their rivals, the Corthocs included, from the field and give the Thamnos a clearer path to power.

Oh, there would have to be compromises. The Family had already extended feelers to the Trade Commission, offering to make a deal and to participate in the transition to a more democratic form of government. But even an occupying power still needed to rely on existing local authority structures for day-to-day rule, so the Thamnos could survive by making themselves indispensable to the new regime, playing along with its reforms while continuing to accumulate wealth and power through *sub rosa* means. Retifel's yearning for open rule of two worlds would have to give way to a more clandestine form of power on the margins of society—the very situation Retifel had hoped to avoid.

But she had gambled and lost, and she was a good enough sport to accept the consequences. What mattered was that, one way or another, the Family would survive.

June 28, 2164
Tregon, Rigel V

"On behalf of all Rigel, I hereby thank you." Adren Kospar, the round-eared Zami male who had been hurriedly sworn in as the new Rigel V representative to the Rigelian Trade Commission, gestured expansively at the two Starfleet captains who sat before the board of directors in the council hall. "Captain Malcolm Reed of Earth, Captain T'Pol of Vulcan—it is thanks to you and the heroic efforts of your crews that the Rigelian society and economy have been spared a true disaster."

T'Pol leaned forward. "Thank you, Director, but we require no accolades. Our purpose is to serve."

"And so you have," Director Sajithen intoned, her words pitched toward the Rigelian masses viewing the live broadcast. "Indeed, recent events have served to open our eyes to a fundamental weakness in our system. We built Rigel's economy on license and indulgence—valuing freedom, yes, but hypocritical in our tolerance of those who would exploit their own freedom to impinge on the freedom of others. We now see that the balance of secrets and threats we used to maintain order left us teetering on the edge of a knife. And so the people now clamor for reform."

Jemer Zehron spoke with more reluctance. "Yes, indeed. Though war has been averted, we have seen sectors of the economy destabilized, public officials disgraced, trust in the system badly undermined. We must act to restore the public's faith in our institutions." He fidgeted. "It seems likely that . . . some of us will not survive the referendum our shareholder-voters have called for. And perhaps that is as it should be. But if nothing else, we should do what we can to minimize the damage our choices have caused.

"I opposed Federation membership because I believed it was in the best interest of my . . . supporters," Zehron went on, though T'Pol was sure he was not referring to his electoral base. "But none of us can thrive unless confidence in our basic institutions is restored. The public increasingly sees Federation law and Starfleet protection as the keys to our future stability. Thus, I will oppose their will no longer."

T'Pol and Reed exchanged a look, aware that there may have been an ulterior motive underlying Zehron's calculations. Garos's revelation of the First Family's secrets had led to the arrests of their operatives and puppets throughout the system, crippling their off-world criminal operations and their ability to buy politicians' votes. Garos himself had gotten away cleanly, and the Commission showed no interest in pursuing him. No doubt buying immunity had been part of his intent. Although T'Pol believed that Garos was not above taking such actions out of sheer vindictiveness.

"I applaud my colleague's support for admission," Kospar put in. "I am convinced that, whatever my predecessor's First Family ties may have compelled her to do against her preference, Director Hemnask's true belief was that Rigel would be stronger and better as a member of the Federation. And I hear support for that belief from an ever larger number of her former constituents. I consider it my place to honor that side of her legacy."

"And I think we all know where I stand," Sajithen said.

Nop Tenott looked around uneasily. "I still have my doubts about the cost to the liberties of our business interests. I may have been overruled on admission, but if the voters see fit to keep me on this board, I will continue to fight for those liberties."

"If I may," Malcolm Reed said. "Certainly it is the right of all citizens to dissent and disagree peacefully. That is a Federation value and a Rigelian one. But there is a right way and a wrong way to do it." He paused. "I have found over the course of my career that secrets, however benevolent the intentions underlying them, have a tendency to do more harm than good in the long run."

"Indeed," T'Pol added. "It is better to express such disagreements openly, within the framework of mutual transparency and trust. We may disagree with one another on many things . . . but so long as we trust one another, we can work together to resolve those disagreements.

"We hope that Rigel's many worlds and cultures will join the worlds of the United Federation of Planets in a partnership of mutual trust . . . and friendship."

Excerpt of speech by Councilor Anlenthoris ch'Vhendreni, June 30, 2164

. . . The discovery that two of my chief advisors were on the payroll of the Zankor syndicate, and that they arranged for my diversion and delay at Babel in order to set up a false attempt on my life in hopes of discrediting Admiral Jonathan Archer, has prompted me to conduct a fuller investigation of this corruption. And I am now forced to admit that it extends further into the Planetarist movement than I had wanted to believe. While the great majority of Planetarists have legitimate questions and concerns about the haste with which the Federation has centralized power, the evidence I am releasing today will show how their grassroots activism has been co-opted by a self-serving few who do not have the people's best interests at heart, but who instead seek to cripple the Federation in the name of their own selfish, even criminal interests. Legitimate efforts to reform the Federation's laws and secure the liberties of its citizens have been supplanted by cynical manipulation and inflammatory rhetoric designed to undermine the Federation itself and its ability to maintain peace and order. This agenda does not serve the liberties of the Federation's member peoples, and indeed it actively endangers them.

And I must confess that I have let myself be complicit in this manipulation. I have knowingly acted against my own beliefs and advocated positions that I knew were irresponsible and unwise, because I let myself be convinced that it was necessary to score political advantage. I chose to lie to my own constituents, to be untrue to myself, in the name of winning an election. And in so doing, I forgot that the goal of politics is not to win at any cost—the goal is to serve. I have used the good of the people as a justification for my rhetoric, but I have been a hypocrite in doing so, for I believed I had to trick the people into voting me into office, to inflame their resentment and anger against the opposition, rather than inspiring them to strive alongside me for a better future. No one can govern merely by attacking one's political rivals. We compete for office, but our obligation once elected is to work together for the common good. Our different values and priorities allow us to act in concert to serve a wider range of the people than any one faction could do alone. This is the essence of democracy.

I intend to withdraw from the presidential race. I know that many of my fellow Planetarists—and there are still many legitimate ones—may feel that they have lost a voice in this election as a result. But they have not. The truth is, my own beliefs and those of Councilor al-Rashid are not that far apart. We agree on the fundamentals, and only differ on certain matters of emphasis that are well within both our capacities to negotiate. Whatever the rhetoric I have spun in the name of politics and in the unwitting service of those who seek to divide and undermine our state, I agree with Councilor al-Rashid that we, the peoples of the United Federation of Planets, have more uniting us than dividing us; that we all share a common goal of making a better Federation and a better future; and that we can achieve that goal by listening to one another and fairly considering one another's points of view. I believe in the independence, uniqueness, and dignity of the Federation's member species and cultures, but I believe we cannot defend those ideals unless we are united in defending the whole, and joined by certain fundamental principles. Rather than rushing to an extreme of centralization or of individualism, we must find a balance between the two, a balance we can only arrive at by working in partnership with our political opposition. As the Vulcans say, it is our differences working in combination, not at odds, that will give us strength.

We are a Federation of Planets . . . but we must never forget that we are United.

July 1, 2164
Babel Station

Sedra Hemnask rose from her cot as Jonathan Archer arrived outside the transparent door of her cell in Babel's security section. She looked as though she wanted to reach out for him, but the door—and something else—held her back. She waited until Archer activated the intercom, then spoke. "I wasn't sure you'd want to see me again."

"Honestly . . . I wasn't sure either."

Her eyes darted around, staying low. "I heard the news . . . the delegates voted to approve admission. I'm . . . I'm relieved that my sabotage failed. If only . . ."

Some moments after she trailed off, Archer spoke slowly. "I thought you should know that the people of Rigel IV are in open revolt. Many of the First Families have already been overthrown, or have fled the planet with their assets in tow. Others have invited in Trade Commission peacekeepers and advisors to help them transition to a democratic form of government. The Thamnos family is one of them."

She stared at him in fear, wringing her hands. "That would not spare my kin from their wrath."

Archer's tone softened. "We alerted the resistance on Four to get in touch with Voctel Thamnos. It turns out that he already had a plan in place to get his wife, children, and grandchildren to Rigel V so they'd be safe from retribution if you didn't succeed. The resistance ran interference and helped him get them away. They're staying with your mother, Sedra."

She gasped and sobbed in relief. "A great mercy." She caught her breath. "I suppose I'm both grateful that it's over—and so terribly ashamed that I helped them for nothing. Voctel was looking out for his heirs. If I'd defied them from the start, my family would still have been safe."

Archer took pity on her. "You couldn't know that for sure. You made the best decision you thought you could at the time. You acted out of love, Sedra. I can't blame you for that."

She turned back to him, her vast emerald eyes glinting with tears. "Love. Oh, Jonathan, I'm just as ashamed of how I used you. How I hurt you."

After a moment's thought, he put his hand on the door. She placed hers opposite it. "I forgive you, Sedra. Yes, I'm hurt—but I know you thought you had no choice. And really . . ." He laughed, lowering his hand. "It's gotta be the fourth time I've let someone manipulate me like that. If anyone's at fault, it's me for being so damn gullible." They shared a laugh, though it was not without pain.

"You deserve better, Jonathan. I hope those experiences don't harden you to the search for love. I know there must be someone out there you can trust, someone who'll be good for you. Someone who . . . who deserves you."

He held her eyes, but his thoughts were elsewhere. He thought of T'Rama, a Vulcan who seemed to draw strength from the bonds of family on far more than the professional and logical levels she confessed to. He wondered if maybe he'd been wrong all these years to see relationships and professional responsibilities as conflicting forces. Maybe the one could actually reinforce the other.

And once again, he found himself thinking of Danica Erickson. And wondering.

July 3, 2164
Lyaksti, Sauria

Charles "Trip" Tucker had been eagerly awaiting Harris's response for more than a week. Using the real-time subspace relays Starfleet had set up between Sauria and Federation space created too much risk of unwanted attention, so Tucker had needed to bide his time. Time during which the Global League, for all its commendable efforts to distribute the cure (regardless of who took credit for it), had been too paralyzed by political games and collective ass-covering to take any action about the growing oppression in M'Tezir-controlled territory, or to react to the alarming evidence of a massive military buildup beginning in M'Tezir itself. Time during which the Federation government had been just as useless, unwilling to consider intervention when the natives of the planet would not ask for it—and perhaps unwilling to risk the steady flow of dilithium and transuranics from the countries Maltuvis now held in his tightening grip.

In fairness, Tucker could understand the Federation's position. From the beginning of their time together on *Enterprise*, T'Pol had argued against aggressive intervention in the affairs of indigenous cultures, and events had often proven her right. Jonathan Archer had come to embrace the principle himself, and now advocated for it as an admiral, insisting that the Federation's benevolent intentions needed to be balanced by an awareness of the risks of cultural imperialism. To be sure, Federation law was a long way from catching up with that principle—in part due to the growing nation's need for resources from worlds like Sauria— but even so, helping out when invited was a far cry from imposing aid on a planet that didn't welcome it. History showed that such impositions proved hard to distinguish from military occupations.

But Section 31 was another matter. Its whole purpose was to find back-channel solutions to matters too sensitive for overt Federation intervention. Surely with Harris's backing, and the help of good people like Antonio Ruiz, Tucker could organize a local resistance, maybe even suborn M'Tezir officials willing to stage a coup against Maltuvis—ideally one leading to his arrest and imprisonment, but Tucker would take what he could get, given how many other lives were at stake. In the meantime, a small team of section operatives under his lead could infiltrate M'Tezir and sabotage their military buildup, possibly staving off an invasion of the Global League. No doubt Harris would have some suggestions of his own, and Tucker was eager to hear them.

But his hopes fell the moment he decrypted the message and saw the solemn look on the older operative's face. *"Mister Sims. I appreciate your zeal to come to the aid of the Saurian people. I can't disagree with your outrage at the current situation, and I share your concern for the lives on the ground.*

"However . . . the sad reality is, these matters are not our responsibility." He held up a hand, anticipating that Tucker was about to talk back to the recording. *"I know what you're going to say. You've been living among those people for weeks now, and you want to help them. But our organization has a clearly defined purpose, and that is to protect the best interests of the United Federation of Planets."* He sighed. *"And sometimes, the best way to do that . . . is to do nothing. As things stand, M'Tezir is continuing to supply vital mineral resources to the Federation— indeed, now that Maltuvis controls them all, he's given us an even better deal than before."*

Tucker threw up his hands. "Sure, to bribe us into leavin' him alone!"

Harris had continued speaking under him: *"And yes, of course he's done that to buy our complacency. I don't like being* manipulated any more than you do," the career manipulator added without visible irony. "But there's more at stake here. If we stir things up too badly, if Maltuvis suspects the Federation or Starfleet of taking any action against him, then not only could we lose the resources he provides, but he could decide to share them with the Klingons or the Orions instead. And then how many people—Federation citizens included—would suffer?"

Harris leaned forward and gazed intently into the pickup. "This is what we do, Mister Sims. We make the cold calculations, shoulder the ugly choices, so the rest of the Federation can sleep at night. If you had any illusions about that, I suggest you leave them behind on Sauria. Because we need you back here, where you can do some good."

A pause. "And if you're considering some noble gesture like going rogue and staying there to help . . . don't. Not only would you have no support from us, but we'd be obligated to actively work against you to preserve the steady flow of trade. And we have a zero-tolerance policy toward operatives who go off the reservation. I trust I make myself clear.

"Come home. Right away. That's an order. That's your duty . . . to the Federation."

Tucker seethed as he deleted the message from the system memory, wishing it were on some disk or cartridge he could smash. "Come home where I can do good, right—just sit and watch and do nothing!" *Do nothing while a world is threatened with tyranny . . . because we care more about dilithium and duranium.*

Is that what I signed up for?

Tucker found Antonio Ruiz in a sauna bar in Lyaksti's capital—a pale, touristy imitation of the ones in

Narpra, according to Tony, but the closest thing he could find. But Ruiz showed no inclination to go back to the saunas, although he'd clearly been at the bar for a fair amount of time already. Tucker had a long way to go to catch up, but he was willing to try. "I'll have what he's having," he told the bartender.

"Al, how ya doin'?" Ruiz slurred.

"Not great," Tucker said. "I've been recalled. That is . . . I got a new job assignment. I'll be leaving tomorrow night. Goin' back to the Federation."

"Is that so? Hunh. So much for Mister Bond. I guess it's right what they're sayin'—the Feds won't lift a finger to help. Even unoff-unofficially."

Tucker shrugged. "I just got a new job, is all." He tried to put in as much apology as he could without giving anything away. Then he blinked, struck that such a thought had made sense to him before he'd even had anything to drink. Was that what this job was doing to his way of thinking?

"Well, fine. Be that way." Ruiz scoffed. "Me, I got recalled, too. No more alien miners allowed in the mines, no more plague to volunteer for, so the company's shippin' me out to an Earth colony. Zavi . . . Zavijavijavi . . . something. Five." He chuckled, leaning in conspiratorially. "But you know what? I'm not going! I'm gonna stay right here. I'm gonna continue the work you got me started on. I'm gonna raise a fuss, I'm gonna make people see what Malthuselah-two-bits is up to, I'm gonna start a damn revolution if I have to!"

Tucker stared at him, worried. "All by yourself?"

"'It does not matter how small you are if you have faith and a plan of action.' A Cubano said that! And I know there are others who will join me. Others who feel like I do—like I thought we did."

The agent studied the engineer's face carefully. This was no drunken fantasy; Ruiz genuinely planned to stir up the very kind of trouble that Harris had warned Tucker against creating. "Listen," he said to his friend. "I understand why you wanna do this. I swear, I do. We've both lost people. We don't want to see others suffer. But . . . you gotta choose your battles, man. This one—well, if you took it on, you wouldn't be on the Federation's side."

"Yeah? Well, so what? What are they gonna do about it?"

Tucker grabbed his arm. "Listen. It won't go well for you if you don't drop this."

Ruiz stared at the hand on his arm, then at Tucker's face. "Are you . . . are you threatening me?"

"No, I—" He realized what he'd been doing—how easily he'd fallen into the habit of veiled threat and intimidation. How could he talk that way to a friend? He remembered the look in Jonathan Archer's eyes when they'd interrogated that Xarantine pimp last year. The pimp hadn't been the only one afraid of what he might do.

"Look," he went on in what he hoped was a friendlier tone. "I'm just trying to look out for your safety. You need to know that what you're thinking of doing could be dangerous in more ways than you realize."

Ruiz jerked his arm free. "And you'd tell them,

wouldn't you? Be the good little spy boy. I shoulda known. You just used me. Pretended to be my friend."

"No. I didn't have to make friends with you to do my job. I did it because we connected."

"But you'd still throw me to the wolves. Well, fine!" Ruiz punctuated it with a roundhouse punch so sloppy that Tucker could've blocked it with ease. But he didn't try, and ended up on the floor with his jaw throbbing. "Tell them to give it their best shot!" Ruiz went on over the ringing in his ears. "You know where I'll be."

The bouncer came over, ready for trouble, but Tucker held up his hands in an appeasing gesture and let himself be escorted out. He didn't try looking back at Tony Ruiz. He no longer deserved the privilege of calling himself the man's friend.

Freighter *Harryhausen,* outbound from Sauria

T'Pol found him in their shared mindspace that night. "It has been some time," she said tentatively, her figure in stark silhouette against the white space that Trip currently lacked the will to embellish with his own mental imagery. "I had been growing concerned."

Trip stood where he perceived himself to be, a few paces before her. "I've been far away," he said. He fidgeted. "I still am, for the moment, but . . . I guess I needed you tonight."

With the invitation given, it was no time at all before she was in his arms, or so his mind interpreted the comfort and love he felt from her now. "Can you tell me?" she asked.

He just held her for a while, soaking in her warmth against him. Finally he said, "I thought I was doin' some good, T'Pol. I thought that justified all the compromises, the lies . . . the sacrifices. Now I'm not so sure."

"You are no longer convinced that Section Thirty-one acts in the best interests of the Federation?" She kept her tone neutral.

"That's just it," he said. "Protectin' the Federation is all that matters to them. So much so that . . . maybe they're forgetting about protecting what it stands for."

He pulled back just enough to face her. "Is that all we are?" he asked. "Just a place, a bunch o' planets and governments and, and resources to protect? Can you defend a nation without defending its soul?"

· She held his gaze. "I once believed so, when I served the High Command. My time on *Enterprise* showed me I was mistaken."

He took her implied meaning. As a result of those experiences, she had resigned from the Vulcan High Command . . . and eventually played an active role in its dissolution.

Could he follow her example? Could he even survive the attempt?

"I don't know," he told her. "Section Thirty-one isn't that bad."

"Neither was the High Command, when I joined it. Corruption spreads."

"But maybe there's still time. Maybe if I stay in, I can fight the corruption, keep them on the right path."

"Or you could succumb to that corruption. If you make too many compromises to remain, however noble your justifications, you will lose too much of yourself." He felt her hand stroke his cheek. "I have no desire to lose you, Trip. For my sake, if nothing else—get out while you can."

She kissed him, making the rest of her case without words. He responded in kind, giving himself over to the loving embrace he had craved for so long. But one lingering thought remained in the back of his mind: *What if it's already too late?*

16

Maras was awoken from her nap by the sound of Navaar storming into the Sisters' suite, cursing and shouting. She turned her head to gaze sleepily at her eldest sister. D'Nesh, who was getting her hair washed for her by a nude male Risian slave, raised her head in annoyance. "What's going on?"

Navaar strode over to the middle sister and answered her question. "It's that *gisjacheh* human! That scrawny drunkard, Charlemagne Hua."

"What's he done?"

"A new drug has begun to appear on the colonies he supplies. They're calling it the Venus drug. It's said to increase its users' sexual allure and potency. To enhance their masculine or feminine attributes—and make them all but irresistible."

Maras stretched kittenishly on the couch, changing position to give her a better view of D'Nesh's reaction. Her curly-haired sister showed immediate recognition, but then stopped herself and spoke noncommittally. "So that would mean . . ."

"Don't you get it, Neshie? He's using Orion hormones! Selling them to—to rabble as a common street drug! Our gift, *our* sacred gift of power, and he, he, he reduces it to a, a——" She broke off, unable to find the words.

Maras rolled off the couch and slinked over to Navaar, putting her arms on her big sister's shoulders. "You're sad. Can I help?"

Navaar turned into her embrace, her hand reflexively going to clasp Maras's. "Oh, sweetie." They fell into a hug, and Maras felt Navaar's tension easing. "I love you for asking, dear, but no, don't worry about it. This is big-sister stuff."

D'Nesh tossed Maras an annoyed glare that she ignored. "How did he manage to replicate our hormones? It's been tried before—it's not easy."

"I had Honar-Des check the medical supplies," Navaar replied. "His stock of hormonal supplements has been broken into. Half his supply was replaced with placebos." D'Nesh looked worried. When Navaar broke free of Maras's embrace and began to pace the room, her back to D'Nesh, the middle sister grabbed a mirror and looked herself over. After a moment, she sighed, seeming reassured. Not that that proved anything, Maras reflected; it could very well be that the placebo effect had prompted her body to produce more hormones of its own. It had been known to happen.

"I just wish I knew how the *shechjuk* even knew the pills existed. I interrogated Honar-Des thoroughly before I had him perform *Vyun-pa-shan*, and he swore on his children's lives that neither he nor any of his staff had revealed their existence." Maras pouted on hearing that Navaar had ordered her lifelong doctor to kill himself. He'd been kind, and had always given her candy after her exams. But Navaar knew what she was doing. At least *Vyun-pa-shan* was quick and painless. It was the least the old dear had deserved.

"Well, it's easy enough to find out," D'Nesh told her, spreading her hands. "Rip the answers out of Hua before we rip his heart out."

Navaar grimaced. "I can't. We need him as an in-road to Federation space, now that *you've* cost us the Mazarites," she finished pointedly. D'Nesh rolled her eyes. "Don't take this lightly!" Navaar chastised her. "This whole alliance is falling apart. We lost Zankor. Garos has proved unreliable—we can't risk letting him act unsupervised again. And Jofirek is barely worth the effort of keeping around. All while the Federation is getting bigger and stronger. This is not going the way I planned!"

Maras moved up to her again and nuzzled the side of Navaar's head with her own. "Are the purple lizard people still our friends?"

Navaar chuckled, and Maras could feel her cheek pulling back in a smile. "Yes, sweet one. Maltuvis has proven a worthier ally than any of these others."

"Good. They have cute eyes."

Navaar stepped away and sighed, shaking her head at Maras fondly. "I envy you sometimes, baby sister. Life is so simple for you." She tousled the hair atop Maras's head and went back to D'Nesh to begin planning their next move. Maras was glad she'd made her big sister feel better.

After all, the poor dear could be rather slow on the

uptake. She and D'Nesh had gotten where they were through their pheromones, not their intellects. And so they'd failed to notice some important clues. Mainly it was a matter of timing. Maras had noted that D'Nesh was beginning to lose her luster a bit, her control over her slaves weakening. The middle sister had gone to visit Honar-Des (the poor fellow), and since then she'd been as sexy as ever, if not more so. Conclusion: She'd been prescribed a hormonal supplement, the kind Navaar took when she thought Maras wouldn't notice. But Maras noticed everything she could—like the fact that Jofirek had been in the clinic at the same time as D'Nesh's visit. And the elderly Agaron had then brought Charlemagne Hua into the alliance. Navaar had been watching Hua clandestinely during that party where he had first proposed selling Orion hormones as a drug, but Maras, as was her habit, had watched the whole room, and noted Jofirek's body language as Hua made the offer. He had been quite unsurprised and untroubled by the suggestion, unlike everyone else in the room. Which would make perfect sense if he'd overheard something about the hormone supplements while in the clinic, then made Hua an offer afterward.

The question was, what to do about it? It would be easy enough to make some seemingly disingenuous observation that would nudge her sisters' thoughts onto the right track. She knew them well enough to manipulate them easily. But Navaar was so upset by the betrayals and failures of her allies. How hurt would she be to learn of another betrayal? Maras wanted to spare her that pain, or at least find some way to soften the blow.

But she was no stranger to taking care of matters in secret. It was how she'd survived this long. As soon as Maras had hit puberty, it had quickly become evident that her pheromonal potency surpassed even the considerable power of her sisters, and that had made her a potential threat to them both. She knew that Navaar truly loved her, but Navaar was also a pragmatist and a strategist who would do whatever it took to win, and D'Nesh was merciless and ambitious. Had Maras shown comparable ambition and intelligence in addition to her animal allure, it would have made her too great a threat for them to tolerate.

Fortunately, she had always been quiet by nature. And the traditional, structured education she had been given as a scion of a powerful elite lineage had been boring and limited, not firing her curiosity like the antique books her mother had collected as valuable heirlooms without ever reading, or like the history and art and science she discovered while searching the subspace information networks in her private chambers. So she had been easily distracted in her classes, resulting in poor performance. She hadn't cared that her distraction was mistaken for a lack of intelligence—not until adolescence kicked in and cultivating that perception had become her greatest survival skill. In the years since, playing the fool had become a kind of performance art for her, a comedy routine for her private amusement, and for Navaar's in a different way. And often a means to an end. People let things slip in front of her that they'd never reveal to anyone they thought was truly paying attention.

And others' lack of attention could be quite liberating when there was something she needed to get done quietly.

Devna stood outside the door to Jofirek's suite, preparing herself for the detachment she would need to service the ancient Agaron. She could look beyond outward appearance if a bed partner was kind, but Jofirek hadn't lived as long as he had in his line of work by being compassionate. She knew from prior experience that she would have to retreat some distance inside herself.

But before she could go in, a hand fell on her shoulder. She turned to see Maras standing there. "Mistress!" she said, bowing her head. The last thing she wanted was to provoke a Sister, even one as . . . well, innocent as Maras. Not only did it bring the risk of punishment, but it could prompt a release of the pheromones that Orion females could deploy against rivals, causing Devna a headache or—worse, under the impending circumstances—a loss of concentration. True, Devna was attracted to women as well as men, and thus not generally troubled by another Orion female's sex pheromones, but the pheromones of active hostility were another matter.

Maras put a finger under Devna's chin and tilted her head up gently, meeting her eyes. "Don't. I'll take him."

Devna stared, then chose her words and her tone

carefully. "Mistress . . . he is very old. He might not survive you."

Maras smiled slightly. "No. He won't." Her hand rested on Devna's shoulder. "Tell them you had an accident. I wasn't here."

The erstwhile spy didn't understand. Why would Maras want her to take the fall for the death of one of the Sisters' chief remaining allies? Her breathy voice grew agitated. "Mistress, please . . ."

Maras pulled a data crystal from her cleavage and wrapped Devna's fingers around it. "Tell Navaar you found this. She'll understand."

While Maras was inside the bedroom with Jofirek, Devna went to the terminal in the outer room to read the crystal. It revealed files from Jofirek's private database, communications verifying that he had tipped off Charlemagne Hua about the Orions' hormonal enhancement pills and worked with him to steal a supply, in exchange for a share of the profits from the sales of the so-called "Venus drug" that Hua had then reverse-engineered from the pilfered samples. Moreover, there were confidential details about Jofirek's contacts and the logistics and interconnections of his underworld network—just the kind of confidential information the Sisters would need to take over his operation for themselves. Navaar would reward her handsomely for this information—and congratulate her for the death of a traitor. How had Maras, of all people, gotten this?

But after the sounds from the bedroom had finally ceased and Maras emerged freshly showered and contented, Devna had a more pressing question for her. "Why give this to me?"

"You've been punished enough. We could use a good spy."

Devna studied her angular face, seeing depth there she'd never suspected. "Why . . . confide so much in me?"

Maras smiled, moving closer. Even sated and cleansed, she still reeked of pheromones powerful enough to overwhelm Devna's control and arouse her intensely. "You're quiet," she said. "We quiet girls should stick together."

The elite woman's lips captured hers, and the helpless Devna expected to be taken and used. But though the kiss lasted long, Maras let it end softly and pulled away. She gave Devna a tiny smile loaded with meaning and promise, then slinked away.

Devna stared after her for a long time, reflecting that this unexpected and clandestine supporter could prove very valuable to her career—or potentially very dangerous. Either way, change lay in her future, and she welcomed it.

Epilogue

"LADIES AND GENTLEMEN, announcing the first Federation Councilor for the United Rigel Worlds and Colonies: Kishkik Sajithen!"

Jonathan Archer joined in the applause as the regal Chelon stepped into the executive building's reception room, took her bows, and moved to stand alongside her fellow new electees: Councilors Avaranthi sh'Rothress of Andoria, Nasrin Sloane of Alpha Centauri, Zhi Nu Palmer of Vega IX, and the only male in the group, Percival Kimbridge of Earth. The re-elected councilor from Mars, Qaletaqu, stood in the crowd applauding them, while his fellow surviving incumbents T'Maran and Gora bim Gral were still on their homeworlds until the next Council term began. The election had been some two weeks earlier, but it had taken this much time for all the new council members to arrive at Earth for the reception.

Archer was grateful that Sajithen's fortunes had taken this turn. The exposure of her radical ties had cost the Chelon her directorship, just as Zehron's own past secrets had cost him his. But apparently the

Rigelian people had been grateful enough for her assistance in the recent crisis that, following their induction as official Federation members, they had wasted little time in electing her as the system's first representative.

President Thomas Vanderbilt also stood nearby, beaming with pride as he saw his legacy made real before his eyes. The lean, bald man looked comfortable about his imminent retirement, turning to chat happily with the man who would replace him at the start of the new year, President-Elect Haroun al-Rashid. The younger, swarthier man looked confident and excited, but Archer knew he would have his work cut out for him. The Planetarist movement was still strong, and Councilors Sloane, Qaletaqu, and Palmer all supported its principles. Even after Thoris's revelations, many of the more radical Planetarists were denouncing his findings as propaganda to discredit them, and the Andorian Lechebists and Vulcan Anti-revisionists still remained unbowed in their radicalism. Organized crime had suffered a blow from these events, and going forward it would find fewer havens at Beta Rigel, but Archer was still convinced that the Orion Syndicate had a hand in many of the Federation's recent problems. As for Rigel itself, its political and economic reforms would be the work of years, and the economic strength and prosperity that Vanderbilt had sought to bring into the Federation would prove a more tarnished prize than he had hoped. Moreover, the growing dominance of the M'Tezir nation on Sauria was becoming a serious concern, and the incoming president would find himself faced with difficult questions about the standards the Federation applied to its trading partners.

Still, those challenges lay in the future, and this was a time to commemorate battles won. Archer was proudest to see the command crews of *Endeavour* and *Pioneer* standing at his flanks in full dress. It was the closest he'd come in more than a year and a half to reuniting his old crew from *Enterprise*. He could not be more proud of T'Pol, Reed, Sato, Mayweather, Phlox, Kimura, and Cutler, as well as their colleagues Thanien, Williams, Sangupta, Dax, Grev, and Kirk, all valued additions to what he saw as the extended *Enterprise* family—the people who kept the spirit of that ship alive even though its body was now a museum display. The achievement being celebrated this day would not have been possible without their skill, dedication, and courage, and he was proud that the whole Federation could celebrate their victory along with him. His only regret was that Trip Tucker had not found a way to be part of these proceedings in some way.

Well, no: he had one more regret. "Jon? What is it?"

He turned to the one person whose presence in this room he was perhaps most grateful for. Danica Erickson stood there, looking resplendent in a satiny silver gown that highlighted the chocolate richness of her skin. Her warm, dark eyes met his with concern and deep compassion. Those eyes reminded him of someone else's—or maybe, he thought, he had been drawn to that other's eyes because they had reminded him of Dani's.

He gave her a wistful smile, appreciating her instinctive compassion, her ability to read him like few others could. "I was just thinking . . . it's a shame Sedra Hemnask couldn't be here to see this. Whatever she may have done . . . she really loved Rigel and believed it deserved a better future, a future in the Federation." He shook his head. "If only she hadn't been trapped by what she saw as her duty . . . she could've been here to see the culmination of her hopes."

Dani's hand moved to his, their fingers intermingling. "You really cared about her, didn't you?"

"I wanted to. Or maybe . . . maybe she just offered me something at a time when I was ready to look for it. I just wasn't looking in the right place."

"Hm." She kept on holding his hand and rested her head on his shoulder. "Thank you for inviting me to this, Jon," she said after a while. "I'm really glad you finally got up the nerve to ask me out."

He let go of her hand, but only to put his arm around her shoulders. "I wasn't afraid," he said. "I was just too focused on the future to see what was waiting right in front of me."

She gave him a look, reminding him he knew better than to try corny lines on her. "The future's still what matters, Jon."

"Of course it is." Gazing into eyes as dark as space, he couldn't resist one more corny line. "And right now it looks better than ever."

November 18, 2164
Boslic trading vessel *Namkun*, uncharted space

Captain Bievel sobbed as the freighter's deck jolted beneath her feet and warning lights multiplied on her status console. "Please," she begged to her attackers. "We're sorry, we won't tell anyone! Please, just let us go!"

It had started out so invitingly, with that pristine white trading post *Namkun* had found while seeking new trade contacts in the unknown territories that had opened up now that the Romulans had been forced behind the Neutral Zone and the Mutes had stopped hijacking ships. Bievel had known that, with those powers no longer blocking entry into the space beyond, it would not be long before Starfleet explorers and prospectors in the Rigelian trade network would begin expanding here, discovering what resources the region had to offer. She had been determined to beat them to it.

True, the trading post had been entirely automated, and its computer had been a very limited conversationalist. But the outpost had offered resources and comforts irresistible to a crew weary from five weeks of fruitless searching. The station's menus had offered a variety of technologies for sale, including engine components, robotic maintenance drones, and advanced, transporter-based food synthesizers. The barter payments it had demanded had been exorbitant, limiting what Bievel had been able to purchase; and they had lost their life support specialist to a stupid accident during installation of one of the new components.

But that had hardly been the station's fault, she had thought at the time, and if anything it had marginally increased the average competence of her crew. Once *Namkun* had made its payment and undocked, the station had transmitted an advertisement for other, similar facilities in the sector. Intrigued, Bievel had set out in that direction, hoping to learn more about the robot stations and their builders.

Contacts with other travelers and natives of the region turned up stories of other such facilities of various types, and even automated ships of the same make, some ferrying tourists or colonists, others un-occupied but adamant about refusing passage into certain territories. The consensus was that the white robots were useful so long as you respected their restrictions and could afford their fees. Although there were a few spacers' tales of the stations being cursed, demanding blood from those who entered them. Bievel had paused to wonder about that, given her own loss and similar tales of fatal accidents from some of the others she spoke to. But her visits to other white stations had gone smoothly, so she had dismissed the tales as traders' follies or the slander of jealous competitors.

But then she had gone a bit too far into the sector, probed a bit too deeply into the white robots' origins. She had found one of the worlds they had overrun and seen what had happened to its people. And she had made the mistake of trying to warn the next world it was happening to.

Now their orbital patrol ships closed on *Namkun*

with mindless singularity of purpose, firing relentlessly, giving no quarter. Most of her crew was dead already, her beloved freighter was disintegrating around her, and the only thing left for her to try was a distress signal to warn Rigel and the Federation what would face them as they expanded this way. But the subspace transmitter had been damaged, and there was nothing she could do but beg. "Please," she sobbed over the short-range comm, "just tell me, why are you doing this? Who are you?!"

Just before a clean white mechanical arm tore through the cockpit viewport and closed around her, Bievel heard her killers' answer, the only reply they ever gave to the most important questions:

"Your inquiry was not recognized."

STAR TREK: ENTERPRISE
RISE OF THE FEDERATION
will continue

Acknowledgments

I don't have room to recap all the thanks and acknowledgments I made in the previous volume, *A Choice of Futures*, but most of them still apply. Thanks to Ed and Margaret at Pocket Books for letting me continue to develop this story. Thanks to Doug Drexler for technical advice on the *Enterprise* era and to Paul Abell for asteroid expertise. *The Amateur Magician's Handbook* by Henry Hay provided the basic principles from which I derived Tobin's magic trick.

Many things have been asserted about the Rigel system in *Star Trek* episodes and books, and I've tried to reconcile what I could, favoring information from canon and the modern novel continuity. While *Star Trek*'s Rigel has traditionally been assumed to be the blue supergiant star of that name in the constellation Orion, its depiction in *Enterprise*: "Broken Bow" as a nearer, less familiar system led to its reinterpretation as "Beta Rigel" in *Star Trek Star Charts* by Geoffrey Mandel, and the StarMap site at whitten.org/starmap identified Mandel's Beta Rigel with the real star Tau-3 Eridani. The Kandari Sector was mentioned in an onscreen graphic in *The Next Generation*: "Conspiracy" by Tracy Tormé.

By the numbers:

The Trojan asteroids of Rigel I are loosely inspired by the Rigel asteroid belt depicted in *Worlds of the*

Federation by Shane Johnson and in *Star Charts*, but reinterpreted to fit our modern knowledge of the abundance of hot Jovians orbiting close to their stars.

The cabarets of Rigel II were established in *The Original Series*: "Shore Leave" by Theodore Sturgeon. Its seedy reputation and criminal ties were suggested by *The Lost Era: Catalyst of Sorrows* by Margaret Wander Bonanno and IDW Comics's *Alien Spotlight: Orions* by Scott and David Tipton and Elena Casagrande. Kefvenek was alluded to in *Vanguard: Precipice* by David Mack.

The Chelons were introduced as background "Rigellians" [sic] in *Star Trek: The Motion Picture*. Costume designer Robert Fletcher's background notes for the film described them as single-gendered. The *Vanguard* novels by David Mack, Dayton Ward, and Kevin Dilmore established their specific name and characteristics and identified Rigel III as their homeworld, while also giving them two sexes, which I have tried to reconcile. Rigelian hypnoids are from *The Animated Series*: "Mudd's Passion" by Stephen Kandel. My portrayal of the Hainali Basin is heavily informed by the chapter on Amazonia in the fascinating nonfiction book *1491: New Revelations of the Americas Before Columbus* by Charles C. Mann.

The "Vulcanoid" Rigelians were established in TOS: "Journey to Babel" by D.C. Fontana. *Catalyst of Sorrows* established Rigel IV as their native world (drawing on TOS: "Wolf in the Fold" by Robert Bloch) and introduced the First Families (including the Thamnos clan) and the expatriate population on

Rigel V. That novel depicts these Rigelians as human in appearance, while other sources suggest a more Vulcan appearance; I have struck a middle path. The name "Zami" is based on Zamiar, the name for Rigel IV in the Decipher role-playing game. Rigelian fever and ryetalyn are from TOS: "Requiem for Methuselah" by Jerome Bixby.

The craggy-faced, bead-wearing Rigelians were first seen in *Enterprise*: "Demons" by Manny Coto, after being established as four-gendered in ENT: "Cogenitor" by Rick Berman and Brannon Braga. Memory Alpha, the *Star Trek* Wiki, identifies Rigel V as their homeworld, perhaps by the process of elimination. I have chosen to identify their "endosexes" with the silver-skinned, red-eyed Rigelians posited in various novels by Michael Jan Friedman, one of whom, Folanir Pzial, is a member of the *U.S.S. Lovell* crew created by Dayton Ward and Kevin Dilmore and featured in the *Corps of Engineers* and *Vanguard* series.

The Rigel Colonies were mentioned in TOS: "The Doomsday Machine" by Norman Spinrad. My interpretation of them as colonies of alien immigrants identifying as Rigelian was inspired by a comment by David Mack. The presence of major shipyards around Rigel VI is based on a reference to one such shipyard in the *Deep Space Nine Technical Manual* by Herman Zimmerman, Rick Sternbach, and Doug Drexler.

Rigel VII and the Kalar are from TOS: "The Cage" by Gene Roddenberry. My depiction of them is heavily influenced by Marvel Comics's *Star Trek: Early Voyages* #3, "Our Dearest Blood" by Ian Edgington,

Dan Abnett, and Patrick Zircher. The giant cratered world seen in Rigel VII's sky in the famous Albert Whitlock matte painting from "The Cage" has been interpreted as Rigel VI in fan sources, but due to the *DS9 Technical Manual* reference, I made it Rigel VIII instead.

The 1980 *Star Trek Maps* and *Star Charts* both interpreted Rigel VIII as a ringed Jovian, implicitly the one seen in the sky of the "Cage" matte painting. I have followed this precedent but made it Rigel IX instead.

The Rigel X trading outpost was seen in ENT: "Broken Bow" and "These Are the Voyages," and its Orion slave market was established in the ENT novel *The Good That Men Do* by Andy Mangels and Michael A. Martin.

My depiction of the Babel outpost (introduced in "Journey to Babel") is informed primarily by *Myriad Universes: A Less Perfect Union* by William Leisner (which established the Ramatis Choral Debates and the basic station layout) and *Alien Spotlight: Orions* (which established the esplanade). Thoris (Joel Swetow) debuted in ENT: "Demons." Avaranthi sh'Rothress is a historical figure introduced in *Articles of the Federation* by Keith R.A. DeCandido. Selina Rosen and Doctor Sobon are from *Vanguard: Open Secrets* by Dayton Ward. Solkar, father of Skon, was named in *Star Trek III: The Search for Spock* by Harve Bennett and established as Vulcan's first ambassador to Earth in ENT: "The Catwalk" by Mike Sussman and Phyllis Strong. His daughter-in-law T'Rama was created by John Takis in

Star Trek: Strange New Worlds V: "A Girl For Every Star," and established as a member of T'Pau's security force in ENT: *The Romulan War: To Brave the Storm* by Michael A. Martin.

Kaferia was established in TOS: "Where No Man Has Gone Before" by Samuel A. Peeples. *Star Trek Maps* identified it with Tau Ceti III and established its insectoid natives, a precedent I followed in *Department of Temporal Investigations: Watching the Clock.* Yet *The Romulan War: Beneath the Raptor's Wing* by Michael A. Martin identified Kaferia as a human colony on Tau Ceti IV. I have attempted to reconcile this herein.

Harrad-Sar (William Lucking) is from ENT: "Bound" by Manny Coto. The Mazarites are from ENT: "Fallen Hero" by Alan Cross (story by Rick Berman, Brannon Braga, and Chris Black), the Agaron from ENT: "The Seventh" by Berman and Braga. The Venus drug is from TOS: "Mudd's Women" by Stephen Kandel.

Brantik is the name of a Tellarite colony in *Articles of the Federation,* which may be the same Tellarite colony founded herein. Danica Erickson (Leslie Silva) is from ENT: "Daedalus" by Ken LaZebnik and Michael Bryant. Jeremy Lucas (later played by Richard Riehle) was introduced in ENT: "Dear Doctor" by Maria and André Jacquemetton. Section 31 agent Harris (Eric Pierpoint) debuted in ENT: "Affliction" by Mike Sussman (story by Manny Coto).

This was a tough one to get done, so I want to thank my friends at the 2013 Shore Leave convention, my cousins Barb, Mark, and Teddy, their friend

Charles, and the folks at GraphicAudio for helping me recover mentally and Amanda Lass, NP, for helping me recover physically. Thanks to Dave Mack and Kevin Dilmore for moral support, and particularly to Kirsten Beyer for being willing to find the time.

About the Author

Christopher L. Bennett is a lifelong resident of Cincinnati, Ohio, with bachelor's degrees in physics and history from the University of Cincinnati. He has written such critically acclaimed *Star Trek* novels as *Ex Machina*, *The Buried Age*, the *Titan* novels *Orion's Hounds* and *Over a Torrent Sea*, the two *Department of Temporal Investigations* novels *Watching the Clock* and *Forgotten History*, and the *Enterprise* novel *Rise of the Federation: A Choice of Futures*, as well as shorter works including stories in the anniversary anthologies *Constellations*, *The Sky's the Limit*, *Prophecy and Change*, and *Distant Shores*. Beyond *Star Trek*, he has penned the novels *X-Men: Watchers on the Walls* and *Spider-Man: Drowned in Thunder*. His original work includes the hard science fiction superhero novel *Only Superhuman*, as well as several novelettes in *Analog* and other science fiction magazines. More information and annotations can be found at home.fuse.net/ChristopherLBennett, and the author's blog can be found at christopherlbennett.wordpress.com.